CU01461135

ESCAPE FROM ARCADIA

SISTERS OF FATE TRILOGY, BOOK 1

NATHAN SCAMMELL

Copyright © 2021 by Nathan Scammell

All rights reserved.

No part of this book may be reproduced in any form or by any electronic or mechanical means, including information storage and retrieval systems, without written permission from the author, except for the use of brief quotations in a book review.

ISBN: 9798731839716

To Ethan and Amelia.

My children and my biggest fans, not only have you inspired my love of storytelling, but you have inspired my love of life itself.

1

Cad stared down his opponent, looked him in the eye and realised that this would not be much of a fight at all. He would not even meet his gaze. The sword-master yelled to start the duel. Despite how easy he would find this fight; he still gave it his all. He leaped forward, easily ducking a clumsy swing from his opponent. In the same movement he caught his opponent in the side of his leg with the hilt of his sword, causing him to fall to his knees. Cad then delivered a powerful blow to his chest. The vibrations from the blunt sword hitting the armour hurt his hands, but he could see that he had knocked the wind out of his opponent. He fell to the floor as Cad drew his sword with a flourish.

"Stop." Shouted Pike the sword-master. "Once again you've not held back, ending the fight early."

"I don't want to hold back." Cad replied, not meeting Pike's gaze, "I wouldn't in an actual fight."

"But this is not an actual fight."

"Sorry Wil," said Cad, offering his friend a hand to get off the floor.

"I hate this," Wil said, "You always take it so seriously." Cad knew his friend was right, but he had a reputation to uphold. He was the youngest and greatest swordsman ever to come from Arcadia. Cad obviously had not duelled with anyone from past times, but there is no history of anyone being a skilled swordsman in any literature. Few people saw it as an important or even useful skill, they used it mainly for fitness. It frustrated him that all he could fight were the wooden dummies or local opponents who lose quickly. Most of the town now refused to duel with Cad, they could not suffer another defeat and frankly he knew that they were not interested in practicing enough to meet his level.

"Sorry" was all Cad could mumble again, knowing that he would do the same next time.

"It's not normal, you know. You need to find a better way of burning your energy." Wil tried to smirk as he caught his breath, stretching his back from where Cad had winded him. They headed towards the duelling hut to take off their armour.

"I could say the same to you and those books you know." Cad said with a smirk "if you spent more time with a sword in your hand rather than a book, you might actually be a challenge." Cad removed his sparring helmet and swept his sweaty brown fringe out of his eyes, he looked at his friend. Cad had an advantage over him. He was at least a foot taller than Wil and leaner. The height he could not help, but if he spent more time with the drills and sword, then at least he would become as strong. Wil did not have the time that Cad had to practice the sword, he was too invested in his books.

"At least learning about things is useful, besides what is being a swordsman going to achieve? Being a sword-master is the only job that that will get you, and that job is taken. Pike is young, you will be his apprentice until you're an old man." Cad gritted his teeth and wished he had not started this; it was an argument that he and his friend had had time and time again. Cad could not describe the feeling he gets when a sword is in his hand. The excitement, the rush, the challenge. He could not understand how people did not love sword fighting as much as he did. He knew deep down that this is what he wanted to do with his life.

"It may come in useful." Cad said, knowing that this argument would go nowhere, but he could not let it go without trying to get the last word. "When we get outside, or whenever what's outside gets in. Who will fight them off?"

"Nothing is getting in and nothing is getting out. That's the way it is, no one even knows what's out there. What if there are giants and you look like a tiny ant waving a toothpick about with your sword? Won't be much help then." Wil started waving his sword in the air, fighting an invisible giant. Both Cad and Wil laughed.

"I will get out there one day you know." Cad said, staring out of the window, towards the horizon where the magical barrier surrounded their town.

"So, you've said." Replied Wil. Cad wanted nothing more than to get through the barrier. Everyone believed it was to keep out a great evil, but no one knew what that great evil was. There was nothing definitive in the history texts and even if there was something evil out there, the odds were that it was dead by now. What they knew is that the barrier has been up for centuries. Wil was right, nothing got in, nothing got out. Still, Cad lived in hope.

"Come on you two, I want to get home." Pike shouted poking his head in the room. Cad knew Pike disliked him. If he was being honest with himself, he did not really like Pike either. Pike was jealous of Cads ability with a sword, he had been better than the towns sword-master for quite some time. It had even come to the point where Pike refused to duel with Cadderick. He did not like Pike because he had the title and job that Cad wanted, to be known as sword-master would be a dream come true for Cad, but ability has nothing to do with it. In Arcadia you had to be in the right place at the right time. If Cad had been born five years earlier, then he probably would have been made the towns sword-master. Pike was lucky enough to be coming of age, just as the previous sword-master had retired. It annoyed him that neither Pike nor his predecessor Graff took their jobs seriously. Swordplay was a dying art, before long, the town will have no idea how to defend themselves. Not that they were ever likely to get attacked.

Cad and Wil said their farewells to Pike, who was preening

himself in the mirror. He was bigger than Cadderick, more well defined. Pike knew that he had a great physique and showed it off at every opportunity. Another thing that irritated Cad. He knew Pike enjoyed the more fitness and body sculpting side of sword play, focusing more on drills rather than sparring, and he was always too busy sculpting his physique to focus on the skill that was involved. The two friends left him admiring his body and headed towards home. Cad could see Wil was fidgeting and knew what was coming, he prepared himself to become annoyed.

"You really could do with broadening your horizons you know." Wil said. Cad gave him a look warning him to stop, but he carried on, regardless. "I know you don't like to admit it, but there really is no future for a swordsman. At least try to learn something else, otherwise you will be sent to be a mage." Cad pulled a face at the thought.

"Why would I work on keeping up the barrier that's locking me in?" asked Cad.

"You know you'd have no choice. Once they assign your job, you're stuck with it. They will not want you to be an apprentice sword-master when he is so young, and you know it." This was another argument that Cad was fed up with having, not only with Wil but also with his parents, and his tutor. Deep down he knew that they were right, it killed him to admit it but nothing else came to him like sword fighting. Nothing inspired him or excited him anywhere close to whenever he held a sword in his hand. The thought of doing anything else for a job made his stomach turn. Doing something you do not enjoy for the rest of your life, only to fit in with a society that he did not really want to be stuck in. He had read adventure books; they must have based them on some fact, so he knew that there must be a lot more out there than just this little town. It was his dream to discover it and maybe one day be the star of his own book.

"Look, I'm sorry. I just don't want to see you stuck with the mages. They are a strange lot, you must admit." Wil pulled his cheeks down, doing his best impression of the Archmage Urlwin. "Join us, young Cadderick." This brought a smile to Cad's face; he knew that he did not want to be stuck with the mages. They put anyone with no actual skill or trade with the mages. Apparently, many centuries ago, the mages could do powerful magic. Now they struggle to conjure enough heat to boil a teapot. Besides, they spend all their time maintaining the barrier, the total opposite of what Cad would like to do. "At least think about it." Wil said to Cad with a weak smile and stopped outside his home. "Will see you tomorrow ok?"

"Sure thing." Cad said waving to his friend "Maybe we can duel again?" Wil shook his head.

"I am sure we will. Wouldn't want to do anything fun now would we." He said with a laugh.

Cad said goodbye to his friend and then headed towards his home. Just before he got there, he made a turn into the woods and followed the path he had become familiar with. His mind was racing today. He knew Wil and his parents were right. He just did not want them to be. Every time he tried to talk about wanting to get out and explore, they met him with rolled eyes or excuses of it being impossible and from his father just plain laughter. Cad sat on a large log that he had dragged into his makeshift den in the woods. It was right on the edge of town, on the border of the barrier. You could easily see through the barrier, but there was a definite distortion, like everything seemed greyer, with a lack of colour. The same as the sky when he looked up, just grey. He picked up a handful of rocks and started throwing them at the barrier. This was one of his favourite pastimes, his own little way of rebelling against the barrier. It was also fun jumping out of the way of the rocks as the magic in the barrier made them ricochet back towards him.

Cad imagined what kind of force it would take to break through. It embarrassed him thinking about all the attempts he had made trying to run through or push through. He even stole a knife from his parents' kitchen to see if he could cut it, yet nothing even came close. He grabbed the last stone and hurled it towards the barrier with all his might. Lost in his thoughts and frustration, he jumped, but no stone came hurtling back. He stopped and stared at the barrier, no holes. He looked around him, checking to see if it had landed near him. There were a lot of stones on the floor, so he could not be sure.

He walked up to the barrier and stared out. In the distance there was a stone. On the other side of the barrier. Cad's heart raced, had it gone through? He looked around. There were also a few other stones in the area that could have been there before. He was not sure, but his stomach was turning with excitement at the idea of something making it through the barrier.

He picked up another stone and envisioned all of his frustration and desire into the stone. He wanted to will it through the barrier. Cad threw the stone as hard as he could and watched. The stone hit the barrier and ricocheted off at speed. Hitting Cad square on the forehead. He did not think to jump as he was so sure the stone would go through. He returned home with crushed hopes and what felt like a crushed head.

Cad's father looked up from the pot of stew he was making to look at him walk in the door.

"You actually took a hit in sword practice?" His father asked, raising an eyebrow "Hopefully it's knocked some sense into you, but I won't hold my breath." Cad felt his head, there was a large lump where the stone had hit him. Cad just grumbled and sat down. Usually, he was met with lectures about his future. He was almost coming of age, and his parents had been constantly bringing up what he wanted to do for a role in the village. They would set this decision for life. His father sensed his dark mood and decided not to push him today and placed a hot bowl of stew in front of him. "Here you go, freshly made. I got some meat too. Its drying in the yard." Cad looked up at his father in surprise.

"How did you manage that?"

"One cow died giving birth. So, it's not the old tasteless kind we usually get. Being a farmhand has some benefits, you know." Cad was waiting for him to push the subject. His father had been quite vocal about how he wanted Cad to take up farming, as his father and grandfather did. Cad did like the animals but spending so much time with them day after day doing the same chores seemed monotonous and not something he wanted to do every day for the rest of his life. To Cads surprise, his father did not continue the conversation, just sat with down with his own bowl of stew and dropped a large wedge of fresh bread next to Cads.

"Was the calf alright?" Cad asked, he knew that the population of animals was something that they worked hard to maintain, hence the rationing of meat. Losing a cow would cause a lot of worry.

"Yeah, he had no problem, shame really, he would have gone nice in this stew." Cad looked up at his father in shock. His father laughed, "It's ok, I'm joking," he dipped his bread in the stew, "Cassius had a fit about it. He came to see if it was our fault. He doesn't have a clue about the animals though." Cad looked at his father "He didn't actually blame us." His father added. "But I could tell he was suspicious. I think nothing we could have done could have saved that cow. She was weak during the whole pregnancy. I don't think the grain is as nutritious as it once was."

"Back when they ate meat every day, and the vegetables had flavour." Cad imitated his father's favourite thing to moan about. The council rationed the meat long before Cad was born, so he never knew what it was like to eat meat every day. His father claimed to remember those times, although Cad was sure that the meat was rationed before his father was born. It did not stop him from bringing it up at almost every meal though.

"Exactly!" His father laughed. His good mood was infectious, and soon Cad smiled again. "So, do you want to tell me what happened to your head?" His father asked.

"Not really." Cad responded. He could not admit to throwing stones at the barrier to anyone, he could not even tell his father. They would brand him a heretic if they ever found out, the entire town loved the barrier, felt safe by it. If word got out that he actively tried to break it, it would bring shame to him and his family. The only one he trusted with this secret was Wil, and even he thought Cad was not serious about it.

"Ok, but your mother will be home from work soon, you know she is going to ask you all about it. The cow's death has probably caused a lot of drama at the council, so she may not be in the mood for you to avoid her questions."

"I am stuffed." Cad said, pushing aside his empty bowl. "I think I'm going to lie down."

"I think that would be a good idea," his father replied. "I will wake you at sunup. Don't forget you are with me at the farm tomorrow."

Cad sighed before retiring to his room.

2

Cad dreamt of getting through the barrier only to be caught in a smaller one, it disturbed his sleep. Nothing but a dream, he thought to himself as he woke. He sat up in bed just as the sun was rising. His father walked into his room, surprised to see him already awake.

"Stews on if you want food before we go." His father said. Cads least favourite part of stew. It would not last long before it spoiled, so you had to eat it for every meal in the upcoming days. He got himself dressed and ready, forced down a bowl of stew and walked with his father to the farm. Cad worked hard when he was at the farm, not because he enjoyed it but because he liked to build it into a workout. The faster he moved and the heavier the things he lifted, the stronger he would get, and this could benefit his swordplay. He and his father approached the farm and Hamish, the head farmer, came rushing out of one of the barns towards him.

"Gentar, you need to come to the barn. Linus wants to see you; he's asking a lot of questions about the cow."

"Why is a mage getting involved?" Cad's father asked, his eyes narrowed at the word mage. His father was a kind man but even he had a disdain for the mages, he claimed they were all lazy and being a mage meant not doing what he considered to be proper work.

"He's been sent by the Council, by Cassius," Hamish replied, "He is investigating the death." Cad saw his father look worried and he sent Cad to muck out some of the horse stables. Deep down, Cad was grateful it was not a horse that had died. It was probably his least favourite meat, but the one that they had most often. His father was gone longer than expected, when he returned, he looked pale but said nothing to Cad. He decided not to ask questions, so they both worked in silence for a while.

"Let's go take a break." his father said midday. They both walked into a barn. His father made a small fire and got out an iron pan, into the pan he put two delicious looking steaks. Cad's jaw dropped.

"Didn't want to dry it all." his father said in response to his shocked reaction. "I thought it would be nice to enjoy some fresh." Cad said nothing, just watched the steak cook in awe. The aroma filled the barn and Cad's stomach rumbled. He was really excited about this; he could not remember the last time he had had a fresh steak. His father sprinkled some spices over the top and began dishing up. Cad tore into the steak. He could not remember a time where he had tasted something so full of flavour. "Try to savour it, it's ok to chew." His father laughed but he could not resist. He ate the whole steak in record time. Mopping up the grease and fat with a piece of crusty bread. Even that was delicious.

"That was amazing." Cad said, leaning back on the hay bale he used as a seat, rubbing his stomach in satisfaction.

"Now you see why I get so grumpy about having no meat." His father replied. "But let's keep this between us, ok? I don't want anyone getting jealous of our lunch today. That includes your mother."

Cad nodded slowly in agreement. Keeping secrets from his mother was a very unusual request for his father to make. He stood to go to the pump for some water as his mouth was dry.

"Wait," Cad's father said, holding a bottle of amber liquid. "I've got something special to wash that steak down with."

"Is that ale?" Cad asked.

"It sure is." his father said, taking a swig from the bottle and passing it to his son.

"Are you sure?" Cad asked. Ale was made in plenty in the town as they had a lot of grain to make it, but his mother and father had always been against him drinking it until he was older.

"Of course, you're practically a man now." Cad took a swig of the ale, it was not the first time he had drunk it, not that his parents knew that. He was not sure if he liked the taste, although when he drank this, it was refreshing. He passed the bottle back to his father. They took a few more swigs each before his father spoke. "The thing is Cadderick, me and your mother have been treating you like a child. Telling you what you must do instead of treating you like the young man you are."

Cad looked up from the bottle. He was surprised, but also happy. He felt like an adult, and he was getting frustrated about being treated like a child. "The thing is you know what's coming up. If you don't have a plan, you're going to end up being a mage." Cad was about to interrupt, but his father held up his hand and continued. "Your mother and I will still love you, of course, but you know how people look down on the mages and I admit that I am also guilty of that. You are better than that though. Why not speak to Hamish about sponsoring you for the farm?"

Cad was about to argue that he did not want to work on the farm, but he stopped. Deep in thought, he realised that if he did not act now, he would get stuck as a mage. All he wanted to do was be the sword-master, but that would not happen. Even if it did, it would involve Cad following Pike around everywhere and doing what he was told for the next however many years. He did not know what to say. He looked at his feet, avoiding his father's gaze. His mind raced, was this his best option? He felt guilty for not putting more thought into it. He just assumed that everything would work itself out.

"I'll think about it, Dad, I really will. You are right, I should have thought about it sooner. Let me sleep on it."

"OK son, I won't mention it again, it's up to you now, only you can control your future."

Cad knew that it was a lie. He had no say in his future, it would be whatever the council decided for him. Cad carried on working, but it had crushed his spirit. The words from his father had hurt. He knew that he was being irresponsible. Maybe being treated as an adult was not as good as he had thought, all he wanted to do was finish his work and spend a few hours practicing with his sword. That would help him take his mind off things, at least.

He thought about Casilda, his tutor, and his arranged betrothed. He was not happy about the news when he received it, but his parents were over the moon despite her being at least ten years older. People Cad's age were few, in fact, the only person the same age as Cad in the village was Wil. This was probably why they were such close friends as they had little in common apart from their age. He imagined her reaction when she had got the news about him, she could not have been happy about it either. The child that you have been tutoring becoming your husband, with no choice. Cad smirked at his father's words. "Only you can control your future". While you lived in Arcadia, the Council controls your future.

Cad's epiphany came as he was collecting up the horse manure. If he could not control his future, he was going to try and make the best out of it. That is what his parents would want, and deep-down Cad knew it was the best option for him. He put down his pitchfork that he was gathering hay with and went to find Hamish.

"How's the new calf doing?" Hamish asked Cad as he approached, the new calf was the number one priority for the farm today. It needed to be hand reared because of the mother's early death. Only the more experienced farm hands dealt with that.

"She seems good, she's taken well to being fed by hand. The other cows don't seem to notice." He replied.

"Selfish creatures the cows, all they will think of is more grass to graze on for them. Was there something I could help you with, son?" Cad fidgeted; he was nervous.

"I was wondering if you would sponsor me to be a farm hand, you know, as my village role?" Hamish's eyebrows raised, he looked shocked.

"I thought you were only interested in the sword?" Hamish asked.

"No... Well yes, but the sword-master role won't be available for a long time, so I don't think there will be a need for an apprentice, and I don't want to end up...." Cad paused but Hamish understood.

"So, you think it's either do this or become a mage?" He asked, "I see why you came to me." He chuckled. "Well, I know you work hard, you do a fine job when you come to help your Dad, but I will warn you the job gets harder. Your Dad is one of the best so he can tell you what it's like, but I cannot have a farmhand that daydreams about playing with swords all the time, I need you to work hard every day."

"I will." Cad added, "I promise, I will be one of the best."

"Maybe you will, OK, I think I can put a sponsorship in for you. It just so happens I have enough space for one more farmhand. You know that sponsor is all I can do, though? The final decision will be up to the council."

"I know, thank you Hamish, I appreciate it."

"Ok, well best get running along. Your father is probably on edge thinking about how this conversation went," He said, Cad noticed his father watching him intensely and he quickly looked away when he noticed both him and Hamish look towards him. "Give him the news and thank you for your hard work today." He paused "And hopefully to many more days of work." Cad nodded and rushed over to his Dad. They walked towards home while Cad told him everything. His father was beaming with pride.

"I'm proud of you son, I know it isn't exactly what you wanted, but I'm glad you are looking at the bigger picture."

"You're right Dad. I'm going to make a quick stop, see you at home?"

"If you have enough energy for swordplay, I obviously didn't work you hard enough." His father laughed.

"It's not that." Cad replied, although he always had energy for swordplay. "I thought I would drop by on Casilda." His father's jaw dropped; Cad understood why. Any talk of Casilda or the marriage would cause one of Cads major sulks. Cad and his father said their goodbyes, Cad took a detour through the woods, this time not to go to his den, but to collect some wildflowers. If I cannot control the future, I need to make the best of it, he repeated in his head. It would not be good for him or Casilda if he spent the rest of his life sulking about the marriage, and although he had a while before that was going to happen, it was going to happen eventually.

Cad walked along the forest's edge to her house, and he spotted her outside washing her clothes. He looked over towards her. She was quite nice; he thought to himself. It could certainly be worse. He thought of the other women of the village, there really was not much choice. She was a kind woman and was very good to Cad, even though it was in more of a mothering way, probably because of the age difference. Cad made his way towards her. She caught his gaze. She looked shocked to see him, but smiled at him, regardless.

"Hey," She said, "surprised to see you here".

"Yeah, me too." Cad realised his response sounded stupid. He had never felt nervous around her, but he had also never accepted the idea that they were going to be together, before now. He could not think of what to say, so he just held out the flowers. "These are for you."

"Thank you." She took them and blushed as she looked Cad up and down, he wondered if it was because of his change in behaviour.

"Hard day at the farm?" She asked him, with a raised eyebrow.

"Yeah, did you see me there?" Cad wondered how she knew.

"I can tell by the muck on your clothes. Usually, I like my gentleman callers to be clean." She laughed. Cad blushed.

"Sorry." He stammered.

"It's fine." She replied, still giggling. "Get yourself cleaned up, I'm just about to dish up some food. If you'd like to come in for dinner, that is?"

"Please, I'm starving." Cad smiled. He still felt awkward, as it did not feel natural. He gave himself a wash in the river and used one of Casilda's towels to dry off. He followed her into her house, realising that this was the first time he had ever been here when it was not for some lessons. The smell of roasting vegetables permeated the air and Cad's stomach grumbled.

3

C ad tossed and turned that night. He had spent a long time talking with Casilda, talking about the future, what he wanted to do and what he was going to do. It was the first time that they had spoken on the same level, rather than as tutor and student. He did like Casilda, but to spend the rest of his life with her? Cad still thought that it was unfair. He also thought about working at the farm, unsure of how he could get around it, no ideas came to mind. His parents did not ask him about spending time with Casilda, but their broad smiles and their constant winks annoyed him into going to bed early, not that he could sleep. The morning came and Cad dragged himself out of bed and made himself a hot drink. The herbs he used were bitter, but they were good for starting the day. He had no plans, so he would spend most of the day training with his sword, probably. His parents were already at work, so he ate some bread and cheese for breakfast, when there was a knock at the door.

"Hey." Said Wil when Cad answered the door. "Got something to show you, can you get out?"

"Sure, I can." Cad replied, leaving the house immediately. He was wearing yesterday's clothes, but because of his mood he didn't want to get changed. He left the house and followed Wil into the forest. "What are we going to look at?" Cad asked.

"You always wanted to explore; well, I've got you the next best thing," replied Wil, "Just trust me." They walked for a little while longer, in the woodland close to where Wil lived. Cad had explored little of this area. They got to a large hole covered by a wooden grate. "What is in there?" Cad asked.

"No idea," responded Wil, "People are forbidden to go in, but apparently it is tunnels under the town."

"Why are you showing me this?" Cad asked.

"So, we can explore?"

"You want to go in?" His friend surprised Cad. He was a stickler for following the rules.

"I've always wondered what's in there." Wil responded. "I figured this would be the last chance to check it out while we are young, before we get too old and get in real trouble for it." Cad smiled at his friend as they lifted the grate.

"I like this new attitude." Cad responded. "Do you think it leads out of the village?"

"I doubt it very much, but if it does, who knows what could be down there." Cad made a torch out of some wood and travelled down the hole with Wil. It was one long tunnel, they travelled along slowly; their footsteps echoed on the brick floor. This had to have had some use previously, but Cad did not know what, and if Wil did not know, then it must be a big secret.

"Wait, if you have always wanted to come down here. Why didn't you tell me about this before?" Cad asked.

"Because I knew you would make me come down here," laughed Wil, "and I don't know, I just thought we could use a little excitement before we become of age." His friend impressed Cad; this was exciting. Cad could feel and hear his heartbeat in the silence of the tunnels. There were a few turnings Cad tried to focus on in case they got lost. He did not know where they would end up.

"So why are these tunnels forbidden?" Cad asked.

"Apparently someone died down here a long time ago and the

council ruled it dangerous, so no one could use them anymore. Then they just got forgotten about, I suppose."

"How did they die?"

"No idea." Wil responded. It was a long time ago and people don't talk about it. My parents don't remember it, so it must have happened years before they were born. The hairs on Cad's neck stood up. If someone had died, then whatever had killed them could still be down here. Cad shook his head, if it were a creature, it would be long dead by now. Cad imagined it was probably a falling brick or something, as Cad thought this he looked up, checking the bricks above him were stable. Eventually, the two boys came to a trapdoor leading upwards, Cad's heart raced.

"Do you think this will lead us out of the village?"

"I don't think so." Wil responded. "I think we've been walking towards the middle of the village and we haven't walked for long enough to reach the outside. Let's see where we are."

The boys opened the trap door; they were in a basement, but they were not sure where. Cad and Wil quietly looked around for some clues. The air was musty, and the furniture down here was old. Everything in the village was old, but this seemed even older. They walked up some steps and peered into the room above, although Cad had never been here in person before, he knew where he was. The room was a circle and had a large iron plinth in the centre. This was where the mages came to maintain the barrier.

The life of the mages was very boring. They were to come to this room in pairs and hold their hands on the plinth, expelling the little magic that they had. The entire town could do it, but the mages were the only ones who were not fit for a trade. The ones who would not be useful anywhere else and so, they would be sent down here to do the most boring task, maintain the barrier. Although it was important to the town, it required no skill. Cad soon realised something was wrong.

"Shouldn't there be two people at all times in here?" Cad asked Wil. "At least that's what I was taught." The room was completely empty apart from the two boys.

"Yeah, that's what I thought too." said Wil. The boys heard voices in the corridor, so they quickly dashed into the basement and back to the tunnel.

"Keep going?" Asked Cad.

"Maybe another time." Wil replied. "Let's try to make our way back, we will come again tomorrow. This time I will bring some paper and try to do a map as we walk. I don't want to get too lost. I didn't realise there would be so many turns." Cad reluctantly agreed, Wil was right, and there was still the opportunity of coming back. If they got lost for long or popped out somewhere in town, they would have to admit what they had done.

Cad and Wil made their way through the tunnels. Cad was following Wil's lead, but soon he slowed down and ended up coming to a stop. "We should be back by now," Wil said, "but I think we may be lost." Cad did not panic.

"We haven't been out long. Plenty of time to find our way back, let's head down this way." Cad nodded towards another turning. Wil followed. They had come to a few dead ends and had to turn back, but the boys carried on through the maze. They came to a long stretch of tunnel, there was a black lump in the middle, so Cad raised his torch to see. When they walked slowly towards it, both boys held their breaths, afraid of what it was and as they got closer, they could see it was a person.

"Is that the one who died?" Cad asked.

"Can't be, they would have gone a long time ago." Cad pulled the black robe from over the body and there, staring back at him were the eyes of someone he recognised, Linus, one of the mages. His throat had been slit; the blood was fresh; he had been killed recently. Cad threw up at the sight of the dead man. He backed into the wall and one stone came loose and hit the floor with a thud.

"Run." Was all Cad could get out as they sprinted down the tunnel. They took turn after turn, not knowing where they were going, Cad just wanted to put as much distance between them and the body as quick as possible. They found a trap door that they recognised as the one leading to the mage's hall.

"We've gone in a circle!" exclaimed Wil.

"Shall we go through?" Cad asked. He did not want to get into trouble, but he also didn't want to spend any more time down in the tunnel. His heart was hammering in his chest, Wil nodded as they climbed back into the basement. They rushed up the stairs into the round room, still empty, but Cad did not care this time. He rushed into the corridor and saw the exit. He wondered if he could get through the doors with no one seeing. Then he would not have to get into trouble, but what about Linus? He had to tell somebody.

"What are you two up to?" Cad heard the voice and the colour drained from his face. Wil looked as pale as Cad felt. They turned around towards Urlwin, the archmage. "I asked you a question!" He barked.

"It's Linus!" Was all Cad could say. "We saw him. He's dead."

Urlwin looked at the boys with a bemused expression. He ushered them into his room and got them to sit down.

"I think you had better start from the beginning."

Cad and Wil told him everything, everything about the tunnels and their exploring, everything about Linus. Cad felt his stomach turn over every time he heard Linus' name. The dead eyes staring back at him, were all that Cad could picture every time he heard his name.

Urlwin got out of his seat, without saying a word, turned to his cabinet and poured some drinks. He gave one to Cad and Wil. It was a bitter whisky. The two boys coughed.

"After what you boys have been through, I thought you might need that." Said Urlwin with a kind expression, he drank his whisky without it affecting him. He was probably used to it, Cad thought.

"You don't seem very shocked," Wil said eventually. "No one has been murdered here for generations!"

"Saddened yes, shocked no." responded Urlwin. "I have to let you boys in on something. I believe us mages are being sabotaged by the council and I believe they may know who is behind Linus' death." Cad was shocked, but when he caught a glimpse of Wil, he could see he was furious. Cad knew Wil respected the Council; his ambition was to be a part of it. Both boys remained silent, unsure of what to say. "I have a huge favour to ask of you both. I need you to keep this between us, while I investigate, I don't know who I can trust with this." It shocked Cad that Urlwin wanted to keep this quiet, if someone had murdered Linus, surely, he wanted the murderer brought to justice? "And of course, if we keep quiet about it, no one really needs to know what you boys have been doing today. I don't think it will go well for your future, if the council finds out where you have been." Cad could hear Wil's gulp, he was right, they could get into a lot of trouble for this.

"Go home boys, get some rest. Come see me if there is any trouble and I will update you on anything that we find. We will find out who is responsible for Linus' death, I promise."

Cad and Wil stood up to leave. Cad hesitated.

"Why is no one maintaining the shield?" He asked, he could see Urlwin was taken aback by this question. "When we came earlier, there was no one there and when we returned, there was still no one on it. I thought you had to have two people on it at all times?"

"Yes, you are right. It was Linus' shift to work on the shield. Galloway went searching for him. It would take a long time of no one working on the shield, for it to stop working. We have built it up over centuries, a few hours of no one maintaining it will not do any harm. Now come on, I have work to catch up with. I want to investigate this immediately but remember, it is our secret for now."

Cad and Wil left. They both walked in silence, the image of Linus' blank stare burned into his mind. He still felt sick, numb, unsure of what to do and Urlwin's forced smile as they had left sent shivers down Cad's spine.

"Perhaps it is best if we say nothing." Wil said, reading Cad's mind. "We don't want to get into trouble for this. Let the mages do their work."

"Yeah, that's probably for the best. I just cannot get the image of Linus out of my head." They walked on in the rain. Cad found it very odd how heavy it was raining; it never usually rains this hard. The crops could do with it though, the farmer in him thought. They walked through the town and came to the road where they would part ways. "Let's just have a think about it and we can talk tomorrow, OK?" Wil nodded and went off towards his home. Cad thought about going to his den, it was where he thought best, but as his shoes squelched in the mud, he decided against it. He arrived home to his mother and father sat at the table eating their food.

"Haven't seen rain like this since I was a boy" his father laughed at Cads soaking wet body, his mother rushed to get him a towel and started vigorously rubbing his head and hair with it.

"I suppose you've been practicing your sword fighting in this weather, have you?" His mother asked.

"No, I haven't been to the arena today." Cad paused. Where could he say he had been?

"Oh, I see." His mother smiled. "And how is Casilda?"

"Fine." Cad snapped, hoping to end the conversation.

"The weather seems to be improving. I was saying the other day that the sun seemed brighter and now we have some heavy rain. It will be a busy time at the farm for harvest. We might even have some decent vegetables for a change." Cad noticed that the stew he was eating had meat in it.

"Is this more of the beef?" He asked.

"Yes, we decided against drying it." His father responded, "Don't want the town to get jealous of us having extra meat. You know how they are when it comes to surplus."

Cad wolfed down the stew as he realised that he had not eaten all day, and now it was nearing sundown. He desperately wanted to talk to his parents about today but decided against it. He wondered if Wil would also keep it quiet, it could mean big trouble for Cad if he were to be found saying one thing and Wil the other.

"Is everything OK, Cadderick?" His mother asked. She looked concerned, and he knew that she was serious as she had used his full name.

"Yeah, I'm fine, just feeling a little exhausted, busy couple of days." Cad's father laughed and his mother shot him a glare. Cad was confused by what they were implying. "I think I will go to my room to read for a while." Both of his parents cocked their heads at this statement but did not challenge it. Cad went to his room to check through his education books wanting to find out about the history of the shield and how it worked. He discovered it was as he had remembered, two people at all times. Why would they have no one there? Linus being murdered was a good excuse for it, but it just made little sense to Cad. He lay in bed for another night filled with uncomfortable dreams, this time it was Linus' face seared into his mind and Cad imagining him screaming that kept him awake. He wished that he had never went down in those tunnels. Maybe being an explorer was not as great as Cad had imagined.

4

C ad sat with his parents, eating his breakfast. His mother kept fussing over him, Cad felt terrible and according to his mother he looked as bad as he felt. The truth was, he was tired, he could not get the image of Linus' dead body out of his head. Every mouthful of his bread went down in lumps and he could feel his stomach turn with every swallow.

"Dad, when we were at the farm last, what was Linus doing there?" Cad's father dropped his bread and looked at his son quizzically.

"Why do you ask, son?"

"It's just that mages rarely come to the farm and when they do its only to take samples of the soil. I've just been curious, that's all."

"Well, he raised some concerns about the quality of the soil, son. Also, he wanted to see the cow that had died. The council had sent him to investigate whether or not she died of natural causes."

"She died giving birth though, didn't she?" asked Cad

"Yes, but we are under close watch since they suspect we caused it to happen. Linus always was a bit of a busybody and a stickler for the rules. It's no wonder the council sent him, if anybody could find out anything, it would be Linus."

"What would happen if they decided it was your fault?" asked Cad.

"They won't because there is nothing that could have been done." replied his father sharply.

"That's enough of this." His mother interrupted. "What's going on, Cad?"

"Nothing it's just been on my mind."

"Is that what's been worrying you?" His mother asked.

"No. Well, yes. A bit, I guess."

"Well, you need to stop worrying. They have stopped investigating and nothing else has been said about it. You know what this town tends to be like. Gossip spreads fast."

"Besides, I haven't seen Linus since that day, so he's probably come up with nothing to complain about." His father added. That was what Cad was afraid of. Cad knew that there was no way that his father had anything to do with it, but in a town this small they would look for someone to blame and the farm workers would be prime suspects. Then again, many people didn't like Linus. He would be the first person to accuse you of something and then work hard to find any evidence.

"Just stop worrying about it," Cad's mother said, "everything will be fine." Cad wanted to burst and tell them everything, but he knew that it would only make things worse. He needed to see Wil, he needed to talk about it. Cad got up and told his parents he was going for a walk. His mother hesitated as though she was going to stop him, but she let him go.

As Cad was walking towards Wil's house, he spotted Wil hurrying towards him. He was holding paper and his charcoal pens, charcoal wasn't as easy to use as ink, but ink was rationed tightly.

"I've got the stuff to draw a map." Wil said.

"You mean you want to go back down there?" Cad asked, surprised.

"Of course, don't you want to? Something is odd about that place. I thought you would want to find out what." He stammered. Cad hadn't even thought about going back. He was also really surprised by Wil, he hadn't really been affected by the previous day, or at least he didn't seem to be.

"I don't think it's a good idea," responded Cad. "After what happened yesterday, I don't think we should go back. Whoever killed Linus could still be down there."

"I don't think they would be. I think whoever killed Linus put him down there to hide the body rather than they had both just been down there. Don't you think?"

"Yeah, I suppose your right." Cad agreed. "But what are we looking for down there exactly?"

"I'm not sure." replied Wil. "But we won't get lost this time. I will draw our path, so that we know exactly which way it is to get out. I don't think we even saw half of it yesterday." Cad reluctantly agreed and followed Wil to the hole. Cad wondered where the courage from his friend had suddenly come from and why his was fleeting.

"Wait." Cad said. "I'll be right back." Cad ran off back towards his home and returned shortly with his training sword. It wasn't as sharp as some they kept at the training arena, but it could hurt someone if he hit them hard enough or at least stop them from getting too close to him. Wil glanced at his sword and smirked.

"I hope you never have to use it, but I admit it's a good idea. Come on." The two boys crawled into the hole and Cad once again lit a torch. With his sword in one hand, torch in the other, Cad and Wil made their way through the tunnels. After every turn Wil would stop and ask Cad to bring his light over so that he could mark on his parchment which direction they had taken. It was not too long before the boys found themselves outside the door to the mage hall cellar.

"We don't need to go in there." Wil said, but he studied the map for a while. "There are a few turnings that we haven't gone down. We should go back so we can say we have explored every part before the mages hall."

"Why?" Cad asked.

"Just so we know every entrance and exit." Wil replied. "It may come in handy." The boys took one turning they had not gone down before and came across another cellar door.

"I'll have a look. See where we are." Cad said. Wil nodded and studied the map with the torch while Cad climbed up through. As Cad opened the cellar door, he looked around, it was another basement, only this one looked like it was in use. There was food stockpiled. Grains, dried meat and vegetables. Cad had never seen so much food in one place. Even though the food looked delicious Cad couldn't think about eating, he was too nervous and still felt sick. There was noise coming from the door leading above, so he ducked back down into the tunnel and he told Wil what he had seen.

"That's the hall of Council then" he told Cad, marking it on his map. "I can kind of figure out where we are with those two points," he said. "We have two more turns to go and then we've covered everything this side of the mage's hall." he said. The first turn looped around and came back out of the other one. This must be where they got turned around yesterday and got lost. "This must be where we found Linus." Wil pointed to a section on a map.

"But we would have walked past him the first time we came through." Cad responded.

"Well, it means we missed him the first time," Cad knew this was unlikely the thought of seeing Linus' dead body pierced Cad's mind. "Or they put him there after we walked through." Cad felt sick at the thought of the body being brought here at the same time that the boys were walking through the tunnel.

"I don't think we would have walked past without seeing, I know it's dark but..."

"I agree." Said Wil. He was looking nervous, and Cad was glad that he was not the only one.

"Keep going?" Cad asked. He was scared, but deep down he wanted to finish what they had started, find out where the last few tunnels lead. He still hoped that they would lead him out of the town, but he worried more now about what he may find out there, his hand aching from the strength of his grip on his sword.

"Yeah, let's go past the mage hall." Will agreed. They both walked on. When they got past the mage hall, the tunnels stopped branching and at the end was a solid wooden door. Cad's heart raced.

"Do you think it leads out of the town?" Wil looked at his map.

"I don't think so. I think we are too far away from the edge; we seem to be moving towards the centre of town." Cad pushed at the door, it was stiff, but it was unlocked. Cad held his torch up to see what was in the room.

"Looks like a library?" Cad said to Wil. There were books everywhere, some were covered in thick layers of dust. There was a desk and a chair that looked older than any of the ones they had seen in town. Cad put his hand on the chair to test its strength, it was still strong enough to hold people. They continued to study the room, there was writing on the wall in what seemed to be a brown paint. Cad could not read it and looked at Wil, who shrugged.

"I don't think they are using our language," He said, "I don't recognise it." They thumbed through a few books. The books were delicate and aged. Some were in the language they couldn't read but others they could, even so they were very difficult to understand. "Someone has been coming here." Wil said eventually. Cad agreed, he too had noticed the thick layers of dust had been disturbed in some places. The chair and desk were clean as were some of the books. Someone else had been down here. "Bring the torch to me." Wil asked, standing at the table. He flipped over his map and copied the writing on the wall. He picked up a few books. "Lead us out." Wil asked, "I'm struggling with these books."

Cad lead them out of the tunnels, awkwardly holding the map in the same hand that he held his torch. Following Wil's directions, they made it to the exit in the woods with no trouble.

"What are you going to do with those books?" Cad asked.

"I'm going to try to read them, see what they are about. It's quite difficult, the writing is really faded, and they look really complicated."

"Well, if anyone could read them you can, what do you suppose that room is for? Why is there a secret underground library?"

"I don't know. Why would they want to keep it a secret? It doesn't make sense. I've been thinking about something." Cad looked at his friend. "The only exits are the woods, the mage hall, and the council. That means that Linus must have come from either the council or the mage hall. It was a bit too far in to have been dragged from the woods."

"Didn't Urlwin think it was someone from the council?"

"I'm not sure we can trust him Cad." Wil said "I'm not so sure about the council either. Something feels wrong, but I don't know what."

"Should we tell anyone?" Cad asked, thinking of going to his parents.

"I'm not sure, firstly I don't think anyone would believe us. No one has noticed Linus is missing yet, but also if the council is up to something, who do we turn to? Who could protect us from them?"

"Yeah, you're right." Cad said, the thought of the council being corrupt frightened Cad. They were the only authority here. Why would they need to kill Linus, though? There was a piece missing in this puzzle, but Cad couldn't see it.

"I'm going home to make a start on these books," Wil said. "I'll let you know if I find anything."

Cad said his farewells to his friend and was about to go home when he realised that he had not been to the arena in a few days, still holding his training sword, he decided to go and train for a while. Cad trained harder than he had for a long time. Even though he still felt drained and sickened by the thoughts he was having, he put all his effort into it. With every strike his full force, every drill he pushed hoping to block his thoughts and feelings.

When Cad finished, he realised he was drenched in sweat. Pike knew something was wrong and kept his goading to a minimum. Cad thought he caught fear in his eyes with the effort he was putting into his training. He could not quite face his parents yet; he still needed some time alone so went back to his den in the woods. He laid on a log that was the perfect shape for him; he mulled things over in his head, but the thoughts of Linus and the trouble that was happening in town took over. It wasn't long before Cad was throwing rocks at the barrier.

With each throw he imagined he was throwing away a bad thought, but like his thoughts the rocks came bouncing back. Linus dead, throw, bounce. Corrupt council, throw, bounce. Lying to his parents, throw, bounce. Working on the farm for the rest of his life. Throw... And silence. It had happened again; Cad was sure of it. The rock went through the barrier. He didn't see it happen, but he knew it had happened, he was sure of it. He walked right up to the barrier and put his hand on it. He could feel the force pushing him back. The harder he pushed, the more it pushed back, like an unseen version of himself was pushing back against him.

He picked up another rock and pushed it against the barrier; the rock pushed back. "There has to be some way through," he thought to himself. Then it came to him. He knew what he needed to do. He took a few steps back, away from the barrier and then he sprinted. Just as he got close, he jumped forward, pushing his shoulder into the barrier. The force of Cad hitting it sent him flying back and off of his feet. His shoulder was in great pain, his head hurt, and he felt sick. He laid on the floor for a while in pain and embarrassed. Why did I think that would work?

He got to his feet and wiggled his shoulder; it hurt a lot, but at least it wasn't his sword arm; he thought. He made one last attempt at throwing a stone. The pain in his shoulders and the excessive training he had done earlier made his throw pitiful and weak. The stone bounced back. Cad sighed and turned when he noticed something outside the barrier. He saw the shape of a person, a woman. When he glanced back again, she was gone. He was sure that he had seen someone. Then again, he had not long hit his head; he was exhausted and injured; he doubted what he had saw through the barrier.

Cad made his way home from his den, once again embarrassed and in pain. At least he wouldn't have to tell his parents why. As he was walking, he noticed a commotion down at the river. He spotted his parents there, and many others all looking in the river. Cad's stomach turned. What had happened? He began running towards them as he got closer, he realised people were not panicking; they were excited. As Cad approached them, he could see why. The river had creatures in it. He had learnt about them before but had never seen them. The river had fish.

ad and his parents sat at their table eating fish for breakfast. The council took them away to be rationed, but by the time they had arrived there were hardly any fish left. The townsfolk had already grabbed what they could although this caused animosity in the town as some people felt they had not had a fair chance to get the fish. How they got in and where they had come from caused a great debate in the town. Cad plucked the flesh from the fish carcass, he was not fond of it, but he did not dare complain. This seemed to be a once in a lifetime opportunity.

"Where did they come from, Dad?"

"I'm not sure son, some people are saying it's a gift from the creator while other people are worried that the barrier is failing. All I care about is that we get to eat more meat. Beef and fish in the same week, I never thought I'd be so lucky." Cad shifted in his seat when his father mentioned the barrier failing. No one seemed to work on maintaining it when he went there. Could this be a result of that? He got frustrated that he couldn't voice his concern, but then wondered. If the mages are neglecting the barrier, and it fails, then this would be a good chance for him to finally get out, to explore. He considered that maybe the mages wanted the same thing that Cad did, although the thought of working alongside the mages sent a shiver down his spine.

When he went to Casilda for his tutoring, all mention of the evening they had spent together talking person to person was gone and they were back to their student teacher dynamic. Cad found it hard to focus on his lessons as all he could think about was the barrier. He even asked Casilda what she knew about it, but she repeated everything he already knew, Cad got her to reiterate the fact that two people should maintain the barrier at all times. She did question Cad on why he was suddenly interested in the barrier, but he avoided answering the question, instead claiming it was because of his interest in the fish. The rest of the day he spent planning his next move, to go back into the tunnels and check again on the Mages. He knew he needed Wil with him as he had the map.

The end of his lessons couldn't come quick enough for him, but just as he was leaving, Casilda asked him if there was anything he'd like to talk about. Her tone had changed, more sympathetic, and he believed her to be completely genuine. Cad politely declined, but as he left, he wondered what had caused her to say that. He had not been getting much sleep lately. Maybe it was starting to show also, his mother was friendly with her, so they probably shared concerns with one another.

Wil's Mother let Cad in, and he made his way to his room, Wil had his head in one of the books they had brought back. If Cad felt rough, then Wil looked exactly how Cad felt. His face was pale and baggy eyed. Cad hesitated when he walked into the room, Wil didn't even look up from his book.

"Anything interesting?" Cad asked.

"Not yet." Wil replied. "Not much that I can make out, most of it is written in symbols instead of words, it is almost as if they are using pictures instead of words but it's hard to say what they really mean. I've picked up a few bits but nothing of importance, just some notes on people who lived in this town. It's not even dated so I don't know how far it goes back but I don't recognise any of the names so it must be a few generations back." Cad didn't know what to say. He had hoped that the books would answer some questions, but it seems they only asked more.

"I want to go back again." Cad said. Wil did not seem surprised; he still hadn't looked up from the book.

"OK, I'll come too." Said Wil, "I can grab some more books. Wait. Why do you want to go back?" Cad stuttered, he hadn't told Wil about what he was thinking of the barrier, he had told no one. Now that he had to voice it aloud, he felt silly.

"I want to check on the mages," he admitted, "something is odd about the barrier, twice we saw that no one was working on it, and then the fish arrived and also... Other things," Cad didn't want to explain about the rock throwing and Wil didn't push him.

"Yeah, I think your right, something doesn't quite add up with the mage's hall, then again I think something may be up at the council as well. Everything seems a bit of a mess at the minute, and honestly, I thought the fish tasted awful." Cad laughed, he didn't know if Wil had intended to be funny or if he was just rambling, but they both had tears in their eyes from laughing.

"I hated them too." Cad joined in. He could imagine his father's disbelief if he had told him what he had thought. Once they had gotten over their moment of madness, Wil grabbed the map and they headed out, climbing down into the dark tunnel once again.

"We are making a habit of coming down here," Cad said, lighting their torch. They made their way to the mage's hall with relative ease. Most turnings they didn't even require the map now, they had a good sense of where they were going and how to get there. Cad silently climbed into the cellar. The musty air hit him as soon as he had opened the hatch, Wil followed silently. Cad had left his torch burning in the tunnel, he just wanted a quick in and out to find out what was happening. He climbed the steps and peered into the barrier room but once again, no one was in there.

"So much for using Linus as an excuse this time," Cad whispered to Wil, he crept over to the open door, it was coming up to the evening so most of the mages would make their way back to the halls soon. Out in the corridor they spotted the door to Urlwin's quarters, considering he was arch mage, leader of the mages, his room was very modest. The best rooms in the town were those that held the council members, then again for a mage's social standing this was probably appropriate. Cad made a gesture to Wil to go back to the cellar, but Wil had spotted something on a desk in Urlwin's quarters. He edged towards his room as Cad looked up and down the corridor, worried that they could get caught at any moment.

Wil picked up a book from Urlwin's desk and ran his fingers across the cover, Cad didn't know the book but assumed it held some significance. Wil shook as he looked up, almost as if coming out of a trance, and quickly rushed back to Cad, leaving the book behind. They made their way back into the tunnel before Cad spoke.

"What was that book?" he asked.

"I'm not sure." Wil replied. "But I'm pretty sure I saw that book in the library down here, plus it has similar symbols to the ones I have. We must not be the only ones who know about it. If Urlwin knows, how long has he been using it?" Cad didn't know, so he didn't answer, he just stared at his feet until he could see Wil was in deep thought. He waited until Wil gathered his thoughts and they made their way to the library, it was pretty straightforward from here, so Wil didn't even glance at the map.

They took the turning that Cad thought led to the library, but there was a dead end. Wil looked just as confused as Cad. He looked at the map, backtracked a few corners to make sure he knew where he was, and walked back to the dead end.

"It was here." Wil said.

"I thought so." Cad added.

"No, it was definitely right here." Wil almost shouted, frustration in his voice, "The map leads us right to it."

Cad and Wil looked around they studied the surrounding walls; nothing was out of the ordinary. Wil tried to push the bricks at the dead end, they wouldn't even budge. His hands were all dusty and grimy from the old bricks. He wiped them on his clothes. Wil banged the wall with his fist. Cad could sense he was getting frustrated, but nothing was happening.

"Someone is trying to keep us out." Cad said.

"No, look at the wall, its old, no one has built this wall. It definitely wasn't here last time though. What is going on." Wil banged the wall a few more times, even hitting it with another rock he had found on the floor.

"Maybe we should head back?" Said Cad. Wil looked at Cad, then at the wall, then at Cad again. "Your right, we're not getting in. Maybe there is something in the books I've already got, can explain what the hell is going on down here." They both made their way back through the tunnel. Cad didn't speak, he knew Wil was angry. He didn't like not knowing things, and this whole situation was getting to him, and to Cad too. He knew however that Wil's pride took a hit when he couldn't understand the books and couldn't understand what was going on. Cad imagined it would be what he would feel like if he could not beat someone in a duel.

The boys made their way out of the tunnel when Wil spoke.

"I'm going back home to see if I can try these books. Looks like you were right about the mages too, still not working on the barrier. If no one is down there, it will get weaker every day. Looks like you might get what you want too, Cad, you might get free." Cad wasn't sure if Wil was making a friendly comment or adding it with anger but now that Cad thought about it, if the mages were bringing an end to the barrier this could be exciting but why did he feel so sick at the idea. Something was very wrong with the whole situation. Why didn't anyone know about this?

They parted ways, but on his way home Cad took a detour back to his den; he didn't throw rocks at the barrier, instead he stood close to it. Staring out. What is out there, he thought to himself, and why are we hiding from it? He put his hand out to meet the barrier, the usual resistance pushed back. Cad thought, was it the usual resistance or did it feel weaker? Cad pushed and pushed, and the barrier pushed back. He was there for quite a while, just holding the barrier, as though trying to sense a change, but nothing came. Cad became frustrated. He looked at some stones on the floor. No, he would not do that today, mainly because the last few times he had left here with injuries, but now he was not sure what would happen. He was not sure what he wanted to happen either.

He put both his palms flat against the shield, closed his eyes and breathed deeply. He thought about what he wanted, an internal battle in his own head. On one hand, nothing would be more exciting than exploring out there, finding out what was beyond the barrier, but he was safe in this town, and they must have put the barrier up for a reason. His internal battle raged in his head until he decided, no, I don't want to spend the rest of my life in here wondering what is on the other side. I want to see it. I need to see it. Cad opened his eyes, there in front of him was the same old grey haze of the barrier. Cad became annoyed with himself; he did not know why he had expected something to happen, he just did.

Cad made his way towards his home when he saw his friend frantically running from Cad's house. He called to him and Wil came sprinting over.

"Cad, where have you been." Cad hesitated, he didn't want to tell Wil about his den, it was his special place. His place to be alone.

"I just wanted to take a walk." Cad said. "Clear my mind. What's wrong with you?"

"They're gone Cad, all of them." Wil said frantically.

"What are?" Cad asked bewildered at what was going on.

"The books, someone has taken them all."

6

C ad knew he should have been preparing for his council meeting tomorrow, his fate and future were to be decided for him, but all he could think about right now was what was going on in this town. Murder, corruption and now stolen books. He wondered if it was all connected, but he couldn't quite piece it all together. Wil had not yet found much in the books that he had, so they didn't know what the information was that had been stolen. If they knew that, then maybe they could figure out why?

"The Mages have them, I'm sure of it." Cad remembered Wil saying, he lay in bed waiting for everyone to go to sleep. He and Wil were going back to the tunnels to get the books back from the mages, Wil had spotted one book from the secret library on the Arch Mages desk, they are the only ones that could know about Wil's books, he was also the only one that knew the boys knew about the tunnels. Cad was feeling determined tonight, excited even. Although he wasn't going anywhere new, it was a quest like in the stories, he was going to find something lost. It was a minor task, but he had hyped himself up for it. Make the most of what I can get, he thought. He had hidden his sword under his bed, it was blunt, he wouldn't have been able to take a proper sword from the training centre, but it would do.

He hoped he wouldn't need to use it, but there was a sense of danger in the air tonight that made the hairs on the back of his neck stand on end.

Darkness enveloped the town of Arcadia, and Cad carefully sneaked out of his room and out of the house. He had never been out at this time before. There were no lights in the houses illuminating the town. He could hardly see his hand in front of his face, it was more sensing where he was going than seeing it. He didn't dare light a torch from fear of being seen. Luckily, he was very familiar with the route, so he had had little trouble getting there. When he arrived at the hole, he noticed Wil was there waiting; he was breathing heavily, fiddling with the sleeves of his coat. He was glad that Wil looked as nervous as he felt. They climbed into the tunnel before lighting the torch. They silently crept through the tunnels, Wil holding the map but not needing to look at it. Both not daring to speak to each other, Cad could feel his heart thump in his chest. He was a lot more nervous than before, but he was not sure why. Possibly because the stakes were higher than before, they actually intended to steal from the arch mage.

As they neared the passageway to the Mages hall, they heard voices.

"Can we get out of here? This place gives me the creeps." Came a voice. Cad and Wil stopped abruptly, both held their breath not daring to move and Cad quickly extinguished his torch. The voice was familiar, Cad thought.

"No, the Mages know something. We have to find out what they are doing." Came the other voice. Cad recognised them now. It was Meldon and Bryce from the council. It surprised him that the council members were down in these tunnels.

"Come on, we can get in this way." Bryce said, climbing the ladder that led to the mage's hall.

"What are they doing here?" Cad asked Wil. It was pitch black, but Cad could hear Wil's clothes creasing as he shrugged his shoulders.

"I don't know, they know the mages are up to something but what? Should we follow?"

"We may find out if we do, but then it's a gigantic risk if they catch us." Wil moved forward, Cad assumed he was willing to take the risk and followed him. They felt their way to the ladder, not daring to light their torch, and made their way up into the mage-hall basement. The closer they got to the trapdoor leading to the barrier room, the louder the shouting got.

"I allow my mages to take breaks, you know." They heard Urlwin say, the anger in his voice was very apparent.

"Two mages at ALL times." Replied Bryce, just as Angry. "Or do you think you have the authority to change the rules without the council's permission?" He added.

"I rule the mages, I protect the town, I allow my mages to take breaks. It would be inhumane to make them stand here all the time."

"This isn't the first time though is it Urlwin? You have had no one on barrier duty the last time I checked."

"You councillors never leave your comfortable hall," spat Urlwin, "When was the last time you actually came down to see the mages?"

"Almost a week ago." There was a silence that seemed to last forever. Cad could not get close enough to see what was happening, but it seemed Urlwin was lost for words.

"So, you have been spying on us? How? I thought the tunnel was forbidden to be used?"

"I make the rules." Bryce said with a loud, sharp tone. "I am in charge. Who are you to dare challenge me on what is forbidden? Just some lowly mage."

"So, you are above the town law?" Urlwin said, "Is that what why you killed Linus?" There was another brief silence.

"We did not kill Linus."

"I wonder what the town would think if they knew their council was above the rules set specifically by them. I wonder what they would think if they knew their council was murdering anyone who dared speak out against them."

"Now you are twisting my words, mage." Bryce spat, "We have murdered no one."

"No, but the town will think you did. You killed Linus because he heard of your plans to eliminate the mages, to bring down the barrier. I don't think the town will like that."

"Now you listen to me!" Bryce shouted; Cad could hear he was getting flustered.

"Then sneaked into the Mage hall to kill some other mages, but in all the struggle ended up getting killed themselves."

"That's not what is going to happen, that is not why we are here."

"You have forced my hand early, Bryce, now it is the Mages turn to take over." There was a slice and a gurgle, sounds that Cad would never forget. He felt all the colour drain from his face and his legs turn to jelly. What had just happened?

"Throw their bodies into the library," Urlwin said, "Make sure you lock it behind you. It might not have been those two that had taken the books." Cad tugged at Wil's arm.

"We've got to get out of here." Cad whispered frantically. Wil shook himself as though coming out of a trance and rushed behind Cad. Cad jumped down the ladder to save time but realised his mistake when he hit the ground. His ankle started throbbing as he moved aside for Wil to climb down. Cad lit his torch, not caring about being seen, just wanting to find his way out as quick as possible. Wil led him as he hobbled behind. Walking on his twisted ankle. They darted through the corridor and climbed out of the tunnel. They breathed in the outside air deeply. Both were still pale and shaking. Wil vomited on the floor whilst Cad steadied himself against a tree. Cad felt tears sting his eyes and let out a sob, what was he going to do now? He thought, as the boys tried to compose themselves, they heard the sounds of footsteps, then the cracking of branches beneath someone's feet.

"There you are." Someone said as a hand grabbed each of them by the scruff of their necks. Cad knew that he and Wil were done for. The mages had killed two councilmen, and now they were next.

7

They locked Cad in one of the rooms of the council hall, where he was all alone. He did not know where they had taken Wil. It relieved him that it was Cassius from the council rather than a mage, until he began dragging them to the council by the scruffs of their collars. He was unnecessarily rough with them, but they knew that it would not be a good idea to fight back. Cad knew that they were in a lot of trouble, he banged on the door again, frustrated at how long he had been in this room, but no one came. There was no window, and the only light came from a crack in the door. Cad paced back and forth, running his hand through his hair in frustration. He thought of Wil and how he was holding up, he felt as if they were still in danger, even though they were away from the Mages. Out of the cook pot and into the stew, as his Mother would say. Eventually he heard the door. He stepped back, Cassius came in, followed by Urlwin. The sight of Urlwin made the colour drain from Cad's face.

"I think you had better take a seat." Cassius said with bitter anger in his voice. He looked weary, it was probably the early hours of the morning and they had all been up all night. Cad did not feel fatigued, but he put that down to the adrenaline pumping through him. Cad sat on the other side of Cassius and Urlwin. Sitting down had made him realise his legs were tired. "We need to go through what happened last night."

"Where is Wil?" Cad asked, worried for his friend.

"Wil is fine. We have already spoken to him and Dyne is taking him back to his parents." Urlwin showed no emotion on his face, but Cassius was clearly frustrated. "I know what you may think you saw...."

"You Mages murdering two members of the council?" Cad interrupted. His stomach turned over at the thought of the two corpses, probably hidden in the tunnels somewhere.

"Yes, but you have to understand why." Cad gasped, so Cassius knew about Meldon and Bryce but didn't seem to care. Cad was confused about how calmly he was reacting to it. "The barrier needs to come down Cad, it's the only way that we can survive." Cad did a double take.

"You want to take down the barrier?" Cad asked.

"It's more of a need. Food is getting scarce; the crops are getting smaller. Even the animals are thinning out."

"But why did Meldon and Bryce have to die?"

"We tried to reason with them, they had forbidden any more talk about it. They would not listen to reason and would have let this entire town die before going against their beliefs."

"What about everyone else? What do they think of this?" Cad asked.

"Some will not like it of course, but we know what is good for them. Either we face the dangers outside and try to survive it or we remain trapped in here forever and die out in here. Do you understand?" Cad agreed, he had always wanted to go beyond the barrier, yet he thought of his parents. It would petrify them, the thought of the barrier coming down.

"I am not sure." Cad said, trailing off. He didn't know what to think at the moment, he would have preferred to just say yes, I agree, the barrier should come down, but he felt selfish just thinking about it. He knew how everyone else felt. What if he agreed and then it led them to their doom? Cad would be partly responsible for the death of his town. Could he have that on his conscience?

"You remember the fish?" Cassius said. "We did that. We have weakened the barrier enough that small animals can pass through the water. Was that not a good thing? Did that not make people happy? The extra food?"

"I guess so." Said Cad, still unsure of what to make of the whole situation, his head felt like it was at the point of exploding.

"The more we work, the more we will get, first its fish, it won't be long before more animals can make it through and when the barrier comes down there will be more land to grow on. More space to live. Isn't that something you would like? Something that will improve everybody's life?" Cad nodded slowly; it was making sense although Cad never really enjoyed being surrounded by a barrier anyway.

"Why not just take it down?" Cad asked. "Why drag it out like you have?" Cassius sat back in his chair and huffed.

"It's not as simple as we thought, we have been maintaining that barrier for centuries. Strengthening it day by day, we have not got the power to destroy it, but we can wait for it to fade. It may take many months yet, perhaps even years, but during this time we have to get people on our side into wanting the barrier gone. If we went and told all the town now, I don't think they would be too happy, would they? They don't have as much common sense as you or me, they will not see what a benefit it would be for it to be gone." Cad felt a sense of happiness, finally someone who saw like Cad did, it would be a good thing wouldn't it? Perhaps it is the best way to go. "We just need your help, Cad."

"Help?" Cad asked, bolting upright. "What do you need help with?" He felt uneasy about where this conversation was going.

"We need you to not mention what happened tonight. We need you to completely forget about it. We won't tell your parents about your midnight wanders, and we won't put you to trial for it." The talk about the barrier had taken Cad's mind off the two dead councillors, but now he felt guilty as his mind went back to them. The talk of not putting him to trial made him realise he did not really have a choice.

The shame it would bring to his parents was unthinkable. He could not think of a single person who had been brought to trial in his lifetime.

"But what will happen?" Cad asked. "Their families need to know. You can't just have people go missing."

"We will sort all of that out Cad," Cassius said firmly, "We don't expect you to deal with anything like this, all we ask for is your word and your secrecy." Cad stared at him, and then the table. He thought about how he was going to avoid bringing the mages to justice for murder so that he would not get into trouble, was he really going to let murderers walk around the town? Yet for the things they said and their reasons, it made some kind of sense.

"I don't know" Cad mumbled, not daring to look Cassius in the eye. Urlwin cleared his throat and Cad jumped, he had almost forgotten he was in the room as he hadn't spoken until now.

"You have dreams, don't you, Cad? It's no secret that you want to become the town's Sword master."

"Yeah, that's true," said Cad "But Pike is young, and I don't think I will be able to."

"Your judging is today, isn't it?" Urlwin asked. Cad was about to reply tomorrow but he realised he had been out all night and it was morning now.

"With all the events that have happened, I think it is best to reschedule the judging for the boys until tomorrow when we are all thinking a little more clearly." Interrupted Cassius. "But yes, it is soon."

"Well, how about if you keep this secret for us." Urlwin said. "Then we can make it, so you are sword master." Cad noticed Cassius shuffle slightly in his seat, Cad thought he must not agree.

"What about Pike?" Cad asked.

"I'm sure we can find another role for him." Urlwin continued. "We have two empty seats on the council, after all. I will be taking one, but your friend Pike will be well taken care of trust me." Cad's heart started pounding. A way to fulfil his dream, but would Pike want to change and would it be fair to force him? No one had been given the option to change roles in a very long time. Not since Cad had been born, anyway. Again, Cad thought of the two dead councillors and then of Linus.

"Why Linus?" He asked.

"He was another one who didn't believe our cause, I'm afraid." Cassius said. "It was a shame really, but he would have ruined everything. We tried to persuade him; we really did. It was not our intention for anyone to die Cad. We just felt that it was for the good of Arcadia. Do you understand?" Cad nodded, but he wasn't sure they were talking about murder as if it was a necessity. If Cad didn't agree, would they just murder him as part of this plan, the thought of it gave him a cold sweat.

"OK." Cad said, "But I don't want to replace the Swordmaster. I want to work the farm like my Dad." Cad thought that if he had become the Swordmaster because of this, he would always feel the guilt of what he had to do to get the role. It felt as though it should have been a tough decision, he was giving up his dream after all, but he wasn't sure if he could deal with that day in day out. Cassius looked at him, surprised.

"If that's what you want, then fine." Cassius said some warmth returning to his voice. "We can see to it," He paused, "and you will agree to our terms?"

"Yes." Cad said simply, again not making eye contact. He felt sick about what he was doing, but he knew he didn't really have a choice. Besides, this is what would be best for the town. It wouldn't be long before he was free. He then made the snap decision in his head, as soon as that barrier came down, he was off, leaving the town and its people behind. He would miss his parents and Wil, but he would do what he loved and knew that he needed to get away from the truth of what had happened. He didn't think his parents would ever forgive him if they knew.

"Ok, let's get you home." Cassius said getting out of his chair and offering his hand to Cad. "I think we need to have a conversation with your parents." He said shaking his hand firmly.

Cad followed Cassius from the mage hall to his parents' house.

The fatigue had really set in now, Cad could feel how heavy his legs were as he walked. Every blink was a struggle to reopen his eyes. They did not speak on the walk. Cad kept his head low to the ground; it was early morning now and Cad knew his parents would be awake, so there was no escaping being out at night.

Cad put his hand on the door handle to let himself in, but Cassius pulled him back, he rapped on the door three times, Cad's father answered shortly.

"Good morning, Gentar!" Cassius said in a cheery voice.

"Hello Cassius." His father said suspiciously. "Dyne said you would be calling by, what sort of trouble has my boy got himself into." He gestured for them both to come in Cad's father didn't look at him, but he could tell he was furious, his face was bright red, and his forehead wrinkled. Cassius remained in the doorway though.

"Oh, no trouble at all." He said chuckling. "He's just been anxious about his judging today. He tried to sneak into our hall this morning and see if he could get any clues as to what will be happening. There's no harm though. He's not the first to try to find out if we have decided what role to give him, but like I told him, we decide on the day. We've had a good chat about it though, and we both think it would be best to save it until tomorrow. We have had some terrible news last night," Cassius used a more sombre tone. "that we need to deal with today and both Cad and Wil have had restless nights needlessly worrying so could do with a bit more rest."

"Terrible news?" Cad's father asked.

"I cannot go into too much detail right now, but we will call a meeting at midday for everyone to attend.... Probably best if the boys stay home though." He said nodding towards Cad.

"I see, is there anything I can do?" Cad's father asked.

"No no, it's all under control, well as much as it can be. I will see you at midday and Cad, I will see you tomorrow. Try to get some rest and don't worry, come talk to me if you need any more help." He waved goodbye and strolled away. Cad's father shut the door behind him and turned to Cad. His mother stood in the doorway with her arms on her hips.

"Why haven't you talked to us about how worried you were?" Cad's mother asked him. Cad could not answer. His lip wobbled, if he started to speak, he would start crying. He knew it. Partly because of exhaustion, partly because of everything that has happened in the night, but also partly because he was safe at home with his parents. Cad's eyes filled with tears. His mother's face turned from stern to soft. "What happened, my boy? What's wrong?"

"I... Don't... Know," said Cad between sobs. "I'm just so scared."

"Oh honey." His mother said, flattening his hair. He could not remember the last time he had cried in front of his parents. "The judging will not be bad at all; you are worrying over nothing. It's pretty much guaranteed that you will get a farm role. And if you don't, we are proud of you no matter what." Cad just sobbed, holding his mother. He wanted to tell his parents everything and it frustrated him that he couldn't. Would he feel like this forever? "Come on, let's get you into bed. You need some rest." She said pulling Cad up off the couch. Cad spotted his father looking uncomfortable, he didn't know whether to leave them or join in, so he stood in an awkward half getting up pose whilst they went to Cads room.

"What are you like," Cad's mother said pulling the sheets over him in his bed, she stroked his head whilst she embraced him. "Nothing bad will happen you know; it is not as scary as you might think."

"I know mum." Cad said, angry at himself for not explaining. "I think I am just overthinking things. I will be better once I get some sleep."

"That's right," His mother said with a smile, "Now you get some rest, there's some stew in the pot if you want some later while your father and I are at this meeting, do you know what this big news it?" Cad froze, he nodded slowly, his mother sensed how tense the subject made him. "Let's not worry about it right now then, you get some sleep." She kissed Cad on the forehead, "We love you, son."

"Love you mum." Cad replied, it had been a long time since they had said that to each other, Cad didn't have unaffectionate parents, but they knew emotions like this made him feel uneasy, right now though it comforted him. As soon as Cad got himself comfortable, his entire body sunk into the bed. He was so tired. He closed his eyes, but all he could think of was everyone who had died. Would there be more? Three deaths in such a short period would be the biggest news this town has had in generations.

He could hear his parents talk in hushed voices, starting with how worried they were for Cad, ending with speculation for the news. Cad tossed and turned before he entered a dreamless slumber.

8

C ad woke up feeling groggy, he did not know how long he had been asleep; it was light outside but for all he knew he could have slept all the way through given how tired he was. His eyes stung from all of the crying and lack of sleep, he wiped them and pulled himself out of bed, although he still felt tired, and his joints were stiff. He had made himself the stew and looked out of the window. It was close to midday. His parents would be at the council meeting where they would learn about the dead council men. Cad was curious about how they were going to say it, or what they would say had happened. He pushed the thoughts out of his head. It's nothing to do with me. He ate his soup slowly, each mouthful was difficult to swallow, his stomach was still turning, and his mind was full of a million different thoughts. He could feel the tears welling up again. He really didn't know what to do with himself.

Cad got himself changed and walked out of his back door. Just behind his house, he kept his sword and his targets. He had lost his good training sword last night; he could not remember if he had dropped it in the tunnels or when Cassius had grabbed him. His memory was cloudy of that night. He still had another that his father sometimes used when he was practicing with Cad. As he felt the pummel of the sword in his hand, his mind became clearer. He set up his training dummy and worked on some drills. He practiced in silence, the only noise being the whack of his sword on the straw dummy and his footsteps as he glided back and forth ducking and dodging imaginary swipes. He loved duelling; it had been too long since he had done any. Wil was the last time he had duelled anyone. He could duel a lot more if he was the sword master. Bad thought, Cad realised, and started thinking of other things in between his strikes. His arms and legs ached, but he still spun gracefully around the dummy, the air in his lungs made him feel better and his head definitely felt clearer. I need to do more of what I enjoy instead of roaming around the tunnels and finding…. Bad thought, Cad shook his head, pushing himself harder and harder. After a while he was satisfied, and his arms ached so he came back in to wash himself.

The door of his house rattled, and he knew it must be his parents returning. He quickly jumped back into bed and pulled the cover over him. He wasn't quite ready to talk to his parents about things just yet; he wanted a bit more time to just enjoy the rush of the swordplay, pretending that he didn't have a care in the world. He heard his bedroom door creak open but kept his eyes tight shut. He felt someone sit next to him on the bed and jostle his shoulder lightly. Going by the size he could feel it was his father, he opened his eyes slowly pretending to just wake up.

"How are you feeling, son?" His father asked.

"Still a bit run down." Cad replied, he didn't want to elaborate.

"Listen, I know what happened, it can't be easy being the first to see those dead bodies, but no one blames you. Everyone knows Urlwin killed them." Cad shot up in his bed.

"How do they know that?" Cad asked, surprised.

"He told everyone," His father said, "Don't worry about it though."

"Why did he tell everyone? I don't understand."

"Meldon and Bryce had a plan to murder all the mages, Cassius had found some of their documents. Luckily, Urlwin is spryer than you would believe. Between him and Galloway they fought them off, shame they got killed in the process though." Cad tried to process what his father was telling him.

"So, they were planning to kill the mages?" Cad asked. "Why?"

"It scared them that the mages were planning to take over the council, it was just a strong mage prejudice."

"Linus..." Cad began, he found he could not finish. They have spun quite a lie, and now Cad was part of the web. What would his father think if he knew the truth?

"Yes, unfortunately Linus is dead. They have not officially stated that it was Meldon and Bryce, but they are sure. The council is reviewing the evidence and will make the final call tomorrow." Cad could not make sense of what was going on. He tried to wrap his head around the whole situation, his father saw his expression and looked concerned. "It's nothing you need to worry about though boy." His father said ruffling his hair, "you just focus on your judging tomorrow. I know Hamish is definitely going to sponsor you..." Cad's father looked at him. "I know it's not exactly what you want, but it's the best of the situation, I think. Plus, a lot of changes are happening. Who knows what's going to happen next?"

"Changes?" Cad asked

"Yeah, your friend Wil had his judging today, they rushed it through I think because they wanted him on the council."

"Wil's on the council?" Cad shouted, as he jumped up in his bed, "That's great." Cad was genuinely pleased for his friend. He knew that would have been a dream of his but knew that there wouldn't be space on the council for years. Then Cad wondered if Wil had made some sort of deal with Cassius like he had? Was that why?

"Yes, it was a bit of a shock, but with everything going on they wanted to fill the spaces quickly," His father said, "Urlwin has the other seat."

"Urlwin? But he's a mage?" Cad said in disbelief. Now he wasn't as happy for Wil as he had first been. It would probably be a scary experience for him to be working alongside Cassius and Urlwin.

"With everything going on, they thought it would be a good idea to improve relations with mages," Cad's father said, "Not sure if I fully understand myself, if I'm honest." He stroked his beard in thought, "But again, nothing we need to worry about. "How about we go out and practice some duelling?" Cad's father asked. Cad hesitated and his father looked out the window, he laughed. "And I thought you had been sleeping." Cad laughed too. It felt good, it had been so long since he had laughed, I'll tidy that up before your mother sees. Cad smiled at his Dad and laid back down on his pillow before jumping out of bed and following him, helping him put the targets away.

"I'm going to go and see Wil, see if he is back yet, congratulate him on his role."

"No problem but don't be out too long though, your mother will worry. Let's get tomorrow out of the way before we have another adventure?" His father chuckled, Cad nodded and made his way towards Wil's home. He wondered how Wil felt, probably a mixture of happy and scared. Cad wondered how he would feel if he was in his position. He knocked on Wil's door, as the door opened, he noticed Wil looked pale.

"Hey, congratulations on joining the council. How are you feeling?" Cad tried his best to be upbeat. He hadn't seen Wil since they caught them coming out of the tunnel, but if Wil's experience was anything like Cads, then he knew it would have been tough.

"Hey, thanks," Wil said, not meeting Cad's eye, "They have given me a lot of work to get through, so I need to be going."

"Oh OK." Said Cad, "Everything alright?"

"Yeah, yeah, I'll just see you tomorrow, ok?" Wil said still not meeting Cad's eye.

"Sure, see you tomorrow." Cad said deflated, Wil quickly shut the door. Cad became annoyed, it would have been nice to talk things through with him, he thought, but it was quite a difficult evening and Wil copes with things much differently than I do. He still thought his behaviour was strange. Then, with Cassius and Urlwin leaning over his shoulder, Cad would probably be the same. Cad looked at his home and then to the path that took him to his den. Not today, he thought, returning home, he wanted to clear his head, but he also wanted family close by. His Father was right, no adventures.

He returned home and his father gave him a quizzical stare.

"That was quick." He said and Cad shrugged his shoulders.

"Too busy for the likes of me now that he's got a job." Cad laughed. He didn't go in his room but sat near the stove. The warmth from the fire soothed him, and he remained in the company of his parents for the rest of the day. He felt safe here, and this is where he wanted to stay, trying not to think about tomorrow.

9

Cad's mother bounced around the house, preparing for the day.

"Make sure you have your breakfast, I've put out your best clothes, let me sort that hair out." She was hectically running around, Cad smiled, he was relaxed today, even if his mother was not. She had berated him for not moving quick enough, but in a fun way. His father was sat at the table giving him advice.

"Wait until your spoken to before you speak, be polite, listen to what they say, do not argue if you disagree. Keep calm." The words were going in one ear and out the other, though. Cad munched on his bread and focused on anything he could apart from his judging. He should relax. He knew where he was going, which was more than some could say, but he was still on edge. There was a knock at the door, which pulled him out of his thoughts and into the present. His father answered. He could see Freida at the door.

"Hello Gentar, you have been summoned for a meeting at one hour before midday." That was one hour before Cad's judging.

"I'm summoned? What for?" Cad's father asked. Cad's mother had stopped what she was doing and stared at them, Cad had put down his bread and stared at Freida. You can't turn down a summon, and it's never a good thing, Cad thought.

"We will explain it when you arrive at the council, sorry for the short notice but because of new testimony it cannot be delayed." Freida turned and walked off, Cad's father stared at the open door for a while before shutting it and returning to his seat.

"What's going on, Dad?" Cad asked.

"I'm not too sure son," his Father said, "New testimony? I don't even know what it's to do with. I guess we'll find out soon," he said, looking out at the sun. "We are all practically ready, we can all go together," his father said, "I don't want to miss walking with you to your judging, it's a once in a lifetime event." His father said and he smiled, but Cad could tell he was worried, Cad worried too. What could they possibly want with his father?

As they left, they walked together.

"You know Cad, you're officially a man after today." His father said as he stared into the distance. He knew the summoning was troubling him.

"I don't feel any different than I did yesterday." Cad said laughing, but the thought hit him that he was no longer a child, after today, he was a man. They would expect him to do grown-up things.

"So, we will make preparations for you and Casilda." His mother said.

"What, already?" Cad asked, he had completely forgotten about Casilda. He pulled on the sleeves of his jacket. This is the stuff he should have been focusing on rather than the secrets and the murders. They had robbed him of his opportunity to think things through, and now each moment was hitting him like a train.

"Come on, I thought you liked her." His mother nudged him playfully.

"I do its just, I'm not ready."

"But you're a man now, son," His father said, "That's the way it goes. Plus, she will need to have children soon before she gets too old." Cad went pale. He hadn't even thought of being a father. His parents could see how uncomfortable he looked, "Well maybe we don't need to talk about this right now." His father continued. "But these are the things you should have been planning instead of playing with your sword all the time." Cad didn't argue, he was right, he had no one to blame for not thinking about all of this, he should have known. He had just tried so hard to not think about it. It shouldn't be a shock. When they got to the hall, Freida and Cassius stood at the doors.

"We need to speak with you, Gentar." Freida said sternly, "Come with us."

"You two can wait in the hall." Cassius said putting his hand on Cad's shoulder and Cad froze at the touch. He was not very comfortable with what was going on. "Your father will be out to join you soon." Cad and his mother took their seats at the front of the hall. Cad looked nervously at his mother; she just shrugged her shoulders. They sat in silence for a while before his mother spoke.

"You know this thing with Casilda. It will be ok; she is really quite fond of you." Cad just grumbled and looked at the floor. "You know me, and your father didn't feel like we were a suitable match up at first but look at us now. I don't think anyone could make me happier."

"But Casilda is so much older than me, she's almost your age."

"So, she will be sensible and be able to keep you in check. Trust me, young girls aren't that great, and you know how small a number we are, Casilda is the best of the lot, count yourself lucky." She was right there. Cad didn't like to think of women, they were all so much older or so much younger than him. He would have rather been alone. He wondered if he would leave her behind too when the barrier came down. This made him feel guilty, he knew that he wouldn't hesitate and wondered how she would feel about that.

The doors slammed open, and they both jolted around to see the noise, Cad's father stormed towards them, his face was red.

"What happened?" Cad and his mother said in unison.

"They are questioning me about Linus's murder! They think I had something to do with it!"

"What why?" His mother said, all the colour drained from Cad's face. What was going on?

"They found notes in Linus' drawers saying that he had discovered that I had purposely killed that cow and that I am suspected of killing him to cover it up. I mean to take a man's life over something so trivial. It's ridiculous."

"Did you kill the cow?" His mother asked, given the tone in her voice, Cad had a feeling she knew the answer.

"It doesn't matter!" His father was flapping his arms around as he talked, "I wouldn't kill a man to hide it!"

"Did you tell them that you killed the cow?" His mother asked bluntly. His father looked at her stunned for a while, then sunk his head in shame.

"No, I thought that it would make things worse."

"Worse?" His mother was angry. "I knew that something was wrong. Why did you do it?"

"It had been so long since we had had any good meat, I was frustrated. I felt like we hadn't eaten properly in months. I was greedy, but this has nothing to do with the fact that Linus is dead. I would have taken the blame for it."

"But you must be able to see how this looks! Oh Gentar, what have you done." His mother said, putting her face in her hands. Cad was on edge but remained still. They couldn't actually blame his father, could they? He knows that he didn't kill Linus. Cassius and Urlwin know that Cad knows, they would not make him lie to get his father in trouble, would they? They couldn't.

"They are trialling me today. Right now, in fact. There's no way they can blame me for this. I'd never kill someone." Cad's father was shaking, Cad was afraid to move or speak. He knew that he wouldn't let his father get in trouble for this. He would tell everyone the truth about everything before that would happen.

The doors opened, and the six councillors entered. Wil did not look at Cad as he made his way to his seat. Was this why Wil was so dismissive of Cad yesterday, did he know all along?

"Due to Bryce's unfortunate demise, I will lead the council from now on." Cassius said looking at Cads father. "We have reviewed the evidence and the testimonies you have given us. We have concluded that we cannot prove it was you that killed Linus."

"What do you mean you cannot prove? That makes it sound like you're saying it is me anyway?" His father shouted.

"We will not be holding you responsible for the death of Linus, and that is all we are prepared to discuss on the matter." Cad felt relieved, although his father he could tell, was still angry. "However, we have found testimony from Linus's quarters that you were responsible for the death of the mother cow, you purposely let it die and you stole the meat from it for you and your family. Would you call these accusations false?" Cad's father stood in silence for a while.

"No." He said hanging his head.

"Hamish, would you agree on the punishment of allowing Gentar to continue working the farm, but no longer working with the animals." Cad turned, he hadn't even notice Hamish had come in. A few others from the town were in here too. The gossip from this would spread quickly, Cad could feel himself going red. He noticed Casilda was sat not far behind too although she was probably here to see his judging.

"Yup I agree with that, going to need some new farmhands though." Hamish grumbled.

"Then it has been decided," Cassius said, hitting the gong behind his chair, "Now, apologies that we had to do that, let us continue with your judging Cad." Cassius stood and walked to the front of the tables. He held his arms out wide.

"Today marks the day where young Cadderick is no longer a boy, but he has become a man. Cadderick has been a bright child and is well liked by the people in this town. He has shown an exceptional aptitude to duelling and has been extremely useful in supporting the farm. Is there anyone here today who would wish to sponsor Cadderick in providing him a role within the village?" Cad tensed in his seat, waiting for Hamish.

"I would," Hamish spoke, Cad breathed out, "He has worked on my farm before, he knows what he is doing, he would solve my lack of hands."

"Is there anyone else wishing to sponsor Cadderick?" Cassius asked and was met with silence. "Very well. The council will discuss this when we reconvene. Cadderick, do you approve of your future wife that the council has selected?"

"Yes." Cad said.

"And Casilda, do you approve of Cadderick as a future husband?"

"I do." Said Casilda. Cad could read no emotion from her face. Was she truly happy with the situation?

"Very well. The council will now meet to discuss your role in the village and a date for the ceremony. Is there anything else you would like to tell us when making these decisions?" Cad's mind raced. Don't make them, was his initial thought, but he knew that it had to be done.

"No." Cadderick said.

"Then we will discuss and reconvene shortly, please remain in the hall." Cassius said, he walked out of a side door and the five other councillors followed him. Cad sat in silence as his mother patted his shoulder.

"You will be fine." She whispered to him. Cad looked at his father, who was still bright red. Cad thought he may explode. He looked over at Cad.

"Don't worry son, this will all blow over soon." Cad felt ashamed. Could he have stopped this if he had told the truth from the beginning? He felt guilty, he knew the animals were his father's favourite part of working on the farm, he hardly worked the crops anymore because of his gift with the animals. He wondered if he could persuade the Council to change their mind. He may even threaten that he will reveal the truth. Cad began making plans in his head, he could sort this mess out, Hamish would help too. He knew how good his father was. He heard the doors open again; it was a quick discussion and Cad took this as a good sign.

"After meeting we have decided that the wedding will take place one week from today. We will begin preparations tomorrow." Cad smiled at Casilda, more because he had too, he didn't really care about this, although he knew that he should. He just wanted to know what he would spend the rest of his life doing. "Finally due to the nature of Gentar's crime. The council feels that it is not appropriate for you to take a role upon the farm alongside your father." There was an audible gasp from his mother and his father was no longer beet-root red. He glanced back at Hamish in shock. His jaw was clenched and his face red, "Councillor Wil has a new position for Cadderick." Cad relaxed a bit; Wil was deciding where he would go. Where could he put him though, there wasn't a lot left for him to do? Wil stood and took Cassius' place.

"Cad has shown a great aptitude in swordplay," Cad's heart started beating, swordmaster? But what about Pike? "He has however shown little interest in anything else. I am approving Cad for a position with the Mages. To work the barrier and maintain our town's defence." Cad's heart sank. His best friend had just betrayed him, giving him the one job that he knew would bring shame.

"You can't do this!" Cad's father shouted, "Put me with the mages and let Cad work the farm, he will be more useful there." Cad's mother was crying, Cad looked around. This couldn't be happening. They were making him a mage. Urlwin had promised him, this had to be some kind of joke.

"Order," shouted Cassius, "The boy will become a mage, you may take up residence in the mages halls and Casilda can live with you there after the wedding." Cad looked at Casilda. She looked as if she had just stepped in something foul. Cad looked around; someone was going to tell him this was all a joke.

"No." Cad shouted. The hall fell silent. "I won't." Cad's mother tried to pull him back. Urlwin stood up.

"Yes, you will, you will embrace it like the rest of us have. We have already had our fair share of hate towards the mages, and this is the attitude that brings it. You will spend the night with your parents, but tomorrow morning I expect you and your belongings at the mage hall where you WILL work alongside us in maintaining the barrier." Cad looked at his parents. They were both speechless. What was Urlwin trying to do with Cad and his family? Cad could feel himself fill up with tears once again.

"I won't do it." Cad sobbed, and with that he bolted out of the door.

10

Cad ran, tears pouring from his eyes, everything was a mess, and he didn't know what to do. His father had been taken away from the job he loved and accused of murder, and it was all Cad's fault. On top of all that, Cad was now being made to become a mage. The shame his parents must feel and the shame the entire town would throw towards them. He kept running, straight past his house and into the woods, towards his den. He sat on the ground and put his head in his hands, he hated this place. Everything that happened here was making things worse and worse. He wanted to get out. He needed to get out.

"I hate you." Cad shouted at the barrier. He started beating it with his fists. The force pushing back hurt his knuckles, but he didn't care. He picked up a large stick and hit the barrier with it. "Stupid." Whack "Barrier." Whack. "Hate." Whack "Being trapped." Whack. The force of hitting the barrier the last time caused Cad to lose his balance. He fell on his back and threw the stick in a tantrum. He cried into his hands again.

Cad didn't know how long he sat there for. He was regaining some control of his emotions. He wiped the tears from his eyes and just sat there, staring beyond the barrier. It made everything on the outside look grey and dull. He wondered if that was the barrier or if it was the colour of things on the outside. His attention caught something on the other side of the barrier.

There was a woman, Cad had never seen someone so attractive. Her hair was bright pink and well maintained, not wild and tangled like he was used to. She appeared to be floating whilst walking, her clothes were not modest, and a lot of her body was showing, the dress she had on seemed to be made of bright materials. He was mesmerised; he was sure this was the woman he had seen before. She made her way towards the barrier facing him; he did the same.

She held out her hand and placed her palm flat on the barrier. Cad slowly lifted his hand to meet hers. He placed it on the barrier. There was no resistance pushing him back. The lady smiled at Cad and he blushed. He closed his eyes and felt an odd sensation surround his body. He couldn't breathe. He fought for air; he couldn't see, he was trapped. Then as quickly as it went, it all came back. He opened his eyes and took a deep breath. His hand was still up and against the barrier, but something was odd. He looked through the barrier, that was his den. He turned around slowly. Forests as far as the eye could see, a deeper green than he was used to and mountains in the near distance. His heart raced. He was on the other side of the barrier.

Cad smiled. He did it; he didn't know how, but he was out. Then the crushing realisation hit him. Now where? He had nowhere to go; he pushed at the barrier but couldn't get back in. He panicked.

"I'm sorry." He shouted trying to push his way back in, but the barrier pushed him back. "Let me in!" he said, beating it with his fists. He gave up, his heart still racing. He did not know where to go or what was out here, he had no food, no water, and no sword. He had no chance. He did the only thing he thought was sensible and started to make his way through the forest and towards the mountain. His mind numb, he just walked forwards. The woods were denser on this side, the trees greener, everything seemed much brighter. Even the sun felt hotter than it had. Did the barrier stop all this? He ambled through the woods, stepping over branches and logs. He walked in a trance, not taking in the luscious fields and woods that surrounded him.

"Get down on the ground and put your arms on your head!" A voice shouted, pulling Cad out of his trance. He looked around to see who had spoken. "I said down on the ground, hands on your head or you will lose it." Cad saw the speaker; they had a metal armour surrounding their body and face. More importantly, they had one of the longest swords Cad had ever seen, and it was pointing straight at him.

Urlwin sat at his desk, pouring himself a glass of whisky. He had chosen one of his oldest and most favourite malt tonight. He was celebrating. The entire plan is coming together better than I imagined, he thought to himself. With him taking place on the council, Cassius acting like a lapdog and Wil in his pocket, he had pretty much majority control of the town. It wouldn't be long before he made his next move. The last loose thread was Cadderick. He wondered what the best way to deal with him would be, but that time would come. Comply or Die were the choices he would give. He had his father as leverage though, his place within Arcadia was on a knifes edge. The boy was still to be found, but there was not a lot of places to hide in this town. It wouldn't be long and if Teague and Zane got to him first, well, that would make things a lot easier for him.

He took a sip of the whisky and savoured the taste; they don't make it like this anymore. He imagined Cassius's face if he knew Urlwin's actual plan and it made him chuckle. He pulled out an old book from under the floorboard and continued studying it. The library had taught him everything, all about the town, the people who made it and why they were here. If people knew, they would be as angry as he was. Perhaps if the people of the town didn't look down on him as they did, he would consider working with them instead of following his own destiny.

It wouldn't be long before he was rid of this filthy place and could restore the full power that he should have been born with, the power that he deserved. Then everyone would regret ever treating him the way that they did. Sneering at him, classing him as a useless dolt. They would pay. That's if they survived what he had planned. He would deal with this town first, then the people who had trapped him in here.

11

"How did you get all the way out here? You don't even have any supplies. What are you running from?" The plated stranger asked.

"I don't know." Was all Cad could say, laying on the ground with his hands on his head. The figure walked around him, studying him and then they picked him up.

"What do you mean you don't know?" The stranger asked, removing their helmet. It shocked Cad to see that it was a woman, but not like any woman he had ever seen before. She was big, not fat, but even with the plate mail on he could tell that this was a well-built woman. Much bigger than Pike, even. He lost trail of his thoughts looking at this woman, he struggled to focus, he wasn't really sure what had happened, or even what was happening now. "What's your name?" She asked.

"Cad, I'm Cad."

"And your family name?" she asked.

"Err Cadderick." He answered, not really sure what she meant by family name.

"Your name is Cad Cadderick?"

"No, just Cadderick, but everyone calls me Cad." The stranger tilted her head, looking at him bemused. Cad was just as confused as she looked.

"Which city are you from?" she asked. Cad looked back at his town, he could just make out the barrier through the trees, he hadn't got as far as he had thought. He just pointed. "Arcadia?" She asked and Cad nodded, finally something they both understood.

"What are you hiding?" the stranger said, pulling out her sword. "I'm not as stupid as you think. Arcadia has been sealed for centuries."

"I know!" Cad said, swallowing hard whilst looking at the point of the sword, "One minute I was in there, the next I was on the other side." He had decided not to mention the lady with the pink hair. Cad wasn't exactly sure that he hadn't imagined it. She stared at him for a while.

"For some reason, I believe you." She said, putting her sword in her sheath. "You know how crazy that sounds though? No one has gotten in or out of that place in centuries."

"I know." Cad replied. "I lived there." She grabbed a rope and tied Cads hands together. He tried to pull away, but she was a lot stronger than him. "What are you doing?" He shouted.

"If you really are from Arcadia," She said, "Then that means you're dangerous. I'm not taking any chances." Her tone had changed from bemused to stern. She pulled tightly on the ropes around his hands, and they hurt.

"I'm not dangerous, I don't have a weapon, you could easily defeat me." Cad pleaded; he didn't know where this was going to lead.

"I know all about you lot, the mages." She said pulling him along. Cad gulped, how did she know he was a mage and why did she think that made him dangerous? Cad had no clue how to respond, so he just followed her in silence. They reached a clearing in the woods where he could see a pair of horses, one of them was huge, bigger than any he had seen before or even could have imagined, it was almost a silver colour and Cad could tell that this was a strong horse, it was lean, and he could see the horse's muscles. The other horse was much different, it was a lot smaller, its hair was a dark grey, it even looked unfocused, it was stocky but far from toned. It had lots of bags strapped to his back and it hadn't even noticed the two newcomers walk into the clearing, it just carried on eating.

The stranger picked Cad up before putting him onto the small horse; he gave no resistance.

"Where are we going?" He asked.

"Well, if you are from Arcadia, I'm sure you will be worth a lot. The king will pay handsomely for you." And with that, the stranger tied Cads leg around the small horse before fastening his chest with rope so that he was lying on the animal. She then emptied what looked like food out of a cloth bag and put it over Cad's head. He could see nothing, and there was a strong smell of cheese. Cad just lay there, not making a sound. He closed his eyes and wished he had just stayed home. The further away he got from Arcadia, the more he wanted to be back.

Cad lay on the horse, his stomach hurting from both hunger and from being led awkwardly on the horse. Every footstep taken jolted him, and he could feel it shake through his body. Cad had no more tears left to cry, he just felt empty. He did not know what to do, where to go or what was happening. The first-person Cad had met had treated him like a dangerous person, and yet she was the one in armour holding a sword. He thought about who this King was and why he would pay for Cad, what would he be paying for exactly? His head hurt with all the thoughts going through his head.

Cad suddenly realised that they had come to a stop, he could hear nothing, and he wondered where his jailor was. What was she doing? He tried to scuffle slightly, turned his head to get the sack off his head, but he was tied too tightly. He gasped as the bag came off his head and a hand around his mouth. It was the lady who had captured him; he knew that he should be more worried but was relieved it was a familiar face; she looked at him with a finger to her lips.

"I'm going to release you, but you need to listen carefully." She whispered. "There's a large clan of Elfkins tracking us. I don't know why they are coming, but we need to outrun them. There are too many to fight and I don't think we can avoid them. I've never seen so many in one place." Cad nodded but didn't really understand what an Elfkin was, but he assumed that meant they were in trouble. "If it comes down to it, can you fight?" The woman asked and Cad nodded.

"Yeah, I'm feeling quite weak, but I imagine I could probably put up a bit of a fight." He said, looking at her sword. "I was the best in my town." She looked at him with concern.

"If you try any funny business, I will cut your head off before you'd even raise your hand, and if you think getting rid of me will help then God help you if the Elfkin catch you." Cad looked at her as she said this, their eyes met, although she was being quite threatening, he was relaxed, Cad nodded. They seemed to be at an understanding. He noticed she was no longer wearing her metal armour but was in a lighter leathery one. "Can you ride?" She asked. Cad shook his head.

"We only had a couple, they just pulled carts." Cad responded and his captor sighed.

"Just hold on tight and try not to fall off. I'm not going to leave you to their mercy like I should, but I'm not going to sacrifice myself for you either. Understand?" Again, Cad nodded, his jaw was agape, he did not know what to say, he did not know what was chasing them but a part of him was excited about finally being in a fight, a life-or-death situation. It was what he yearned for, but his stomach was turning in anticipation. Would his first real swordfight be his last? He had never had stakes that were life and death before. He sat on the horse, his companion shouted, and the two horses ran.

Cad struggled to grip the reigns, his heart was beating fast, and he was struggling to maintain balance on the horse. He thought he could hear noises behind him, but he was not willing to look back in case he lost his balance; he closed his eyes and leant forward. He wondered where he would get his sword from, but he could only see the one that she was carrying. He assumed it would be a much shorter sword in one of the bags. Cad felt a whistle behind him, and in the corner of his eye he saw an arrow hit a tree to the left of him. They were being chased. He felt as though he was going to be sick.

What if one of those arrows hit him in the back? He would be dead before he even had a chance to fight.

"Keep going!" He heard his companion shout from in front of him, he knew that his horse was struggling, he was carrying both Cad and the supplies, although he had noticed that they had lost a lot of their bags. Cad gripped the reigns tighter and pushed on. He still focussed on trying to keep his balance and watching where his companion was going. They were running through a woodland path, so they kept pushing on straight. Suddenly the horse in front shot off to a path on the right and his horse followed, Cad was not prepared for this and the momentum flung him off the horse.

He hit the ground with a thud and landed on a soft mossy bank but still he felt his body judder at the impact, it knocked the wind out of him, and he hit his head on something hard. The pain immediately rushed to his head. He heard the sounds of many footsteps approaching and then everything faded to black.

12

Cad came to, his vision was blurry, and he could hear a commotion around him, he grabbed his head where it hurt, there was a large lump. His senses came back, and he could tell that there was a fight going on. He got to his feet. He could see the creatures that were chasing him. They stood like humans but were covered in red fur; they wore loose leathery vests and trousers. They had no shoes but had giant paws for feet. He sniffed at Cad with its snout and stared, the creature's eyes were a piercing blue colour as he inched towards him and Cad stood frozen in fear. He couldn't move away, his legs had decided not to listen to his brain, all he could do was stare at the creature as it approached. There was a loud crack and the creature's head came tumbling from his shoulders next to Cad. The headless body fell to its knees before laying on the floor. Cad still looked on in shock.

"A little help would be nice!" He heard, he noticed his captor was fighting the creatures, bodies lay on the floor as she danced around, slicing limbs off, stabbing at those who got too close, there was a lot for her to handle as they closed in. Cad panicked, he had no weapon, he looked at the headless torso on the floor, it had a crude axe still in its closed hand. Cad pulled it out, which surprisingly gave some resistance. The axe was too heavy for Cad to swing comfortably, so he had to hold it in two hands. He took a swing at the creature closest to him. It was concentrating on his captor. He swung the axe with all of his might and hit the creature right between the shoulder blades. The axe made a sickening crack as Cad could only assume it broke some bones as it became lodged deep within its back, he tried to pick the axe back up, but he couldn't pry it from the creature, it had gone in too deep.

The noise caused the creatures to turn towards him to see what had just happened. This short moment gave his friend enough time to break out of the circle surrounding her, and Cad heard more limbs fall to the floor. He looked around for another weapon; he picked up a similar axe when an arrow just narrowly missed his hand, hitting the axe and causing him to drop it. He looked to see where the arrow had come from when he saw the creature going for another arrow, a small axe hit him straight in the head, it had come from his captor. There was only one of the creatures left, and it had pinned her to the ground, she was stopping it from driving a sword into her chest, holding the dagger the creature held as much as strongly as she could. She looked at Cad.

"Please," She gasped, almost pleading, "Help me." Cad panicked, he didn't know what to do, so he just charged, he tackled the creature with such force they both began rolling on the floor, Cad's head was still throbbing. When he pinned the creature to the floor, they both struggled until his captor came along and drove her own dagger through its head. Cad rolled off the creature, panting, exhausted. He felt sick at the smell and the sight of the surrounding blood. He sat there trying to catch his breath.

"You made that a lot more difficult than it needed to be." The woman said to him, readjusting her own leather armour, and wiping the blood from her sword.

"Couldn't find a weapon." Cad puffed, sitting up. Trying not to look at all of the dismembered body parts that surrounded him.

"Couldn't you have just used your magic?" She asked.

"What use would that do?" Cad asked confused.

"I don't know, fireball? Lightning? What can you do?"

"Nothing like that!" Cad said, almost laughing.

"I thought you were a mage from Arcadia?" The woman asked. "Or was that a lie? I knew there was something strange about your story. No one comes and goes to Arcadia."

"I am a mage from Arcadia." Cad said, feeling unhappy to admit it. "But mages can't do much, they can only make heat, but everyone can do that."

"Like fire?" The woman asked, "Show me"

"Not quite fire." Cad explained, he held out his hands and used his focus to generate the heat in his hands. "Come here, I'll show you." He moved closer to her and held out his hands to grab hers. She hesitated at first but put her hands in his.

"What that's it?" The woman laughed.

"That's all any of us can do." Cad said. "We just create warmth into a panel and that keeps the barrier strong."

"Well, if I ever need to keep my mead warm, I'll make sure that you're holding it." She laughed and she sat down, trying to rub some blood from her face. "So, you're sure that's all anyone from Arcadia can do? It's not anything like the stories that I've heard at all."

"What have you heard?" Cad asked.

"Well, Arcadia is supposed to be a prison of the world's most dangerous mages. Whose magic is unmatched. The prison was created years ago though, so it was more of a myth than fact. There are lots of different versions, but that's the most accepted one." Cad didn't know what to say, he just laughed.

"No, we don't have any dangerous magic, we can barely boil a kettle, and it's not a prison. We keep the barrier to keep away the evil."

"What evil?" The woman asked. Cad paused, unable to answer.

"No one really knows, but I've only met you and those creatures, the creatures tried to kill us, and you tied me up. So probably that." Cad couldn't help but laugh. He even saw this woman smiling. Cad couldn't help noticing that even though she was covered in sweat and blood, he could see she had a beauty about her. Not like any woman he had ever seen in his village, she was stronger than any man he knew and although he was her prisoner, he felt safe with her around. Suddenly a realisation hit him.

"You came back for me?" He said surprised.

"Well, I noticed you fall off the horse, and I did kind of feel guilty about leaving you, you didn't seem like a bad guy, but I was wary."

"Well thank you, I'm not an evil person, I'm just lost, and I can't get back home." Cad's thoughts trailed off, he looked at the ground, the thought filled him with sadness.

"Well Cad Cadderick," The woman said getting to her feet, "I still think our best chance is to go to the king, he will have advisors and scholars who would be better suited to help you. I can show you the way if you'd like, and I promise to not tie you up again. Unless you become a pain in the arse again." She chuckled. Cad nodded, it was a plan and the only plan he had right now so he thought it would be best. "There's a stream just through that clearing that we can use to get ourselves washed up. The horse should be back soon, I trained them to stay away from battle and return when it gets quiet. That's if they survived. The donkey is not so bright, but he should follow." Cad assumed the donkey was the smaller of the two horses, judging from the vacant expression on its face. She pulled Cad up to his feet and they walked towards the stream.

"What are these things?" Cad asked, picking up a small sword from one of the creature's hands. He cleaned it on the grass, trying not to look at the blood surrounding him.

"These are Elfkin." The woman said, "They don't normally organise themselves like this though, something is very strange about it."

"Are they like people?" Cad asked.

"They used to be, a long time ago. They were civilised, again a very long time so its unsure how much of this is fact but they burnt themselves out with magic, they lost their minds and survive on basic instincts of food and aggression, they usually live, in colonies, and come out to get food, but this seemed like an organised attack, they don't normally have the brains to organise something like this. I need to warn the king."

"Who is the king?" Cad asked, he was listening to her but was having a hard time taking it all in. He felt stupid.

"King Rodderick." She laughed. "I forget how isolated from the world you have been." Cad blushed at this. He felt even more stupid. "He is the King of Roshir, his palace is about a four-day ride from here." She looked at the sky. "Straight up that way." She said pointing past the stream. Cad did not want to ask any more questions, he already felt stupid enough. His new friend began taking off her leather armour. Cad admired her physique, she was large but muscular, very well defined. He felt his cheeks burn, and his erection pressing against his trousers.

"I'm sorry I don't even know your name." Cad said.

"You can call me Gwen, and if it helps, maybe don't stare." She laughed, unashamedly washing herself in the spring. Cad tried to cover it up, but he too needed to get clean. He faced away from her and cleaned himself.

13

C ad was enjoying travelling with Gwen, he was still getting used to riding the donkey, who thankfully showed up along with the horse while they bathed and he was enjoying learning about the world, although he was still upset about not being able to return home, this was more what he was looking for. He was in awe of how big the world actually was, he could easily travel the whole of Arcadia in less than a day and now they had been travelling for three days straight, on horseback, in a straight line and they hadn't even gotten out of the woodlands, although the trees were a lot more spaced apart now and they could pick the pace up slightly.

He had learnt that Gwen was a bounty hunter, a very good one apparently as she worked directly for the king. When Cad asked her who she was looking for near Arcadia, she dodged the question, apparently being on a personal errand. Cad didn't push further, but he found it odd that she would be out so far. Then again, he found a lot of things odd in this unknown world but what he was enjoying the most, was the food. Gwen had a selection of dried meats in her sack, and they tasted so much more tender than Cad had experienced. Apparently, they killed the animals young, which gave them a better taste rather than waiting for them to die. Cad thought it was a waste to kill animals so young, but then they had a vast supply that would never run out, so to him it made some sense. He had also enjoyed the cheeses that she had brought; he had never tasted cheese before, which came as a bit of a shock to Gwen, but apart from the meat they were his new favourite food. Gwen kept telling him that these foods were nothing compared to what he could get in the city. His stomach growled every time he thought about the new tastes that he was going to experience.

He had his new sword, which was shorter than he was used to, more like a long knife, dangling from a belt that he had taken off of one of the Elfkin. He felt comfortable having it by his side, although he hoped he would not have reason to use it. It dangled at his side and he thought about Gwen and her sword, and how for a woman of her size, moved so quickly and nimbly, it was almost as if she danced with the sword rather than fought. He admired how good she was with the sword and hoped that he could duel with her; he thought he was a good sword fighter but wondered what it would be like to clash with her, excited for a proper challenge at last.

"Do you think the king can get me home?" Cad asked?

"I'm not sure," Gwen said, "Like I say, no one has been in or out in centuries, but if anyone can find out, it will be him."

"What if he can't?" Cad asked, "What can I do then?"

"You will have to get a job, I suppose. Start a new life. What are you good at? What can you do?"

"I'm good with a sword." Cad added quicky.

"You didn't seem it when the Elfkin attacked." Gwen laughed.

"I didn't have a sword! Remember!" Cad shouted. He didn't want her to think he was not a good fighter. It was the one thing that he knew he was good at.

"Yeah, yeah, I know, don't panic." She laughed. "The Army is always looking for more soldiers." Cad remembered learning about armies and soldiers from Casilda, Large groups of men would show up with weapons and battle. Lots of people would die, but whoever died the least, won. This didn't appeal to Cad.

"I'm more of a one on one, I like to duel." Cad said.

"Well, there's not much call for one-on-one fighting, unless you go to the coliseum, but they are the best of the best. I think you would need some training." Cad got excited.

"Coliseum? What's that?" He asked.

"It's where all the duels happen, usually poor people fight to the death and rich people go to watch. Sometimes they will let people fight for gold or for freedom. It's a really grim experience. I've never enjoyed watching." Cad felt a bit deflated. The way Gwen described it did not sound fun at all.

"If all else fails, I can farm." Cad laughed.

"How can you farm? You don't know any of the animals?" Gwen laughed.

"I know enough!" They both laughed, Cad had stopped feeling embarrassed about not knowing much about this place, which was a good job because Gwen was always reminding him. "What are you going to do?"

"Well, I will carry on hunting bounties for the king. I like it, I don't stay in one place for too long, and the pay is good, as long as I can catch them." Cad felt sad thinking that she would leave him once they got to Roshir.

"Maybe I could work with you?" Cad asked. Gwen hesitated.

"Thing is I only work alone, one bounty, one payment you see. Plus, it's much easier moving around unseen when there's only one of you. I'm sorry." Cad felt disappointed. Truth was, it scared him to be away from Gwen. She was the only person he knew, and he had become attached to her. "You wouldn't want to do it anyway, its hard sometimes, never settling down, not having a home, always on the road."

"I don't have a home either, or I do, I just can't get there." Cad said.

"Well, maybe we are getting ahead of ourselves, maybe the King can help you get back home." Cad thought that is what he wanted, but why didn't he feel happy when he thought of it. It was almost like he was enjoying not being trapped in Arcadia. He hadn't been out enough to think about it, though. Gwen sensed his silence. "Let's stop and make camp." She said and Cad's stomach grumbled as he thought of what meal they would have when they settled.

Cad made a small fire for cooking while Gwen unpacked her things. It was earlier than they would normally camp, but Cad was not complaining. Gwen prepared two rabbits that she had caught earlier that day. Cad enjoyed the rabbit, but it was not his favourite meat. He did however find it difficult to eat something that was alive just moments ago. Killing to eat seemed so harsh, but being out in the middle of nowhere, he didn't really have much of a choice. As Gwen was stirring the rabbit stew, she suddenly jerked upwards, Cad had been staring at her and also jumped when she made this movement. Her hand went to reach for her sword, before she relaxed again and carried on stirring.

"Hello Dyne." She said, Cad did not know who she was talking to, when suddenly a small figure stepped out from behind the bushes, causing Cad to jump.

"Ahh goddamit! If my bounties were like you, I'd make no bloody money. Who is the kid?" He asked, looking at Cad.

"That's my Nephew Cad. Leave him be, he's quite quiet. I'm taking him to Roshir." Cad and the figure stared at each other. He was just over half the size of Cad; he was stocky but if it hadn't had been for his wild beard Cad would assume he was a child. Dyne grunted; Cad could not help but stifle a smirk at how ridiculous it looked to him.

"Something funny boy?" Dyne asked and Cad went white.

"Leave him, I said. He's been through a lot. What are you doing here?" Dyne stared at Cad for a little while longer, Cad stared at his feet, not wishing to upset him further.

"Just seen, there was a huge Elfkin attack about 20 leagues south of here. Very unusual to see so many dead in one place, wasn't in a colony either."

"Yeah, that was us." Gwen replied.

"Shoulda known you had summit to do with it. Where did they all come from?"

"No idea, they just surrounded us, they had been tracking us too, I thought we had outrun them." Said Gwen.

"I was going to inform Rodderick, but I assume that's what you're on your way to do?" Said Dyne.

"Yes, I'm going to tell KING Rodderick." Said Gwen, emphasising the King. If Dyne had noticed, he didn't show it.

"Well, I might as well come with you, got my bounty to turn in." Dyne said, sitting next to Cad. He put his hand in his pocket and pulled out something that looked like beans. He ate them, waving some in Cad's face before offering them. Cad just shook his head. He was still wondering who this strange little man was.

"Where?" Asked Gwen. Dyne opened the sack he was carrying and pulled out a man's head. It had a shocked expression on his face, Cad looked away, it made him feel sick. Dyne laughed as he held the head out at arm's length. Proud of his trophy. "For god's sake put it away, man. You know they are worth more alive."

"I know, it's just their heads come off so easy." The dwarf chuckled, putting the head back in the sack with a chuckle.

"This is Dyne, by the way." Gwen said to Cad. "He's another bounty hunter, a little less.... refined than most of us, but he does the job."

"Less refined? I don't know what you mean." Laughed the dwarf as he tied the sack back up and carried on munching his beans. "So where are you from, boy?"

"Arcadia." Cad said simply. As he did, Gwen turned quickly to shush him, but she knew it was too late.

"And I'm from the fuckin rainbow forest." He said turning to Gwen, "Gwen, I don't like your nephew, he is a dick." Gwen did not know what to say, she just looked at Cad and then at Dyne and back again, Cad was also lost for words, he didn't know what to say. "What's going on?" Dyne asked looking at her suspiciously whilst munching his beans.

"Ok, he is from Arcadia. He's trapped outside. Apparently, he fell through the barrier." Dyne stood up, edging away from Cad.

"And you believe that nonsense. If he was from Arcadia, he'd have killed you by now." Cad felt himself go red, another person who believed that he was dangerous just because he was from Arcadia, would everyone think that?

"I believe him, and they are not like we thought, they don't even have magic. He nearly died fighting the Elfkin, if he could do magic, he would have used it to save himself. No one has magic in Arcadia."

"Then why are they all locked up." Dyne asked.

"They don't think that they are they think that they are protecting themselves from us." Cad wondered what she meant by that. Was Arcadia a jail? Why would they all be imprisoned, none of them did anything wrong?

"Seems strange to me." Dyne said, eyeing up Cad once more.

"Just shut up and have some stew." Gwen said putting a bowl in his hands. She then gave Cad a bowl, and they ate in silence for a while. "I don't suppose you've seen a dwarf before either, have you?" Gwen asked Cad, Cad shook his head. Dyne's jaw dropped.

"Well, you've started with the best lad. You won't find another dwarf quite like me." Dyne laughed and patted Cad on the back. Not a soft pat. More like a whack, Cad struggled to keep hold of his stew. "So, what's the plan."

"I'm taking him to the King, see if he can get him home."

"Better make sure you keep quiet about Arcadia boy; people will think you are mad." Dyne said. "I think maybe we are the mad ones for believing him."

"Thank you," Said Gwen, "For believing."

"Well, it's a tough one, but you've never steered me wrong before. And even if it is a bag of bollocks, well, it will be an interesting story. I'm coming with you, of course." Cad felt like he should be part of the conversation, they were discussing him of course, he did not know what to say. So, he just continued to eat his stew in silence. "Have you got any mead to go with this stew?" Gwen stared at him, "Ahhh ok but I've been sober, for three days now, things are hurting." He said guzzling down the last of his stew. Dyne stood up and emptied another sack, getting out some old green blanket to make a bed, Cad noticed that he had a pair of metal gloves. Bigger than any that he'd seen before. As Dyne laid in his makeshift bed, he caught Cad looking at them. "You like them boy?"

"What are they?" Cad asked.

"These are my gauntlets. I prefer to deal with my enemies' hand to hand. I'm not a fan of blades like our friend Gwen."

"That's only because you are too stupid not to cut yourself with them." Gwen laughed.

"But if you don't use blades, then how did you cut that guy's head off?" Asked Cad, nodding at the sack containing the dismembered head.

"I didn't cut it off," Dyne said, "I pulled it off." And with that, Dyne rolled over and started snoring straight away. Cad looked at Gwen, who just shrugged her shoulders and smiled. Cad lay down in his own bed, trying not to think of the horrific image of Dyne pulling the head off of the body. He wondered if the man was alive or dead when he did it, but judging by the expression on the dismembered head, Cad knew the answer.

14

C ad was not comfortable sleeping that night with a stranger so close, and his snoring echoed throughout the camp, but Gwen trusted him, so Cad tried his best. He was feeling a little jealous as the three of them rode onwards. They laughed and joked together while Cad felt a little left out; he preferred it when it was just him and Gwen.

"Remember boy, if anyone asks, you are from Hawks rift, and you are coming to look for work." This was the cover story they had come up with in the morning. Gwen thought it was a good idea not to let anyone know he was from Arcadia. Cad nodded in agreement but felt resentful taking instructions from Dyne. This was supposed to be him and Gwen, but he pressed on and tried to push feelings of jealousy away. They had chatted more, and Cad couldn't think of any reason not to like the dwarf, apart from him taking away his time with Gwen. She had gotten Cad to show Dyne the warming magic, which sent him into fits of hysterics. Laughing that this is the power that people are afraid of. Cad didn't laugh with them. He did not want people to be afraid of him.

They had made their way out of the woodlands, and Cad could smell the familiar smell of manure. They were on a farm; the farm went as far as the eye could see, vegetables growing in blocks bigger than the entire farm in Arcadia, many of which he didn't recognise. There were also animals, more animals than he had ever seen in his life. They walked their horses along the outskirts of the farm. It amazed him at how big it all was and how many people were working there. He noticed a lot of different people, different sizes, different hair and more peculiarly, different colours of their skin. There were some who had darker skin than he had ever seen, and also, he spotted two people whose skin was bright blue, almost glowing. It all amazed him.

"There's always plenty of work here if you need it." Gwen said. "Just have a word with the head farmer and he can usually give you some work, he has some rooms too and many people work for the room, if you needed a place to stay. Of course, if you joined the army like you said then you would live in the barracks, so don't worry about not having a roof over your head just yet." Cad knew she was trying to be helpful, but he didn't want to think of that. Now that he was out, he wanted to explore more. He wanted to stay with Gwen. He didn't want to settle into the first farm he saw and spend the rest of his life here. Then again, he knew he would need money.

Gwen had told him all about how everything here costs money. You can't just get your rations, you have to buy it, but there's no limit on what you can buy. Cad was excited about being able to have as much as he wanted. He knew he needed a job for money, but if he settled into a job, he would have no time to use that money doing what he wanted. Still, it was much better than being a mage. The more time he spent out of Arcadia, the less he wanted to go back. Although sometimes feelings of guilt would hit him, he knew his father was still in trouble and that him and his mother would be going out of their minds with worry. He felt sad that he never got to say goodbye.

They soon approached a large city gate, it was opened and when Cad looked through; it amazed him at what he was seeing, buildings made of bricks, people everywhere, it was so busy. Cad imagined the entire town of Arcadia could fit in one of the bigger houses.

"Welcome to Roshir." Dyne said, smacking Cad on the back. "It's a shit hole."

"It's amazing." Cad said. They didn't go through the gate just yet, they went to a man just outside the gate, Gwen talked to him, but Cad wasn't listening, he was too busy looking at the hustle and bustle of the town. Gwen extended her hand to help Cad down from the donkey, and the man led the horses away.

"He looks after the horses for us when we are in town, shall we have a look around before we go to the palace?" Gwen asked.

"Yes, please." Said Cad enthusiastically. He heard Dyne sigh.

"We can always show Cad what the taverns are like?" Gwen said to him. The Dwarf gave a big cheesy smile. "You have a tavern in Arcadia?" Cad shook his head, "I think we should visit one first." Gwen led Cad down the streets, Cad was looking left and right, trying to soak in every shop. There were shops for everything Cad could think of, clothes, shoes, furniture, food. He wanted to look inside every one of them but knew he needed money. The thought depressed him that there was so much here to have but no money to buy it. "Here we go." Gwen said, opening a door to a small building. The sign outside said, 'The Huntsman's Arms' "This is where we go to relax." Gwen said.

"Well, one of the places." said Dyne. "Three meads please." Said the dwarf with joy in his voice. "And what are you two having?" He chuckled.

"I'll have a mead too." Laughed Gwen. "Cad, do you like mead."

"Never tried it." Cad admitted.

"Another two meads Barkeep." Shouted Dyne. Let's get these down us. The dwarf skilfully carried his three glasses while Cad and Gwen followed him. They sat at an empty table.

"There's not many people here." Said Cad.

"It's early." Gwen told him. "Most will be working. This place will be packed later." Cad sipped his mead. It was strong but soothing. He enjoyed it and downed it. Dyne had drunk his three in the same amount of time that it took Cad to drink his one.

"That's my boy." Dyne shouted, smacking him on the back. "More?"

"Sure." Cad laughed, enjoying the warmth of the tavern and the feeling the mead was giving him. "Gwen?" Asked Dyne. Cad noticed she had only drunk a little of hers.

"We need to go see the king." Gwen said sternly, "We can't go see him steaming drunk."

"Come on, Gwen. Come on Gwen." Chanted Dyne banging his fists on the table. Cad laughed and joined in, both of them chanting.

"Aww hell." Said Gwen, downing her drink. "We can always see the king tomorrow." Dyne and Cad cheered as she finished her drink. Dyne sprang out of his seat.

"Another round barkeep." Shouted Dyne from the table as he went over with the empty glasses. He returned with another five meads.

"I think I had better get us a room for the night." Gwen said drinking her mead and walking to the bar. She shortly returned with more mead for everyone. "They've only got one room, so we all got to share." A young boy came to pick up all of their belongings. They handed over their weapons. Cad reluctantly gave over his sword.

"Sorry, you should have given them in when you come in." The young boy said, embarrassed to be taking their weapons.

"They know us here, so they are a little loose on the rules." Gwen said to Cad. "But it's not good to be drunk and handling weapons. They will take them to our rooms, though don't worry." Cad nodded to say he understood, then drank another mead. As soon as he had finished, Dyne placed another one in front of him.

"So, lad, what do they have to drink in Arcadia?" Dyne asked. Gwen hushed him.

"Keep it down."

"I know, I know, I'm just curious." He said, with a shrug of his shoulders.

"Well, we only have some ale and whisky, but we can very rarely have it. I've never had much.

"Well, tonight will be a lesson for you, my boy." The dwarf chuckled. "Hurry up." He said collecting all the empty glasses before going for more. Cad finished the drink as quick as he could, it was harder than the first, but he was enjoying himself none the less. He could feel his head spinning.

"So, you've never been drunk before?" Gwen asked.

"No. I know my dad has been a couple of times, but it's hard to get enough ale or whisky, and when you do you need to ration it out."

"Well, the good thing about a tavern." Said Gwen, "Is that the taps never run dry!"

"Wayyyyyyy." Shouted Dyne as he walked over skilfully holding five glasses of mead at once. "And I am extremely grateful." He said clinking glasses with Gwen and then Cad. The tavern filled up as the evening went on. Cad and his friends were the loudest by far, and he was loving every minute of it. They danced when the music played, Cad didn't recognise any of the songs or even the instruments, but the beat made him want to get out of his seat and dance, luckily Dyne was the first one dancing so he didn't feel silly, Gwen joined them shortly after.

Cad had forgotten all about his troubles. He wasn't thinking of Arcadia and his parents; he wasn't thinking of being a mage; he was just enjoying his time. Dancing with his two new friends. The tavern started spinning, and he felt unsteady on his feet, so he sat back down.

"A little too much?" Said Gwen sitting beside him. "It's ok, we have been putting it away."

"Just feeling dizzy, that's all." Cad slurred. Gwen chuckled.

"It's a natural part of being drunk, enjoy it." Said Gwen resting an arm on his shoulder.

"I want to keep doing this." Cad said.

"Well, we got all night, although slow the drinking down If you want to last the night."

"No, I mean after tonight, I want to stay with you, hell I even want to stay with Dyne." He admitted.

"You must be drunk," Gwen laughed. "You'd have to be to want to stay with Dyne."

"I like you." Cad admitted looking at Gwen, not knowing where this courage was coming from.

"I noticed." She said at him, smiling. "When we bathed in the stream, you made it clearly obvious." Cad felt embarrassed and put his head in his hands. "Look, I'm very flattered, but am I the only woman you know right now? It wouldn't work. There is a lot more, beautiful women out there. I told you I have no plans of settling down. So, try not to think about it."

"I've seen other women." Cad argued, "There's even some in here. I still prefer you." Cad said, gesturing to the two women who were dancing with Dyne.

"You're serious?" Gwen asked. "Look your young and drunk, it wouldn't be right. You're very sweet though, thank you." She leaned in to kiss his cheek but ended up kissing him passionately on the lips. She pulled away. "Sorry, I know I'm giving mixed signals, maybe I've had too much mead too. Let's forget that happened." She said before getting up and staggering towards the bar. Cad watched her go and wiped his lips. She was amazing, Cad really didn't want to leave her. She returned to the table with more glasses, Dyne shortly sat with them, sweating from all the dancing, he also brought a handful of glasses, the table was full of glasses of mead.

"Well, we may as well make it a memorable one if it's our only one." Dyne said, drinking his mead. Cad didn't know what to say. He thought it would be best to keep quiet and keep drinking. He enjoyed himself again, quickly getting over the embarrassment. The night faded in his head and he could not remember much of what was happening. Just that he was having a good time.

15

C ad woke up confused. He wasn't sure where he was, his mouth was dry, and his head was hurting. What worried him the most though was that he was not wearing any clothes. He sat up; he was in a comfortable bed. He looked around; Gwen lay next to him facing away. His foot touched something. He looked down and saw Dyne was also sleeping in the bed. Cad looked around and saw his clothes all mixed up on the floor. He looked at them; they were in a state, not just from last night, but he had been wearing them for well over a week now. There were stains covering them, he needed new ones. He quietly changed to hide his modesty.

Dyne stirred before opening his eyes. He got out of the bed, also completely naked. He didn't even try to hide it. He stretched, yawned and smacked his chops.

"What a night!" He laughed too loudly for Cad. "For a young one, you know how to drink. Hair of the Dog, I think. Shall I get you one?"

"Hair of the Dog?" Cad asked. His mouth was so dry all he wanted was a drink.

"It means another mead; shall I get you one? It will stop your head from hurting."

"Oh, no." Said Cad, the thought of mead right now turned his stomach. "I won't be drinking that for a while." Dyne laughed.

"Gwen, drink?" He said again, loudly, Cad's head was ringing.

"God no." Said Gwen, "I think I will die."

"Just me then." Said Dyne cheerfully as he walked out of the door.

"So, if that was your first time drunk, I assume this is your first hangover?" Gwen asked him, getting out of bed.

"Yes…" Cad answered but was interrupted by the door shooting open and Dyne rushing back in.

"Forgot my clothes." He was bright red as he hurriedly put on his clothes from last night. Cad laughed, but he regretted it. Laughing hurt his head and his stomach turned more. He was holding back having to vomit.

"It will pass." Said Gwen, "I don't know if you remember much of last night?" she asked.

"Not really," said Cad, "Just a lot of dancing and…" He remembered kissing her, how warm it felt, how much he had wanted it. "That's pretty much it." He lied.

"Nothing happened." Gwen said pointing at the bed, "If that's what you're thinking."

"Oh no, not at all." Cad said the thought hadn't even occurred to him. Especially with Dyne in the same room.

"OK, so don't worry yeah, it was a fun night for all of us. Now you may want to turn around while I get dressed." Cad blushed and apologised. He was staring again; he couldn't help it. Luckily Gwen didn't get annoyed at him, she just thought it was funny. She had no shame being naked around him, anyway. "I'll go and see about getting us some baths." Said Gwen as she left the room. Cad sat alone on the bed, holding his head in his hands. It was pounding. He just wanted to lay there and stay in bed forever. It wasn't long before Dyne walked in holding three glasses of mead.

"Oh, I said I didn't want one." Said Cad, looking at the mead as though it was poisonous. The sight of it making him want to vomit.

"I didn't get you one." Said Dyne as he downed all three, Cad looked on in disgust. "If you're going to be a wimp about it, get your-self a water." He flicked a coin towards Cad. His reactions were extremely slow. He missed the coin completely and had to pick it up from the floor.

"I think I may need one." He said, thanking Dyne for the coin and heading to the door. He walked down the stairs and into the main room of the tavern. He didn't even remember coming up those stairs last night. He walked to the bar; he saw the barkeep who was there the night before.

"Hope you're not going to redecorate my bathroom again." The barkeep said.

"Uh pardon?" Cad asked, confused.

"Still struggling to remember, are you?" The barkeep laughed. "You vomited everywhere. Took old Fran a while to clean up, I would try not to bump into her today if I were you."

"I'm so sorry." Cad said extremely embarrassed.

"It's no harm, you three put so much money behind the bar last night it's hard to be annoyed. Dyne is always welcome here, and I've never seen Gwen drink so much, very rare anyone tries to keep up with Dyne. Anyway, what can I get you." He said nodding at the coin Cad is holding.

"Oh, just some water, please."

"Excellent choice." The barkeep says filling up a glass for him and giving him some smaller coins back. "So how come I've never seen you before, where are you from?" Cad froze. He couldn't remember the story.

"I'm not from around here." Cad said, hesitating. He was trying to think of the name of the town. His head hurt as he tried to think about it. He couldn't think how to respond so he just looked down and drank his water, even that made his stomach turn but his mouth felt much better.

"It's ok if you want to be mysterious." The barkeep laughed. "But any friend of Dyne is a friend of mine. Half of my takings come out of his pocket; it seems. Can you share your name? My name's Arthur, but most people just call me keep."

"I'm Cad."

"Well, nice to meet you, Cad. Any time you are travelling through your always welcome at the Huntsman's Arms."

"Thank you." Said Cad, finishing his water. Just then Gwen walked through the door. She nodded at Arthur, who gave a cheery wave. Then turned to Cad.

"Let's take a quick walk." She said ushering him out of the tavern. The brightness of the sun burned Cad's eyes. His head still throbbed, but it was milder than before. "We need to go to the King today. Maybe don't mention last night if it comes up." She said, Cad just nodded in agreement. He was nervous about this King. "We need you to get ready to see him. You can't go walking into the palace dressed like that." Cad looked down. His clothes were tattered and stained. He looked around at the people in the town, their outfits were all so bright. He wasn't sure if it was the hangover, but he remembered when he saw them yesterday it was full of colours. Some colours Cad had never even seen before. All the clothes in Arcadia were grey, brown or black.

"But I haven't got any money." Cad said.

"It's ok it's on me." Gwen said.

"No please, I forget about the whole money thing. You and Dyne spent money on me all night last night. I didn't even have anything to give."

"Call it payment for saving my life from the Elfkin."

"I wouldn't have needed to save your life if you hadn't come back for me, so I should owe you." Cad protested.

"Listen, we need to get you ready for the king. You have no money. So, you are going to shut up and take my money. Use it to buy some-thing nice. We can figure out repayment another time if it bothers you that much." Cad straightened up at her abruptness.

"OK, thanks... I appreciate it." He said weakly.

"I know you do, now let's go find something in here." She opened the door to a shop. Inside, were so many clothes like Cad had never seen, all different colours and styles. He did not know what to do. The shop keeper looked him up and down in disgust. Cad pretended not to notice. Gwen called the shopkeeper over, handed him some money and spoke.

"He's seeing the king today; he needs something new to wear."

"You're telling me." The shopkeeper said. "Very well," he rushed around the shop like a madman, "Red is in season so you will need something red." He muttered to himself. He picked up a red coat with gold buttons. "Yes, this will do now let's see." He grabbed a piece of string and pulled Cad's arms up, so that they were straight, then held the string against him. "Yes, yes, and the leg." He said crouching down and pushing the string against the side of Cad's buttocks and foot. Cad blushed; he was not sure he liked this man. He rushed around, picking up a few other clothes. "Black trousers, white shirt. Hm I suppose you will need new underwear too? Don't answer that, I don't want to know." He muttered, piling them all into a sack. "Now I would like you to try them on before I give them to you, but I must insist that you wash first. And if there's anything that doesn't fit, bring it back and I will adjust it for you. Now off you go." He waved Cad and Gwen out of the shop. Cad thought the man was quite rude. Nothing like Arthur. "And please, when you take off those old clothes. Burn them." And with that, the shop keep shut the door behind them.

Cad looked up at Gwen.

"Thank you, I guess."

"Don't mind him, it's just his way." She laughed. "When it comes to style, he knows what's best. Now let's go back and have that bath."

When they got back to the tavern Dyne greeted them, sat at a table with three glasses, one full of mead and two empty ones.

"Care for a drink." He raised his last glass to them and drank it. Arthur followed up with three more without Dyne even asking. Gwen shook her head.

"Why do you always drink three at a time?" Cad asked, he thought it was strange.

"I'm just being nice to Arthur, saving his shoe leather." He chuckled before starting on a fresh glass. Cad noticed his hair was under control now, he had smartened up.

"How was the bath?" Cad asked.

"Good, now, if you're not going to drink, I suggest you get up there and have one, otherwise everyone's going to assume that everyone from Arcadia smells like my morning breath." Gwen glanced at Arthur, who wasn't listening before slamming her hand on the table and pointing.

"Quiet." She said jabbing him with her finger. "But he's right. Have a bath, we will wait here. Take these clothes with you, get dressed. And you don't have to burn those clothes, but I would suggest you get rid of them." Cad nodded; she was right. Some of these stains would never come out.

He followed the signs to the bathroom and found the bath already prepared for him. The water was scalding. Much hotter than he had been able to bathe in before. It took him a while to get in, but once he did, it felt amazing. He laid there for a while, his headache subsiding. He scrubbed himself. It was much easier to get clean in this scorching water. He didn't want to get out. He found some cream on the side of the bath that smelt like flowers. He rubbed it on himself, assuming that was what it was for, and rubbed some in his hair. His hair was thick and matted, he had never cleaned it as thoroughly as he did now; he felt a softness to it. He had finished his bath and dried himself. He tried on the new clothes. The clothes were so much softer than he was used to. They clung to his body comfortably. They were the perfect fit. He put on his coat and had to admit; he looked nothing like the boy who left Arcadia. He was a new man.

16

"Looking smart lad!" Dyne said, holding his glass of mead up to him before drinking it. "Shall we get going?" Gwen looked Cad up and down with a slight smile.

"You scrub up well." She said, still smiling.

"Thanks." Cad said, feeling his cheeks flush red. "Maybe I should have one drink before I go, settle my nerves."

"No chance of that today." Said Gwen. "Can't have you slurring in front of the king. Let's go." She said practically dragging Dyne. The three friends bid their farewells to Arthur and made their way out of the tavern and back into the town. As they were walking through, Cad was still amazed by all the shops. He regretted not getting a good look around before, but he had really enjoyed his night and he figured that there would be plenty more time to explore. That's if the King couldn't get him back home, though. He wasn't sure what he wanted anymore. He had a taste of this new life and he loved it, he wondered if he could cope with being trapped back in Arcadia. Then again, if they are still working to lower the barrier then it wouldn't be too long before the entire town was out, and Cad could tell them all what it was like out here. There were things to be feared, but overall, nothing compared to what they all feared. They could all build a new life out here. Cad's mind was working, thinking of all the opportunities.

"Don't worry about it, Cad. Once we get over this, then you can start thinking about the future. Let's just take each moment as it comes." Gwen said, patting him on the shoulder.

"Either way, there's going to be plenty of times for us to get drunk together, lad." He whacked Cad on the back and laughed. Cad wasn't so sure that was true, but he thought he would be grateful if Dyne had stopped hitting him. His back was getting sore from all the friendly back pats from him.

Cad could see the palace in the distance, it was the biggest building Cad had ever seen. Made of smooth stone and the windows were all coloured. It was possibly one of the most beautiful things he had ever seen.

"That's where the king is right?" Said Cad, pointing at the building.

"Yeah, that's where he does all his poncing around." Dyne said as Gwen hit him.

"Don't go getting us into trouble dwarf." She said sternly. "Yeah, that's the palace. Most people are not allowed in unless it's by appointment and then it's usually something bad."

"No one enjoys being summoned." Dyne followed up. It reminded him of his Dad getting summoned which made him feel sick.

"Can we go in?" Cad asked, confused.

"Yes, me and Dyne work directly for the king. There are a lot of bounty hunters, most of them work for local people or smaller villages. Me and Dyne do the bounties that get escalated to the king. There's five of us in total."

"Four now." Said Dyne. "Anders is dead. Long story, basically his fault." He held up the bag that Cad had recognised as the one with the head.

"Well, there's four of us" Gwen said. "Even though we work directly for the king, it's hard to keep his attention. Normally he gets one steward to deal with us." Cad didn't ask what a steward was. He

would be here all day if he asked about everything he didn't understand. He found it strange that only one man ruled all of this. When
in Arcadia, it was a council of six ruling a small town, and even then,
they struggled to keep order sometimes.

"So, there's a job opening?" Cad asked hopefully. Gwen smiled.

"You would be very lucky. The king is... peculiar about who he
has work for him."

"Really?" Cad said looking at Dyne who had burped loudly.

"Don't let his mannerisms fool you. He is quite a proficient
bounty hunter." She said to him quietly. "Don't tell him I said that."
Dyne had not noticed their private conversation. He was too busy
picking his nose.

As they got closer to the palace, there were a lot more people, and
it got a lot more crowded. There were stalls on the street of people
selling things. Someone caught Cad's eye and was holding up some
jewellery.

"You will look good in this." She shouted. "Come take a look, try it
on." She said about grabbing Cad. Gwen pulled him away.

"Try not to look at them, vultures pedalling shit around here."
Gwen said as they got to the doors. The doors were made of solid
wood and were twice as tall as Cad. He felt that was unnecessarily
big, as Cad still hadn't seen many people that much taller than him.
Two men stood on either side of the door, they were fully armoured
and held long swords pointing towards the ground. They nodded as
the three approached and Gwen and Dyne nodded back, Cad nodded
too but was a little delayed. By this point, the guards were already
looking away and Cad felt silly.

"Who are they?" Cad asked.

"They are the guards, there are loads of them around, I'm
surprised you didn't see them in the town. They keep order around
here. If there is any trouble, they are the ones who stop it." Cad
thought about how sharp their swords looked. He didn't want to be
on the wrong side of them. He was too busy looking at all the shops
to notice any in the town. "Just let us do the talking, keep quiet until
you're spoken to." Cad didn't reply, he was in awe. This was so much

bigger than the council hall, and so much grander. There was colour everywhere. The hall stretched out long, and at the end Cad instantly knew who was king. His chair was magnificent, it was the nicest chair Cad had ever seen. The man looked amazing. He wore a golden crown adorned with jewels and a red cape that matched with Cad's coat and a coat that looked as golden as his crown. He was sat talking to a small group of people. One Cad noticed, was dressed similar to the mages of Arcadia. Only his robe was a deep purple rather than a faded black. Cad wondered if they had mages here too, he had never thought to ask. There was so much he wanted to learn. Gwen and Dyne stood back a distance and waited, holding an arm out for Cad to stop too. The king waved away some people. The man dressed like a mage and another man wearing a coat similar to Cad's with more of a white fluffy collar and trimmings remained.

"The king has been expecting you." The man in the red coat said loudly. Gwen and Dyne approached the King with Cad in tow, Gwen bowed, Cad followed awkwardly after, he noticed Dyne only gave a slight nod of his head.

"Gwen, I've been wondering when you would return, I had to outsource my bounties to lower ranks." The king said with his lip curled.

"Sorry my liege." Gwen said, bowing. "I have had to attend a personal matter."

"Remember who you work for." The king said, not quite a shout, but not softly either. "Remember who puts the gold in your pocket." Gwen apologised again; Cad felt quite sorry for her. Is this how the King treats her? Cad was very curious what her personal errand was, to bring her all the way out to Arcadia. Especially if it wasn't to hunt a bounty. Cad thought he would try to ask her again if he got the chance.

"I hope you have some good news for me dwarf." The king said, addressing Dyne.

"I have avenged Anders. I'm here to collect the bounty." Dyne said, emptying the sack onto the floor. The head looked more disgusting than Cad had remembered. He had tried very hard to forget. He looked away in disgust but noticed the King and the two men around him did the same.

"I prefer them alive." The King said, "This will only be a half payment."

"He wouldn't co-operate." Dyne said simply, "I'll have what I can get." The king looked at the man in the red coat.

"Get rid of that thing." He said gesturing at the head. The man did a double take, it was clear that he did not want to touch it. Dyne had stuffed the sack into his trousers, so the man had to handle the head with his hands. Cad tried so hard not to look, but he could not help himself. The man picked the head by holding a tuft of his hair and promptly rushed out of the room.

"And who is this that you bring before me?" The King asked, "I am assuming you don't let your bounties walk around so freely."

"He's not a bounty, sire." Gwen said. "He's uh. This is Cad. He's from Arcadia." The king leaned forward, looking at Cad. The man dressed as a mage instantly stood up very straight, staring at him. There was a moment of silence as they stared, Cad stared at his feet unsure what to do.

"Are you being serious? I expect this sort of nonsense from the dwarf, but from you Gwendoline?" The king looked angry. It took a second for Cad to realise that Gwendoline would have been Gwen's full name.

"Its true sire. I know it sounds strange, I found him outside the barrier. He wants to get back home, I thought you would be the best person to help him."

"You boy, you are from Arcadia? Answer me truthfully, if I find that you are lying, I will cut off your head myself."

"Yes, sire." Cad said weakly.

"So let me understand this." The king said standing up. The man in the red coat had returned. "You were travelling along the barrier of Arcadia, when you found someone claiming to be from inside there, when no one has gotten in or out for centuries. A prison designed to hold the world's most powerful mages and you decide to bring him to the palace. Have you gone mad?" The King shouted.

"No, my king…." Gwen said.

"First you go missing from your line of duty and now you do this, Gwen, I expect so much more from you. I should have you locked up with him. Guards take him to the cells, tie up his hands quickly."

"He's not dangerous!" Gwen shouted.

"No." Shouted Dyne. Cad was too dumbstruck to even argue. They were locking him up. He moved towards the guards to stop them, but Gwen held him back.

"Don't touch him." Shouted Dyne. He's not like you think.

"I will be the judge of that." Cad heard the king say as the two guards dragged him off. Cad didn't put up any resistance. He knew it would be no good, there would be too many guards.

"I'm sorry, Cad." He heard Gwen shout. "I didn't think this would happen." Was the last thing he heard before he got dragged off. Cad did not speak; he did not fight. He knew it would be of no use. The guards bound his hands and threw him in a cold, dark cell. Once again, Cad was trapped.

17

Cad paced his cell. It was horrible. It was draughty, and it smelled. He was grateful that he still had his coat, but the rope around his hands made them ache. He had been in here overnight, and now most of the day had passed. Not a single person had come to see him, to tell him what was going on. The only person he had spoken to is the guard who brought him some food, and even he ignored him. He thought of Gwen and Dyne. How they had walked him straight into the king. It hurt him, this hurt more than Wil's betrayal, even though he had not known them for long. They must have known all along that they would lock him up, and now they couldn't even face coming to see him. He felt like crying, but he couldn't bring himself to do it. He was feeling angry more than anything else. He should have run, tried to make a life for himself. Now he will remain here, and no one will even tell him for how long.

A noise caught his attention, a guard was bringing another man in, Cad noticed they were not as rough with him, and they had not bound his hands together. The man was quite large and looked much more dangerous than Cad. They put him in the cell next to Cad and without another word they left.

The man paced around his cell, Cad was uncomfortable that

there were only bars between them, he would be in full sight of this man at all times. The man sat on his bed before addressing Cad.

"So, what are you in for?" The man growled. Cad could tell this was a powerful man, he was almost as muscular as Gwen, his shirt was tight around his top showing off his defined muscles, Cad was afraid of this stranger, but he did not know how to answer.

"I uh, I'm not really sure. No one's really explained anything to me." The man looked Cad up and down.

"Hey, aren't you that kid from Arcadia?" He asked, "There's a lot of talk about you."

"Yeah, that's me." Cad said with a sigh. "Everyone thinks I'm dangerous."

"Are you?" The man said.

"No. Although I wish I was, then maybe I could get out of here. What about you, who are you?" Cad tried to change the subject; he knew people would be uncomfortable around the subject.

"My name's Skorn, and I think I might be able to get us out of here." He said to Cad.

"How?" Cad asked, wondering if this would be a good idea. Then again, it couldn't be worse than sitting here alone for the rest of his life.

"The guards won't be back for a while. If I can get your hands untied through the bars. You can use your magic on the locks. You can set us both free. I know the perfect way to escape from there."

"I can't do magic." Cad said frustrated. "No one in Arcadia can." Skorn looked at him surprised.

"I thought you were all mages in there?" he asked.

"You thought wrong, everyone thinks it." Cad said. "We have mages, but they don't do magic, they can't. Not in the way you all think, anyway."

"Well, we've got to try." Skorn said impatiently. "You don't want to spend the rest of your life here, do you?" Cad slowly shook his head. "Come over here." Cad was nervous approaching the bars, but he figured he had no choice. He turned away and could feel Skorn fiddling with the roped around his hand. He felt them loosen up, then his hands were free. Cad shook and rubbed his hands. Feeling was coming back into them, they ached from being tied so tight, but Cad was grateful they were free now. "Now try to undo the lock." Skorn said.

"But I told you I can't." Responded Cad.

"Just try." Skorn snapped, making Cad jump a little. He approached the lock on the cell. He put his hands around it and focussed, he could feel the air around his hands warm up, it felt soothing as his hands were freezing and still aching. He put all his effort into the heat. He did not know what he was planning to do. Melt the lock? Cad couldn't create near enough energy to do that, but Skorn was watching. The least he could do was try. "Hmm," He said, "Whatever you're doing isn't working."

"I did say." Cad added before sitting back on his bed. "I can't do magic." He put his head in his hands. Skorn remained silent.

Cad heard the doors open once again, and it was a guard bringing them food. The food was not very substantial, Cad was still hungry after he ate it. He felt sorry for Skorn, as a man of his size would probably want to eat a lot more. Cad spent the rest of the day talking with Skorn, he was interested in Arcadia and Cad was happy to tell him. It helped pass the time having someone to talk to, and although Skorn looked scary; he was actually quite friendly. Cad opened up to him, telling him all about Gwen and Dyne, about how he fell through the barrier of Arcadia. All about the town's politics and the betrayal of the arch mage and his friend Wil. Cad realised he had been talking a long time. He was grateful to finally get it off his chest to someone. He was happy that Skorn listened, and no longer seemed to be scared by him. Skorn was particularly interested in how Cad had managed to get out of Arcadia and asked lots of questions about the woman he had seen. Cad explained it was probably a hallucination. He had not seen that woman before or since, but when he described her Skorn seemed surprised, as though he recognised her but denied it when Cad asked. He realised he had not even told Gwen about this.

"That is quite the story." Skorn said when Cad finished talking.

"You don't believe me, do you?" Cad asked.

"I'm pretty good at telling when someone is hiding something from me, and by what you've just said, I'm shocked, more so because I believe it."

"Thanks." Cad said. "I know how crazy it sounds but trust me its crazier to live through it." He smirked, a smile for the first time. He laid on his bed and carried on talking to Skorn through the night. They discussed a few things. It annoyed Cad that he would avoid answering questions about himself, when Cad had opened himself up so freely to him, but again he was grateful for the company and for someone to pass the time with. Cad nodded off to sleep before a pair of guards woke him.

"You, time to go." One of the guards said, opening Skorn's cell. Cad kept his hands hidden, he did not want them being tied up again, he watched as they lead Skorn out of the cells, he said nothing, just nodded to Cad as he left. He wondered where they were taking him. Once again, he was alone in his cell, still not one person able to tell him when he could leave or even if he could.

18

Cad lay on the stiff mattress, not even getting up to eat the food that the guards had brought him. He had tried once more to use the magic that everyone thought he had on the lock but could do nothing more than warm it slightly. He was frustrated and angry, he had decided that he was staying in bed until someone would tell him what was going on or if they would let him go. It was the only act of defiance he could manage. The guards still ignored him when he tried to speak to them, so he decided he would not talk or eat until someone told him something, anything. A guard came bringing lunch, Cad watched him out of the corner of his eye, he pulled the full tray of breakfast back through the slot and replaced it with the lunch, again not saying a word and leaving promptly. Cad's stomach grumbled, but he would not give in.

Shortly after, two guards came in opening Cad's cell. Cad wondered if his plan had worked.

"Up." The guards said. Cad hesitated, his hands were still unbound, and he didn't want them to see them. Cad continued to lie there. He was sticking with his plan. The guards didn't care. One pulled him out of the bed and they both grabbed an arm each. They dragged him out of the cell and up the stairs. Cad remained limp, he would not try fighting his way back to the cell. He tried asking where they were taking him, but again there was no answer. They pulled him into a room that he didn't recognise. There was a small stage, and he had an audience. The king was sat there on a large chair, there were a few people he recognised, the two men who were with the king on the day he arrived. He spotted Dyne sat there too, he tried to make eye contact to ask what was going on, Dyne would not look at him. He couldn't spot Gwen anywhere, which saddened him slightly, but it hurt every time he thought of her. That she would let him get imprisoned like this. Cad was silent as he looked around, trying to get a hint of what was going to happen. The King stood and his voice filled the room.

"Arcadia has been used as a jail to keep the most dangerous and evil mages away from society. Today we have in front of us the first person to escape since they created the jail centuries ago. I hereby announce that the sentence for breaking free, to be death." Cad looked around. No one was shocked and Dyne would still not look at Cad.

"I'm not dangerous." Cad said softly. Two guards brought in a large contraption that had a sharp blade at the top. Cad saw it and all feeling went from his legs. He would have crumpled to the ground if the guards were not holding him so tightly. "I'm not dangerous!" He shouted, he tried to wriggle away from the guards. Pleading and shouting. "You're wrong! Stop!" He pulled and pulled, struggling against the guards. He kicked and shouted. "Please, you've got it all wrong, we are not powerful mages. Stop! I don't want to die!" Cad screamed and cried; he sobbed as the guards put his head into the lock of the bottom of the contraption. Cad knew the blade was going to be used to cut off his head. There was nothing he could do about it. "Please!" he pleaded in between sobs. "I promise, you've got it wrong. Tell them Dyne. Dyne please!" He shouted out, he could not tell if Dyne was even looking, all Cad could see was the floor, he couldn't move his head.

"Let this be a lesson to any future escapees planning on coming out of Arcadia." The King said, no hint of emotion in his voice. "Be done with it." Cad could see out of the corner of his eye, one guard flipped a switch next to him, everything was going in slow motion. He could hear the blade speed towards his neck. Then he felt a pain. Not a pain of being cut, but a ringing pain. The metal blade clashed with something else, causing the whole thing to vibrate hard. It hurt Cad's head, but he was grateful that he still had one. The guards unlocked him, Cad looked around confused at what was going on, his eyes stung with tears and he couldn't help but let out a sob. The King looked at him.

"It seems you were telling the truth, Cadderick of Arcadia. I am sure you have many questions. Go with Dyne, rest up in a room I have prepared for you. Do not attempt to leave the castle. We have much to discuss, however I know that this has been particularly traumatic." The king spoke, Dyne interrupted.

"Traumatic! Look at the poor boy!" The king ignored Dyne and continued.

"Go and rest, we will carry on this discussion when your minds are clearer." With that, the guards released Cad. He looked around. Dyne was stood up.

"Come on, lad." He said, gently patting him on the back. "Let's get you some food." Dyne lead him through the palace in silence. They came to a door and as Dyne opened it, Cad saw Gwen inside. She had tears in her eyes.

"I'm so sorry, Cad. We had no choice." She said trying to dry her tears. Cad could do nothing but cry. He held Gwen and sobbed unashamedly. Dyne looked around awkwardly before muttering.

"I had better get us some drinks." leaving the room. Cad sat in his embrace with Gwen. He felt comfortable, he did not want to let go, even though he hated her right now.

"Why didn't you come to see me?" Cad asked between sobs.

"I wanted to; I really did. The king wouldn't allow me or Dyne down, he was worried we would tell you his plan, but you don't know how badly I wanted to come down, to reassure you."

"The king's plan?" Cad asked, pulling away from the embrace. "What plan?"

"He wanted to push you to use your magic, to see if you were lying. He sent Skorn down to try and push you, but when that didn't work, he resorted to extreme measures. He was not intending to kill you. That's why he put a barrier on the guillotine, so that it wouldn't actually cut off your head. He wanted to see if you could use magic if your life was in danger."

"But I don't have any magic, I've been telling you that." Cad said, wiping the tears from his eyes.

"Yes, we knew that. The king wanted to see it for himself. I hope you can forgive us. We had no choice." Replied Gwen.

"I'm just grateful to still have my head." Rubbing his neck as though soothing the injury he almost had. "I really thought you'd left me."

"I know," Gwen sighed, "We tried everything, this was the only way the King would believe us." Dyne entered holding three glasses of mead.

"Didn't get us a drink?" Cad asked. Dyne looked from Cad to Gwen and back again, shocked that he had just made a joke. He laughed loudly.

"I drank them on the way aha," Dyne laughed. "It's good to have you back, lad. We were worried out of our minds."

"So, what's going to happen to me now?" Cad asked taking a sip of his mead, it warmed his cold body, his stomach grumbled, he had had nothing to eat since the day before.

"Well, you need to get some rest, we can have some food sent up to you. Just relax, there's some books to have a read through. Some of them will teach you a lot about the world. Then the king's going to want to talk to you. He wants to know about Arcadia. Then he will see if he can get you home, but..." Gwen hesitated. "He doesn't think it's likely, he has called for some historians to come to talk about Arcadia. Most of what we know is just a myth."

"You mean you're not staying?" Cad asked, caring more about that than not being able to get home.

"We both have work to do, we have to investigate some of these

Elfkin attacks, different to bounty hunting I suppose, but we will be back."

"There's been more?" Cad asked.

"Yes, it's been happening all over the land, no one knows what has caused it, but it's not for you to worry about right now. I'll get them to bring you some food. Don't worry, we will come to see you before we go." Gwen said, she gave Cad an awkward hug, as though she didn't want to pull away.

"You'll be ok lad." Dyne said, getting out of his seat. "Better have some drinks for me when I get back." He whacked Cad on the back as he laughed and got up to leave. It hurt Cad, but he enjoyed it, he had missed it, he knew it was Dyne's way of showing affection. He laid on the bed and closed his eyes. This bed was so much more comfortable than the prison bed. His stomach turned through nervousness and hunger. Things should get better from here, he thought.

19

Cad had been staying at the castle for just over a week now. He was enjoying it; the food was amazing, his room was comfortable, and all he had to do was discuss Arcadia with the King. He found the meetings unnerving at first, as there were scholars all making notes, hanging onto his every word. Even the most mundane things like how they farm and how they ration out the food. They were particularly interested in the mages and how they maintained the barrier, particularly as Cad explained it wasn't the job anyone wanted. Apparently, the mages here were much stronger and could do magic that Cad could only dream of, and yet they were afraid of him. It shocked everyone to know that people in Arcadia could not do magic. He had become a bit of a local celebrity, some people would come to gawk at him, others brought small gifts. Others would completely avoid him, avoid eye contact and completely run the other way. He had gotten used to the people who stared and the people who tried so hard not to look. He had also bumped into Skorn a few times; he knew he worked for the King; he remembered Gwen telling him that but was still shocked when he saw it himself.

He had not seen Gwen since they had both left, although he saw Dyne once, but he was gone the same day. It was a busy time. The king had shown Cad a map of the world. It surprised him to see that Arcadia was just a small dot on the map, and the kingdom he was in was not the biggest country on the map. There were several more, and the King mentioned a war brewing with the people from the west. Apparently, war was normal around here but not on this scale and this had happened suddenly, so the kingdom was currently in uproar. As the days went on Cad noticed the King looking worse, his eyes were baggy and he looked tired, Cad couldn't imagine all the responsibilities of one man running a Kingdom this big. Still, with everything going on, he still made the time to interview Cad.

It was his third meeting where the king started asking about Cad himself. What he enjoyed doing, Cad knew instantly.

"Duelling." He said, "With swords." he added, just in case there were other forms of duelling that he was not aware of. The king lifted his head with a smirk.

"Are you any good?" The king asked.

"The best." Cad said with pride.

"Sounds like a challenge to me." A voice said, it was the king's son Fenton, who had also been sitting in on the meeting but rarely spoke. Cad did not like him, he reminded him too much of Pike. The king was friendly considering his status, but Prince Fenton walked around with a sneer that was fixed to his face.

"No Fenton, I want to keep the boy alive." He said with a chuckle. "You," he said, nodding at a guard. "You can duel." The guard stood forward proudly.

"I can take him." Cad said, nodding at Fenton. At least this way I can start making a name for myself, he thought.

"Very well," The king waved the guard back and sat with a smile, "Get them geared up." He said to Skorn.

"What's your weapon of choice?" The king asked him.

"Sword," Cad replied with confidence. The king rolled his eyes.

"Of course, what kind?"

"Um," Cad didn't know there were different swords. "A duelling sword."

"Just bring him a long sword." The king said. Before Cad could reply, people had surrounded him, attaching heavy armour to him. He was not used to the weight. Someone handed him a sword. It was much the same as the one Gwen had used, and much bigger than what he was used to. He held it up, but it felt awkward in his hands.

Fenton stared through his visor. He could tell from his eyes that he was smiling, obviously confident. Cad struggled to meet his gaze.

"Go." The king shouted, Cad went straight on the offensive, to try to get an early hit. He swung the sword clumsily, the extra weight causing him an unsteady momentum. Fenton ducked gracefully under the swing before hitting Cad in the side of the leg with his sword before swiftly spinning and delivering a powerful blow to his chest winding him.

"You could have at least made it last a little longer." The king said disappointed. Cad lay there trying to catch his breath. Now he knew how Wil felt. He really didn't like it.

On the next of these meetings, Cad was asked to lie on the table in nothing but his underwear. He was very weary. The king assured him that he had nothing to worry about and that they just wanted to inspect him. Cad had developed a trust for the king, so he lay there. Three of the scholars who Cad did not know the names of because not once did they speak or introduce themselves. They just frantically scribbled notes whenever Cad would talk, started poking and prodding him, lifting his arms and his legs, inspecting them as though they had never seen the body parts before. They stopped working without a word and retreated, Cad lifted his head up to check if he gets up, but he saw Randle approach, Cad tensed up, He didn't trust Randle, although he was the Kings head mage, just the thought of mages still gave Cad a weird feeling.

Randle placed his hands over Cad's chest, he got extremely uncomfortable and tensed. The mage pulled his hands away as though he had placed his hands into a fire. He looked at the king.

"There is more power here than I have ever seen, the stories are true." He did not wait for the king to respond; he turned back to Cad and eased his hands towards him much slower than last time. "Yes, you have great power, but why can't you use it?" He asked, Cad wasn't sure if he was suspecting an answer or not. "Yes, this is odd, I've not encountered this before, this is beyond my knowledge. You've got a filter."

"A filter?" Cad asked, but he got no response.

"I can't remove it; I wouldn't even know where to begin. We have not needed filters to be used in a long time. Its old and of no use now we can drain people." Cad did not know what he meant. He didn't bother asking because he knew that he wouldn't be answered. He didn't even know if Randle was talking to him, the king or himself. He pulled out a small knife and pricked Cad's arm. Cad yelped in surprise. Randle continued, ignoring Cad, scooped up the blood he drew into a small vial and put it in his pocket. "I will need to run some tests." He said looking at the King. "The only idea I have at the moment would be to drain the power and hope that releases the filter. Of course, the danger is that he will be completely drained. A partial draining has never been done." The King stared for a while before answering.

"Run your tests, I want to know as much as we can before we actually do anything that we cannot reverse." Cad just lay there. He was used to the King talking to others about him without actually addressing him. He was a little annoyed today. He felt like he was there to be experimented on. The King had dismissed everyone including Cad, as he got himself up off the table, they had laid him on, a soldier burst through the door.

"Sire, there are guardians of Dunhallow here, they request an audience." Cad heard a lot of chattering and whispers from around the room. He recognised Dunhallow as the lands to the west. They would have made quite a journey to get here. Before the King could move or say anything, three large men walked through the door. They were a good two feet taller than most people, and much wider. Their skin was a golden brown and most peculiarly they had two bright white wings on their back like a bird, Cad wondered if they could actually lift the weight of the men. Ignoring the soldier's protests. They stood in a line in front of the King. They obviously did not understand the protocols here, Cad had the impression that they wouldn't care for them even if they knew.

"Three guardians enter my hall uninvited. Perhaps you come to further ignite the war, I assure you we have plenty of strength left to fight you off." At this remark, the soldiers all moved their hands to their swords. Cad knew he should leave, but he was too curious to see what was going to happen. They had forgotten him in the corner. If the guardians noticed the change in hostility, they did not show it. They spoke slowly.

"We have come to collect the chosen one." The guardian in the middle spoke.

"Chosen one? In case you haven't noticed, we," he said, pointing at them and then back at himself, "are currently on the brink of war. I have no time for meddling in Dunhallow prophecies." The king said.

"The war will be tiny compared to what has been foreseen. The chosen one has been revealed, the sisters have revealed themselves. We are here to collect him, to prepare him for the end."

"The sisters have revealed themselves?" The King slouched in his throne. "Then it is worse than I thought. I'm afraid I cannot let you take who it is you seek. We all know when the end is to come, we will need him for protection."

"No!" The guardian shouted, "He must come with us. Only we train him. He will fight with Dunhallow behind him."

"And should I refuse?" The King asked.

"That would be foolish. We have seen the chosen one, we know his destiny. The threat in the north grows stronger. We will have a better chance united, but to do that, the chosen one must come with us."

Cad's hair stood up on the back of his neck. Were they discussing him? The king looked very nervous. Did he know? Is this why he was keeping him around. A lot of things made sense. He wondered why they were so interested in him. Now he knew. Cad did not know whether he should say something, just then he felt a hand on his mouth and an arm on his neck as they pulled him back, he tried to resist but they were much stronger than him; he was dragged out of the hall silently. The king and the guardians did not notice he was there, let alone that he had disappeared.

They dragged him through one of the side doors; he panicked when he had seen a guard lying on the ground and started thrashing around in the stranger's arms, trying his hardest to pull away. They grabbed him and spun him around, hand still covering his mouth. He was shocked to find it was Skorn. He held a finger to his lips, Cad didn't think he could say anything if he wanted to, he was in shock.

"Follow me." Skorn whispered. Cad nodded and silently followed him, as they walked down one corridor Cad could hear a fighting in the distance, a guard came rushing towards them.

"Skorn! Elfkin! In the Castle." He puffed, running towards them. Skorn punched the guard directly in the face, knocking him to the ground. Cad let out a yelp. He had turned white at the word Elfkin. What were they doing here, and why was Skorn attacking the guards? Cad felt a sense of foreboding. He didn't know if he could trust Skorn, but with all the chaos going on around him, this was the only thing he could think of doing. The pair walked deeper into the castle, they had seen a few dead guards, they were getting close to the dungeon. Cad felt sick at the thought of going back down there, coming from the door to the dungeons was an Elfkin, its eyes were red and fiercer than Cad had remembered. Skorn did not break stride and carried on marching towards it, the Elfkin charged, in one swift movement Skorn had impaled the creature with his sword that Cad did not even notice him draw and pushed the body to the floor and continued walking. Cad went to pick up the Elfkin's dagger.

"Leave it." Skorn commanded, "it won't do you any good." Cad hesitated but followed the instruction. Skorn did not look behind to see if Cad had obeyed, or even if Cad was still following. He did a little dash to catch up. In the dungeon, Skorn walked to one of the cells in the far corner, the door was open. He pushed a series of bricks that slid into the wall, as he did the remaining bricks unfolded, the wall moving by itself revealing a door. "In." Skorn said, nodding towards the newly made entrance. Cad walked through, Skorn followed, closing the door behind them, it was dark and reminded

Cad of the tunnels below Arcadia, there was a faint glow of light ahead.

"Where are we?" Cad asked.

"Just keep going, I will explain shortly." His tone made Cad think he was in control, like the chaos seemed normal to him. Cad hurried along the corridor, not running but not walking either. The light got brighter the closer they got to it. As the light began to take shape, he realised the light source was a fire. It was in a large cross section of tunnels. Around the campfire stood three people, two of which Cad was extremely happy to recognise.

"Is this all of us lad?" Dyne asked addressing Skorn, "Now are you going to tell us what is bloody going on around here?"

20

"What is going on?" Gwen asked, they both looked apprehensive, Cad was glad that they were as clueless as him. Cad stared at the stranger in the corner. She was thin, almost sickly looking, she wore a tight tunic that didn't help with her thin looking figure.

"The castle is under attack, the chosen one has been revealed." Skorn said simply. No one moved or spoke for a while. As though expecting Skorn to follow up.

"Chosen for what?" Dyne asked. Not trying to hide his annoyance at the situation.

"The end days. The shadow prophecy."

"The shadow bloody prophecy. What nonsense is this?" Dyne said in anger.

"I am a brother of the Shadowclan." Skorn said simply, "So is Faendal." He said gesturing to the sickly-looking woman.

"The Shadowclan are real then," Gwen said, nodding her head. "I always wondered if it was more than just a legend."

"And what makes you think Cad is the chosen one?" Dyne asked.

"He has seen Argona. He has had the vision." Cad stepped into the circle, fed up with everyone talking about him and not to him.

"What are you all talking about?" Cad shouted, he was embarrassed, he had not meant to shout, he continued speaking quieter than he should have. "Shadowclan? Shadow prophecy? What is all that? And who the hell is Argona?" Cad asked. Skorn kneeled to address him.

"The Shadowclan used to be a large group many centuries ago. Our number has dwindled, and there's even fewer left that I can trust. We have been keepers of the Shadow prophecy. A telling of a future where darkness will rise, and only the chosen one can defeat it. The prophecy has no ending, so we do not know if darkness will win. Only that you will be the one to fight it. The chosen one will be revealed when they see one of the sisters of fate. They control how the world works, the actions we take and basically everything that happens. When we were in the cells together, you told me of a vision of a woman, outside the barrier of Arcadia. Just before you got through?" Cad nodded, "With that description you gave me, the pink hair, the mysteriousness of it all, it must be Argona."

"You didn't tell me you saw her?" Gwen said to Cad sharply.

"I uh... Didn't want you to think that I was crazy." Cad responded, "I wasn't even sure if what I saw was real, let alone her being a sister of fate. So basically, they control everything that I do? Everywhere I go?" Cad asked, frustrated by the idea of him being controlled.

"In a way, yes." Replied Skorn. Cad's heart sank, just when he thought he was free to do whatever he wanted he was once again being controlled, first his family and Arcadia, next the king. Now this. He wondered if he would ever be free to do what he wanted. "You must take him to the Mistpeak Mountains." He spoke to the others in the room, "to the World's Eye." Dyne laughed.

"Oh, a short journey then, a popular tourist destination. Somewhere easily accessible." Skorn frowned at his sarcasm. "Shall we ask someone whose been there before what it's like? Oh, that's right, no one ever goes there, no one's ever seen the world's eye."

"Not with the chosen one, it won't be." Skorn replied.

"And if he's not?" Dyne asked, "All we have to go on is that he saw some crazy woman before he passed out."

"It is a risk we have to take, to see the fate sisters, they can tell us if he is the chosen one and can give him the guidance he needs."

"It gets better!" Dyne shouted, "lets climb to the most unreachable place in the world! Talk to the Gods, perhaps invite them for a drink?"

"What does the king make of all this?" Gwen asked.

"The King does not know, if the King still lives, he will assume the Guardians have taken Cad."

"If the King lives?" Gwen asked.

"Elfkin, has attacked the castle, whether it's the Guardians or something else, something is happening at the castle. Which is why you must leave now, and in secret. The fewer people who know, the better. They will want to use Cad for their own gains." Gwen looked uncomfortable, Cad knew she was loyal to the King, but apparently much bigger things were at stake here.

"And what about our pay?" Dyne asked. "It's no simple journey. Impossible even, if I'm going to certain death, I at least want the pay to be good."

"Is preventing the end of the world not enough?" Skorn asked. "I thought as much," He threw a large bag to Dyne. He opened it up, took a coin out of the bag and inspected it in the light.

"Let's go team!" He said in a cheery voice.

"Why us?" Gwen asked, "What part of the shadow prophecy to we fall into?"

"None," Skorn admitted, "But you have shown loyalty towards Cad, and I know you have moral character." He glanced at Dyne. "Somewhat. Faendal will guide you, she will fight alongside you should there be any trouble."

"You want us to take someone we've never met and expect us to trust her?" Gwen asked. Dyne had different concerns.

"Fight alongside us? A slight breeze is going to knock her over!" He shouted, as he finished his sentence an arrow pierced the water-skin Dyne was holding, he looked at his broken water skin, then at Faendal, then back again, Cad had not even seen her draw the arrow, she was quick. "Fair enough." Dyne said. "You can come with us, but you need to buy me some more mead." He said holding his waterskin up.

"Mead, in your waterskin..." Skorn paused. "I don't want to know. You need to leave now. Try not to talk to anyone or let anyone know what your plans are. Remember, the fewer people that know the better, we don't want anyone to interfere."

"Ready to face certain death lad?" Dyne asked Cad with a huge grin, Cad didn't know if he was trying to be supportive.

"I had nothing better to do today." Cad laughed. Gwen shook her head but hid a small smile, Faendal rolled her eyes.

"Let's go." She said, it was the first time Cad had heard her speak, her voice was raspy, it made Cad feel uneasy. "You might want to suit up." she said pointing behind Cad. Cad saw a light chain-mail armour. It was beautiful.

"For me?" Cad asked.

"Specially made." Skorn said, we've been preparing. "There is a decent sword there too, I just hope you use it better than you did against Fenton." Cad blushed, but his embarrassment faded quickly when he saw the sword.

Cad beamed as he put on his armour and held his sword. He finally felt like something good was happening. He felt like a man, no longer a little boy from Arcadia.

"Thank you." Cad said facing Skorn, but he had already gone.

"Let's make haste." Faendal said. She walked sloppily, Cad couldn't tell if it was an injury or if she just walked funny, but she hobbled through the corridors, although the limp had not slowed down her pace. Cad and the others walked fast to keep up.

"Are you not wearing armour?" Cad asked her.

"No, I travel light, I don't like to be seen." This made sense to Cad. He, Dyne and Gwen stuck out like a sore thumb where you wouldn't be able to spot Faendal in a crowded street.

"How far away are these misty mountains?" Cad asked.

"Mistpeak." Faendal said. "If all goes well, about four weeks travel, we will go cross-country. There should be some horses ready for us when we get out."

"How did you get to become a brother of the Shadowclan?" Gwen asked.

"Sister." Faendal snapped, "My job is to get you to the eyes of the world in one piece. Not to tell you my life story."

"If we're going to be spending weeks on end together, I suggest maybe being a bit more joyful to be around." Dyne said. "Especially if I'm sober, you may end up with my fist embedded in your skull." If Faendal cared or even heard the remark, she didn't show it, she just carried on. Cad looked at Dyne and shrugged. Cad could not help but be excited. He was going on a quest with Gwen and Dyne. Exploring more of this unknown world. The guilt and the thought of returning home had grown very small. He knew that this was where he belonged and now, he felt like he was going to be part of something great. The chosen one, defeating darkness. Now that had a nice ring to it. If his parents knew, they would be proud. They would have to be. He wondered what would be happening in the town right now, but no matter what, it would be nowhere near as exciting as this.

They came to a dead end, Faendal pushed the bricks into the walls just as Skorn did earlier, creating another doorway.

"And how many people know about these secret tunnels?" Gwen asked.

"Just the Shadowclan and now you." said Faendal, closing the door behind them.

"And how many other secret tunnels do you have?" She asked.

"Enough." Faendal snapped, Cad could sense Gwen tensing, he knew she would like nothing more at that moment than to destroy her, but he heard her exhale deeply. She was doing her best to remain calm. "We will be a good twenty leagues outside of the town, we get on our horses and ride east, we don't stop until we reach Shoreville where we stop to rest." Cad could feel the burning looks from Gwen and Dyne, they were not used to being ordered around like this. They emerged from a small cave in the woods, Faendal held her hand up in a stop motion. Cad looked at the floor. There were five horses laid on the floor, in a pool of blood. Something was very wrong.

21

F aendal ducked and disappeared among the trees.

"Where ya going you coward?" Dyne grunted, tightening the straps on his gauntlets, Cad looked around, his sword drawn. There was an eery silence. Cad spotted a movement in the trees ahead and an Elfkin appeared and shrieked. An arrow hit him square in the head and he fell to the floor slowly. Cad could see more movement surrounding him. The Elfkin knew where they were now, so they charged. Cad held his stance and breathed deeply. Two of the creatures at the front fell before they got close, arrows sticking out of their head. They fought, Cad swung his sword, cutting at the Elfkin. He felt awkward and clunky, the blade not bouncing off them as it often did in practice but sinking into their bodies. Cad had to pull the sword out with more force than he was used to. The Elfkin were not excellent fighters, but their numbers could easily overwhelm them. Cad was blocking a hit from his fourth Elfkin, and an arrow hit it in the head, causing it to hit the floor. Cad looked up. There were easily twenty bodies. Cad had barely made a dent, at least this time he actually got to fight. The adrenaline rushed in his body; he was excited. He wanted to fight more. He was bouncing on the balls of his feet.

Faendal reappeared out from the trees, and started pulling the arrows from the dead, putting them back in her quiver.

"Either someone knows what we are doing, or we got really unlucky." She said whilst pulling an arrow from the face of an Elfkin, Cad had to look away.

"Four weeks, was that with horses or without?" Dyne asked.

"Looks like we are walking." Gwen interrupted before Faendal could upset them with the answer. Let's take what we can. One of the animals killed was a donkey, was going to help them carry their gear. Cad sighed, looks like they would have to carry it themselves. He put as much food and water in his satchel as he could. The straps pained his shoulder, along with his armour as well it was heavy. This was going to be a painful journey. They marched through the woods; Cad looked back towards the city. There was a lot of smoke from all different areas. There must have been a lot of fires. Cad hoped everyone was ok. He wondered what would happen if the King had died. Would Fenton take over?

"There's a Hamlet. Before we get to Shoreville. Dwarven clan, we can stop and rest." Dyne said. "It will be safe there."

"Nowhere is safe right now." Faendal said, she paused for a while. "But you're right, will be a good place to stop and stock up."

They marched until nightfall, Cad's shoulders ached, and his legs felt like jelly, he had only been travelling for half a day; he was not sure he could manage a full day like this tomorrow. He was staring at the fire, eating a stew that had been prepared. Gwen came and sat close to him.

"You've been unusually quiet." She stated.

"Just a lot to take in at the moment, one minute I'm forced to be a mage in a town I want to leave, then I'm forced to go to the king's castle, now I'm told I'm the chosen one, forced to go and complete this quest and defeat the darkness, I don't even know what the darkness is. My dad always said you take charge of your own future, but I've never had a chance to. Every turn I take seems to be forced by someone."

"Would you prefer to be back in Arcadia?" Gwen asked.

"No." Cad quickly replied. "I mean I'd much rather be doing this, don't get me wrong, I'm excited, I just wish I could do things off my own back. I guess I have a problem being told what to do all the time."

"I think we all struggle with that sometimes." Gwen said, staring at Faendal. "Look at it this way, you've had your beginning, the end is inevitable for all of us. It's the bit in the middle that our actions impact. You may not be in control of the destination, but you control the journey." Cad smiled at Gwen. It had been a long time since they had talked like this. He missed this. She always made him feel better. She had taken her armour off, he admired the size of her frame, she was strong, and it comforted him to be close to her.

"I was supposed to marry someone, but that's in Arcadia. I don't think that's going to happen now." Cad murmured. Gwen chuckled.

"You mentioned something about that before."

"Are you married, or arranged to be married?" He asked.

"I'm not." Gwen replied. "Not the marrying type. I don't think that a lot of men like my type."

"Your type?" Cad asked. Gwen simply flexed her arm.

"Powerful women, they like a nice, homely woman, staying at home, cooking a stew. I couldn't think of anything worse."

"I like it." Cad said quickly. "I mean the size; I like your strength." He got embarrassed.

"You like my strength?" She chuckled. "You're very sweet. I don't think you could be with a woman my age, I'm easily ten years older."

"Doesn't bother me." Cad responded quickly. "The woman I was arranged to marry, she was much older." Gwen raised an eyebrow and went silent for a while.

"Let's focus on the task at hand." She said, "You can think about dating once you've saved the world. Plenty of time, aye." She laughed and patted him on the back. Cad smiled, but his face flushed red with embarrassment. He wondered if he could ever convince Gwen he genuinely was interested in her. Every time they discussed it, she brushed it off, pretending that he was joking.

"Are you married, Dyne?" Cad asked.

"No, why? Are you asking? You're not my type." He chuckled. Cad blushed further.

"No just interested, all I know about you is how much you like mead."

"Aye, if I could marry the mead, I probably would. Truth is, I used to be married. A group of thieves killed her. Was my first bounty hunting them down and my most satisfying. Still don't bring her back." He said laying down next to the fire. Cad didn't know what to say, he knew Dyne wasn't the type to talk about emotions, so he quickly moved on.

"What about you, Faendal, you married?" Faendal paused for a moment, as though contemplating whether to answer the question.

"Yes, as it so happens. Although with everything that went on in the castle today, I'm not sure if she would have survived." Faendal did not look at Cad when she said this. Cad was confused.

"She?" Cad asked.

"Yes, my wife." Faendal said.

"You can marry women?" Cad asked, surprised.

"Forgive him." Gwen said. "They only do arranged marriage in Arcadia. The idea of choosing love is new to him." She turned to Cad. "You can choose whoever you want to marry, you're not forced here. Men marry women, women marry women, and men marry men. You can't choose who you love, love is fluid." Cad paused, trying to think it all through.

"How do they have babies?" Cad asked, everyone around the campfire chuckled, he blushed at how rude that must have seemed.

"Some people don't need to have children Cad. It's not for everyone. I take it you could only love to procreate in Arcadia?"

"Well, we had to have one child. We were not allowed more."

"Well, it will please you to know you can have as many or as few babies as you want out here. It's not forced. Another bonus about the journey." Gwen said, winking at him. Cad blushed.

"Sorry, guess I'm a little behind with what's normal out here." Cad said.

"Nothing's normal, that's the beauty of it. When everything is strange, normal becomes weird. You are free to live however you want."

"As much as I'd like to debate topics such as free will and lifestyle choices, I think I'd struggle to do it with a clear head and since there's no mead about thanks to quick draw over there, I'm heading to sleep." Dyne said rolling over facing away.

"He's right, we should rest. I shall take first watch." Faendal said. She climbed into a nearby tree and Cad lost sight of her. Cad covered himself in a blanket, the hard floor not helping his aching back, and drifted off to sleep.

22

C ad ached all over. This was the third day that they had been travelling. He stifled the moans that he wanted to make; the others did not complain, and Cad did not want to appear weak. His back and his shoulders burned. It filled him with relief when they saw a small town in the distance.

"That's Scagg's Rock." Dyne commented, seeing Cad's face light up. "Don't expect an entirely warm welcome, dwarven settlements get suspicious of big folk visiting." Cad nodded, as they got closer, a trio of dwarves approached them stopping them in their path. They nodded at Dyne.

"What business do you have at Scagg's Rock?" The one in the middle asked.

"We have come to rest." Dyne said. His voice was different, more defined, clearer. "We would like to purchase some supplies and lots of mead." Gwen hit his arm. "And possibly some horses, if you have any." The three dwarves looked at each other before nodding.

"You may enter." The middle Dwarf said. Sheathing their daggers, Cad had not even realised they were holding them. He assumed that was the point.

"Don't cause no trouble and no trouble will find you." The dwarf on the left said.

"Don't you know them?" Cad asked confused.

"Just because I'm a dwarf lad, doesn't mean I know every dwarf. I tend to avoid dwarf settlements. The whole settling down thing and living in the same town thing gives me the shivers." They walked into the town, everyone they passed gave them looks, Cad felt uneasy, he knew he didn't belong here, but he could do without everyone making him feel unwelcome. "Ahh here we go. The Scagg's Head." Dyne said, "a good place to begin, don't you think." He chuckled, walking through the door, not waiting for their answers. A dwarf in an apron stood at the bar, looked up as they entered. He almost jumped when he saw the three non-dwarves.

"What can I do for you, gentlemen?" He said scanning them. "Oh, and ladies, my apologies." He said with a low bow.

"We are looking for a room for the night." Dyne said. Cad still couldn't work out what was wrong, Dyne's voice almost sounded posh. He was not used to hearing it. "Also, enough mead to sink a boat." He chuckled, slamming some gold on the table. The bartender looked at the three others.

"Will you be staying also?" He asked.

"Please." Gwen said with a smile.

"Uh, I haven't really got the space, I mean we could have the children sleep... Hm I don't know." He eyed the gold on the table, Dyne placed another few coin down. "I'll work something out. You're going to have to share rooms, though. I will only be able to have two available. We don't get a lot of visitors here, you see."

"That's no problem." Said Gwen, smiling.

"Now about that mead." Dyne said with a grin.

The four sat at a table drinking their mead. Faendal had chosen a wine instead. Commenting that mead was a peasant drink. The tables and chairs were built for dwarves, Cad felt very out of place, his knees came up almost to his chest, Faendal and Gwen suffered similarly. At least the glasses were regularly sized.

After finishing their drinks, Faendal decided to go and restock on some supplies and Dyne regretfully went to find some horses to purchase. Leaving Cad and Gwen alone.

"Do you want to go out and explore the town?" She asked. "I've never been in a dwarven town before. Makes me feel even bigger." She laughed.

"I'd rather not." Cad said. "Everyone stares, it makes me really uncomfortable."

"I know what you mean," She replied, "You get used to it. I always get stared at because of my size. You learn to ignore it after a while." They let the barkeeper show them to the room so that they could take off their armour. Cad looked at the bed.

"It's quite small." Cad said. "Probably enough for Dwarves, I guess."

"Yeah, everything here is a reminder that we are not welcome." Gwen said, removing her armour. "It's ok, I can sleep on the floor its comfortable enough for me." Cad thought for a moment. He really wanted a night on the soft bed, his back and shoulders ached, it was such a relief to be out of his armour and not carrying his satchel. He felt lighter. He bounced and stretched.

"No, it's ok, you can take the bed." He tried to think of a polite reason why. Because she's a woman? Because of her age? He decided to just shut up.

"We will see what happens." She said smiling. Cad blushed. They ventured into the town, ducking their heads through the low doorways. The town was not much bigger than Arcadia. A bit of a bustle around the markets, where dwarves were selling their wears, food, clothing. Cad looked through some clothes, disappointed but not surprised that nothing would fit him. They stopped by a meat stall; Cad saw they had jerky stocked. It had been a long time since he had eaten dried meat.

"I'll take a bag of jerky please." He looked at the price and was pleasantly surprised compared to the price in Roshir and got coins out of his pocket.

"That's dwarf prices. Outsiders pay double." The Dwarf stated. Cad sighed and got a few extra out. He chewed on the jerky as they walked through. It was more flavoursome than what they had in Arcadia, but it reminded him of home. He no longer felt sad when thinking about it. He still missed the people, his parents, even Wil, but he no longer yearned to go back. He was happy where he was. He saw some dwarves scowling at him. Well, not exactly where he was, but he didn't want to go back. As they got to the end of the town, no more than half hours walk, they came across a large mine built into a giant rock. The rock was shaped like an animal, he could make out the 4 legs and the body and head, almost like a giant cat, but fierce looking.

"Scagg's rock?" He asked Gwen.

"Must be why they named the town that." She added.

"What is a Scagg?" Cad asked.

"Big creatures, not that big mind, very vicious. Few of them about now, they are mainly found to the south. You would be very unlucky to come across any around here."

"So, we will be fighting one tomorrow then with our luck." Cad laughed; Gwen gave a little chuckle.

"Let's head back to the bar, the jerky has made me thirsty." Cad nodded and followed her back. The dwarf's eyes followed them as they walked.

"I'm sorry." Cad stopped and asked someone staring at him. "Have we done something to upset you?" Cad did not know where this newfound bravado had come from, and Gwen looked more embarrassed than impressed.

"You, no." The dwarf said. "You people, yes."

"Us people?" Cad asked.

"Big folk. You come here, steal our wares and send Elfkin to destroy us in our sleep."

"Elfkin?" Gwen asked. "Elfkin attacked you? When?"

"Just two nights ago, not all of us made it. So, I apologise for our hostility, but with big folk comes trouble."

"That's the night after they attacked Roshir." Gwen said looking at Cad. "Where did they go after that?" Gwen asked.

"Straight to the underworld." He said proudly, "I don't think any of them survived. People always underestimate the dwarves. That's where you go wrong."

"Thank you." Said Gwen, "We will try to be more understanding now that we know." She tossed him a coin, grabbed Cad by the hand and power walked back to the tavern.

"They must have been looking for us," She said to Cad, "Someone knows and is sending the Elfkin to hunt us. That must be why the Dwarves defeated them so easily, must have been rushed after the battle of Roshir." Cad felt the colour leave his face.

"Why are they hunting us?" Cad asked.

"I don't know." Said Gwen. "Maybe we aren't the only ones who know who you are or what you are."

"I don't even know what I am." Cad said. "I still don't know what I'm supposed to be doing."

"We need to warn the others." Said Gwen. They arrived back at the Tavern. It had gotten much busier now that the day was ending. They made eye contact with Faendal and Dyne. Faendal rushed over to them.

"Elfkin attacked here. The night after they attacked Roshir."

"We know." Gwen said. "Do you think they know?"

"I'm not sure." Faendal said. "It's unlike them to be so organised. Someone must be controlling them, though I don't know how."

"Do you think more will come?" Cad asked.

"Possibly. They must be looking for us, they won't come back to places they've checked so soon. Either way, we need to be cautious. They must think we are ahead of them."

"I need a drink." Cad said, he was shaking with nerves. Was this his life now, forever being hunted?

"Good idea." Gwen said. They both ordered a drink and sat with Dyne. He was his usual cheery drunken self, Cad wondered if he knew. Until he noticed he was not drinking his mead like he usually does, only one at a time. He wanted to remain in control. He knew.

Cad took a sip of the mead. It went down in lumps; he was not enjoying it; he was too nervous.

"I think I'm going to head to bed." He said, getting up and walking to his room, leaving almost a full glass of mead on the table.

He laid on the bed, his feet dangling off the end. Staring at the ceiling. Someone knew who he was, although he didn't know how. Even he wasn't completely sure. If it was Skorn, then why would he send him away. He wondered who he could trust. His door opened and his head shot up from the bed. It was Gwen.

"Hey, everything ok?" Gwen asked.

"No." Cad admitted. "I'm tired, I ache. I'm being hunted by Elfkin and I do not know who I am or what I'm supposed to do. Apart from speaking to some Gods of fate on some unclimbable mountain. It's a little stressed to tell you the truth."

"I admit it's a lot to take on. Just try to relax for a while, things will be ok." Gwen said.

"I don't know if I can relax." Cad said. "It's just one thing after another,"

"I know something that can help." Gwen said, slowly removing her clothes. Cad felt his erection press against his trousers immediately.

"I thought you weren't the marrying type?" Cad asked. Gwen laughed.

"Another rule about this big old world. You don't have to be married to have some fun." She kissed Cad passionately before they melted into each other's arms.

23

C ad had woken up with a spring in his step, he was a lot more relaxed, and his aches felt much better. He had slept well during the night and had to be woken in the morning. He was grateful that Dyne had managed to purchase a selection of horses. Apparently, they weren't the best, but anything was better than walking and carrying a heavy load. Cad sympathised with the animals, as they had to carry them and their load, but he knew that they were built for it.

"You seem a lot cheerier this morning, lad." Dyne commented, Cad saw Gwen look away quickly.

"Just slept really well, that's all." Cad smiled.

"Wish I could say the same." Faendal said. "You should have warned me that Dyne's a snorer. Next time we're swapping." Cad almost went to argue, but he knew Gwen wouldn't want them knowing about their night-time activities, so he kept quiet. "We still need to go to Shoreville. There is a shadow brother there awaiting our arrival. He will send word back to Roshir that we have made it that far."

"How many shadow brothers are there?" Cad asked.

"Very few," Faendal replied. "And fewer we can trust." Cad recognised Skorn had said the same thing.

"How do you know we can trust this man in Shoreville?" Cad asked.

"It's a woman, and we don't know. That's why we must be vigilant." Faendal replied.

"And how do we know we can trust you then?" Dyne asked. Cad was glad he was thinking the same thing.

"You don't know, that's why you must be vigilant." She repeated.

"If they are members of the Shadowclan, then why can't we trust them?" Cad asked.

"Many people want to control you, to use you for their own end. You have a lot of power. If they can utilise it, they will. Just because we know the prophecy doesn't mean we all want to see it played out to the end."

"And you want to see it played out?" Cad asked.

"No, I'd rather it had not happened at all in my lifetime, for there will be hard times ahead, but we must press on. I'd rather a chance of defeating the darkness than living under its rule."

"What is the darkness, anyway?" Cad asked. "I can't defeat something if I don't know what it is."

"We don't know either." Faendal said. "It's not clear, although I'm sure it will only be a matter of time before it's revealed now that you are. There are theories, of course. Guardians, demons, gods and Elfkin, depending on who you ask, but they deal with belief and not fact."

"So, the prophecy is fact?" Cad asked.

"The key points are." Said Faendal. "The chosen one revealed, the darkness rising and the last battle. The journey is where we decide how these events go." Cad looked at Gwen and she nodded at him knowingly.

"And if I don't fight?" Asked Cad.

"Then Darkness will come for you, it will destroy you and it will win. Then the prophecy will be fulfilled."

"So, I really have no choice." Said Cad.

"Of course, there's a choice." Faendal said. "It depends on how you want the ending to play out." It did not sound like much of a choice to Cad, either he defeats the darkness or he and everyone he knows gets killed by it. The conversation had dampened Cad's spirits slightly, but nevertheless he kept smiling. He was enjoying the company he kept more and more. Even Faendal had started to grow on him, although she was much more open with Cad than the other two which annoyed him slightly. They were all a team, and he wanted them all to get along.

The more Cad rode the horse the more he enjoyed it, he no longer feared being flung off the back of it. He kept his head up and held his balance well. He was pleased with how quickly he had learned, which was a good job, he couldn't be falling off at every turn. They stuck to the road to make better time, when they were about half a day away from the town, they came across a selection of caravans.

"Hold!" The caravan leader held out his hand to stop the group. "Where are you headed?"

"What business is it of yours?" Faendal snapped. Cad noticed something odd about the caravans. He had seen some before coming and going from Roshir, usually full of goods and trading supplies. These caravans were full of people. Women and children mainly looking distressed. Cad put his hand on his sword. Something was wrong here.

"No business of mine," The man said plainly, "Although I'd advise against going to Shoreville if that's where you're heading." The man was old and plump, the sun was making him sweat, he wore a regal coat, Cad imagined he had an important job.

"Why would you advise that?" Faendal said, Cad could tell that she too was wary. Dyne and Gwen both seemed perplexed by the situation. It seemed dangerous, but the people seemed harmless.

"Because we are all what's left." The man spoke. "We were attacked by Elfkin. We are the only ones who managed to escape. The men and the healthy stayed to fight. We are just the weak, the women and the children. He could see Gwen tense when he mentioned the women along with the weak."

"When was the attack?" Cad asked.

"Last night. They came in the night. We did all that we could. We are heading to Roshir in hope of shelter."

"I doubt you will find it." Faendal said. "Roshir was attacked too, we do not know what state it is in." The plump man took off his hat and held it to his chest. His grey hair flopped over his eyes, drenched in sweat.

"Then it is worse than I thought. I have never seen bands of Elfkin as organised as that."

"Neither have we." Gwen said, "This is the third attack we know of. Roshir being the first. Scagg's Rock being another."

"So, it appears there will be more." The portly man said. "Trouble is coming. I pray we can stop it."

"Do you know of Zaylen? Is she among you?" Faendal asked, looking at the caravans.

"No, she disappeared earlier in the day. What is your business with her?" The man asked suspiciously.

"She is a friend, and the reason we are visiting Shoreville." Faendal said abruptly. "If you know of her whereabouts, I will demand that you tell us."

"As I said, she disappeared. I do not know. I do know that four 'friends' came to visit her before she disappeared. A strange bunch they were."

"What was wrong with them?" Cad asked, thinking back to the dwarf at Scagg's Rock.

"No respect for the law. They were rude, arrogant, and picked things up from the market stall without paying. I was glad to see the back of them, to tell you the truth." Cad and Gwen looked at each other.

"Can you tell us anymore about them?" Cad asked, "it may be important." Faendal looked at him quizzically.

"Not much, just that they asked to see Zaylen, well not so much asked as demanded. I didn't get their names, didn't think it important to ask. I just wanted them gone. They left just before nightfall, and just before the attack."

"You didn't think to arrest them for stealing? You just willingly gave them a lady's address because they demanded?" Faendal spoke, she was sitting high on her horse, looking down on the man, anger in her eyes. She no longer looked pale and sickly, she now looked far grander and intimidating, Cad flinched slightly.

"I didn't want to deal with the hassle." The man said. "I just wanted them to move on. If I'd have known, or even thought they had anything to do with this, of course I would have stopped them. I just thought..." He bowed his head shamefully. "I am sorry. I have failed the town, maybe I do not deserve to lead them, but I am the one that they chose, and now I am the one leading them to safety or so I thought."

"Continue to Roshir." Gwen said, "They will be rebuilding after the attack. They took them by surprise but there is no way they will all be wiped out, I'm sure they will be grateful for any hands they can get."

"Will you join us?" The man asked. "God knows I could do with a few more able bodies for the journey, just in case there are anymore out there. I fear we cannot defend ourselves as well as I'd like."

"Your women seem able." Snapped Gwen, "ensure they are armed." The leader just looked at his feet whilst some women who were close enough to hear the conversation looked aghast at the idea.

"We have our own business to attend to." Faendal said, interrupting. "But good luck, if you meet a man named Skorn, tell him we have made it. He will know what we mean."

"I will do ma'am." The man said. "And who shall I say is sending this message."

"No need for names. He will understand." The man looked quizzically at her for a while.

"Very well, safe travels." The man said, starting up his convoy of caravans again.

"And to you." Gwen said as they continued towards Shoreville.

"What of these four people?" Faendal said to Cad, "you seemed to know something."

"A group of people stayed at Scagg's rock the day before their attack, too. One dwarf said they stole some of their things, that's why they were so mistrusting of us. I don't recall him saying how many, but it seems suspicious."

"So, these four are controlling the Elfkin?" Dyne asked, seemingly waking up.

"It seems so, I wonder how they knew of Zaylen. We need to go and see if we can work it out." Faendal said as he kicked the sides of his horse into a fast gallop. They headed towards the small town of Shoreville.

Cad could see small fires surrounding the town, bodies littered the floor, both Elfkin and men, if there were any survivors they were not here. They stepped through, houses were abandoned, doors were left open, there was an eery silence in the town broken only by the crackling of the smouldering fires. Dyne looked up at a tavern sign called the White Fang and sighed as he walked past. Cad knew he would be disappointed. Faendal led them towards a house on the outskirts of town. The door was locked. She knocked. Cad was not sure if she was expecting an answer.

She waited a little before she jiggled the handle; she turned to Dyne.

"Would you mind?" Dyne nodded understanding. He kicked the door, and it came crashing down off of its hinges. The team walked through the door. Cad could smell something awful. They saw in the kitchen a woman with a sword piercing her skull and nailing it to the table, dried blood covering it and flies hovering around the body. Cad could not help himself, he vomited. The smell was overwhelming. Faendal didn't move any closer, Cad could see a tear in her eye. This was her friend. Dyne walked up to the body, unfazed by the sight or smell, and pulled the sword out. It made a sickening squelch as he removed it from the head and the force caused the body to roll over. That's when Cad noticed the writing on the wall.

"For the chosen one." Cad read the writing aloud. "What do they mean?"

"I don't know." Faendal said, looking away. "They know about you, and I take it they know about the Shadowclan too. Whoever they are, they left this as a message."

"Did they leave this for us?" Cad asked, "If they knew that we were coming, why not wait for us." There was a noise at the door. They all turned to face it, drawing their weapons.

"Maybe they did," Gwen said. A man staggered through the door. He was wounded. His tunic was covered in blood and Cad could see there was a gash down his chest. He staggered past them, madness in his eyes, paying them no attention. He fell to his knees as he saw the body.

"Zaylen. No!" He howled, sobbing into the floor. "Did you do this?" He shouted. Drawing his sword, staggering weakly towards them. "Tell me who did this." He shouted angrier.

"Orrick?" Faendal asked as though she had just recognised him. "It's me. Faendal."

"Oh." Was all the man said as he started sobbing, "I knew the Shadowclan would be the death of her." Cad grabbed a chair and tried to get the man to sit down. "I knew something was strange when she asked me to leave when those men turned up. I shouldn't have left."

"What men?" Faendal asked. "It's important we know." She shook Orrick slightly, but he didn't answer. He had just passed out.

"Who is that?" Cad asked.

"That is Orrick." Faendal said. "Zaylen's husband, and by the sounds of it, the only one who has any idea what happened here."

24

Faendal went out to scout for anymore survivors. Cad and Gwen had dragged the unconscious Orrick to the bedroom and tried to tend to his wounds. He had a heartbeat; it was faint according to Gwen, meaning he was only just hanging on to life. Dyne continued looking in the kitchen, to see if he could find any signs of who the attackers may have been or why they were here. Cad was glad he didn't have to do that. The smell and the sight still disturbed him. He dabbed at Orrick's shoulder wound with a wet cloth, putting pressure on to stop the bleeding, whilst Gwen bandaged him up.

"He has a fever, keep him cool, but not too cold." Gwen said removing the wet sponge that Cad was holding against his head. "We've done all we can for now." She lay him comfortably on the bed and put a sheet over him. She poured some water into his mouth. "He needs to keep his fluids up."

"How did you get to know so much about this?" Cad asked.

"It's just basic medicine." Gwen replied. "I couldn't do much more than make him comfortable and hopefully prevent him from dying. It will take someone much more skilled than me for him to fully recover." It still amazed Cad at how well taught Gwen was, not just about healing, but about everything in general. He felt lucky to know her. His cheeks flushed red as he thought of their night together in Scagg's Rock, they had not talked about it since, and he was unsure about whether he should bring it up. They both stood there in an awkward silence, Cad's cheeks burned, he was thinking about what to say when he was gratefully interrupted.

"We've got company." Faendal's voice echoed through the house as she came rushing in. Cad quickly slipped on his plate armour and grabbed his sword.

"Elfkin?" Gwen asked.

"No, bandits." She said, Cad looked at Gwen, confused.

"Thieves. Come to steal from the dead, no doubt. Suspiciously good timing." She said, the four left the house and stood in an alleyway, watching. Cad didn't notice Faendal leave, just that she was no longer stood with them. A cart pulled up, a group of around twelve men and women jumped off.

"We've got one hour." One of the biggest men snarled. He wore a lot of jewellery. His head was completely bald, and he had patterns all over his skin. Cad wondered if they meant something. "Gold, jewels, cloth. Anything of value straight in the cart, in and out before anyone comes back to investigate." He continued. Jumping off of the back of the wagon last.

"Shall we stop them?" Cad asked. Dyne tensed up and rolled his shoulders.

"Aye, robbing the dead, we need to." He said, stepping out into the street.

"Wait." Gwen hissed at him, pulling him back. "That was Fang, he was in Roshir jail. I collected the bounty on him a long time ago, and that's Lorraine, she was a bounty I collected when Cad was with the king."

"I didn't see them in the jail." Cad said. "I should know, I spent enough time there."

"That's not the jail, Cad." Gwen replied. "That is just where they hold people awaiting trial. The king would not want such a large collection of criminals in the castle with him. These have been released from the jail."

"Aye, I recognise some too." Dyne said. "You might be right."

"But who released them?" Gwen asked, "and why? It's convenient that they show up here shortly after the Elfkin raid." Dyne was bouncing on the balls of his feet. He wanted action. "OK." Gwen said, looking at him. "Keep some alive. We have questions to ask. Try to keep quiet, we don't want to get outnumbered." Dyne rushed off out of the alleyway and into another. Gwen looked down at Cad. "These will not be like Elfkin, these are men and women, trained to fight. Be careful. If things get overwhelming, just run. Ok?" Cad nodded in agreement; his heart was racing, and he held his sword tight.

He shot out of the alley and ran the other way from Gwen, as silently as he could, into another alleyway. He saw one of the bandits entering a house carrying an empty sack. The man looked old; he was missing teeth and had a scar going down the side of his wrinkled face; he was smiling as he went through the door. Cad walked as silently as he could. Try to keep some alive, he thought in his head, although truthfully, he did not know what he was going to do. He crept into the house behind him, checking around to make sure no one was looking at him go into the house. The man's dagger was laid on the table whilst he was searching through cupboards and drawers, Cad looked around for something to restrain him with but could see nothing within easy reach. He had to hurry before the man turned around. In a panic he decided the best thing to do would be to cut the man and hopefully they could question him before he bled out. He swung his sword at great force at the man's leg. He figured it would be the best way to restrain him. The sword hit the man's leg but instead of slicing through soft flesh the sword made a loud clunking sound, burying itself a quarter of the way through the leg. The man jumped back at the sound. With Cad's sword still embedded in his leg, the old man looked at the sword and laughed.

"A hand saw would have been more damaging to a wooden leg idiot." He said in a drawl. Cad looked at him in shock. Sword still sticking out of his leg, he saw the bandit's eyes dart towards the dagger on the table. He made a movement and Cad bounced. Rolling around on the floor with the bandit. He pinned Cad to the floor placing both of his thumbs over Cad's eyes and pushing them in, the pain caused Cad to spasm and push the man off the top, once again they were scuffling on the ground. The bandit was laughing as they fought as though this was a game to him. They exchanged blows with their fists, Cad dared not go for his sword as this would give the bandit an opportunity. He punched the bandit full force in the face. What was left of the man's teeth exploded in a pool of blood in the man's mouth. He looked at him, shocked. The bandit laughed and spat the blood in Cad's face, and he saw red. He punched the bandit repeatedly. Blow after blow, he didn't notice when he had started to cry, but by the end of it he was punching the lifeless face in between sobs. It was not long before he realised what he was doing. Killing a man was very different to killing Elfkin. Those things were animals, that man could have been someone's family. Cad tried to push the thoughts out of his head.

He had to use his foot to hold down the wooden leg whilst he pulled out his sword; it was wedged in tight. He wiped the blood and tears from his face before continuing back outside. There was many more left, he would have to try and show restraint on the next one.

As Cad got to the door, he could hear shouting, we have lost the advantage of surprise he thought to himself as he peered to see where the shouting was coming from.

"You're crazy, stay away from me!" One of the bandits was screaming as he ran into a house, shortly pursued by Dyne chasing after him, growling. Cad would have laughed, had the situation not been so dangerous, to see a man run from someone so small with such fear. Cad noticed two other bandits running towards the house that they had both entered. Three against one, Cad thought. Although he knew Dyne could handle himself, he thought it would be best to help. He too ran towards the house, a steady pace as he was fatigued from his previous encounter.

"Where do you think you're going?" Said another bandit, grabbing Cad around the neck and holding a blade to his throat. "Who sent you, how did you know we would be here?" the man jerked and let go of Cad before he even finished the question and fell to the ground limp. Cad could see an arrow sticking out of the man's head. He nodded to the open space from the direction he thought the arrow must have come from, assuming Faendal had helped him. Almost forgetting where he was going, he ran into the house to help Dyne. As Cad walked in, he could see one man dead on the ground, two of the other men were trying to flank Dyne around the kitchen table.

"We've got questions for you, dwarf." One man said in the same drawling accent as the man Cad had previously encountered. "You will only be able to kill one of us."

"Aye that's true, I'm only going to get to kill one of you." Dyne responded with a smile. "I will let my friend here have the second one. Now lad!" He shouted, jumping towards one of the bandits. Cad jabbed his sword out powerfully into the side of the bandit in front of him, he was aiming to drive the sword into his back, but he turned too quickly in the confusion, it was still a fatal stab. The man fell to his knees, Cad withdrew the sword and hacked off the man's head. It made a squelching noise as it hit the floor, making Cad feel sick. Dyne laughed.

"Yer getting the hang of this lad." He was tying up the man that he had pounced on. He was still alive, looking at Cad in horror at what he had just done. "I'd get you to do the same to this one, but we want to ask him a few questions first. Maybe later, if he doesn't co-operate." He pulled the man's head up by his hair, so that he was looking at him eye to eye, "Please don't co-operate. It will be so much more fun if ya don't." He threw his head down to the ground. "Come on lad, I could have taken them both ya know, but thanks." He laughed as they walked out. They walked back out into the street. There can't be too many remaining, Cad thought. Cad saw the one that seemed to lead them, run into the house where they had started. Fang, he remembered Gwen calling him.

"Orrick," Cad muttered to Dyne and ran. Gwen had also caught sight of what was happening, and they all rushed through the door, one after another. As they got to the doorway of the bedroom, they saw Fang holding up Orrick with a knife to his neck.

"One movement from any of you and he's dead." Fang shouted. "I should have known that you were behind this Gwen, you have always been a thorn in my side."

"How did you get out?" Dyne asked. "You should be rotting away in jail." Faendal had also come into the building and seeing the situation she reached for an arrow.

"Don't even think about it." He said pushing the knife into the neck of Orrick with enough force to release a trickle of blood.

"Shadow fiends." Orrick rasped, blood coming from his throat as he said it. "Shadow fiend." He rasped louder, twisting in the man's grip to face him. Fang was too quick for him and drove the dagger through his chest. In the same swift movement Faendal had already released an arrow catching Fang in the head, both Orrick and Fang fell to the ground. Both were dead.

"Shadow fiend?" Cad asked, but no one replied.

"I've got a couple tied up," Gwen said, "I think they should be OK for questioning."

"We have one too." Cad said, looking at Dyne. He looked around to find Faendal crouched over Orrick's body.

"The members of this family were good friends to me, now they are both dead." If Faendal was upset, Cad could see no emotion on her stony face. "I will avenge you, I promise, but I have duties for now, more important than any revenge. You will understand." She closed Orrick's eyes and laid him on the ground. "Let's get the living ones together. See what they know."

25

Cad and Faendal pushed the furniture against the windows, creating a dark atmosphere. Some rays of light crept through the gaps, but it was still dark enough that you could only just see the silhouettes in the middle of the room. Gwen had instructed them to leave a solitary chair. A table sat next to the chair, a selection of knives, some sharp, some blunt, a long sharp stick and a hammer. Gwen poked her head into the room to see if they set it up. She nodded at them both.

"Let's bring in the first one." She said looking at Cad, gesturing towards the hall. Cad joined her to see three men tied with bags over their heads. One man was sobbing in the sack and shouting.

"Please, don't hurt me. I'll talk." He wriggled in his restraints. Gwen kicked him in the chest.

"You'll get your turn." She said with a harsh tone that he was shocked to hear come from her mouth. She dragged one of the others, with Cad's help, into the room. She used some rope to bind him in the chair.

"Why don't we try the other one first, if he's going to talk?" Cad asked.

"They all say that they will tell you whatever you want to hear in order to live. He will talk, eventually, but I want him scared enough that he won't lie to us." Gwen said, removing the sack that covered the bandit's head. Cad recognised him as the one Dyne had tied up earlier. He looked around at them, his eyes scanning the room, Cad tried his best not to look scared.

"Just kill me," The man said bluntly, "I don't know what you want, but I'm not telling you anything." Gwen leaned in close to him.

"We don't want to kill anyone else today." She said, "We just want to know who sent you, and how you knew to come so soon after the Elfkin attack, and where you are taking all the valuables?" She asked flatly. The man laughed.

"Like I said, I'm not talking. You really think you can hurt me, a pretty girl like you wouldn't want to get her hands dirty." Gwen sighed.

"You're right." She said before punching him straight in the mouth which sent him flying backwards. Still attached to the chair it made a loud smack as it hit the floor. She picked the man and the chair back up into place. "I don't want to, doesn't mean I won't." Cad could see the man's mouth filling with blood from the punch. He spat it at her, Cad remembered the other bandit doing it to him, it made him lose control. Gwen remained calm. "I take no enjoyment out of hurting people." She said emotionless. "But I know a man who does." Dyne stepped out of the darkness with a menacing laugh.

"Not gonna talk aye lad? I told you I'd rather you didn't co-operate. You've just made my day." Dyne said. Cad thought he saw the bandit look worried, but if he did, the expression lasted only for a moment. He kept his stony expression.

"I'm not talking." He said his speech was slightly muffled from the punch he had taken earlier, but he kept his composure.

"Good." Said Dyne, picking up the instruments on the table one by one, holding them up to the man before putting them back down again. Cad was not enjoying this, he knew the bandits would have killed him if they had the chance, but to see them hurt in this way, it made him feel queasy. "Sharp or blunt?" Dyne asked himself, holding a knife in one hand and a hammer in the other. "How did you get out of jail?" Dyne asked, putting the knife down and holding the hammer. The man said nothing. He scrunched up his face, closed his eyes and tensed. Dyne hit his knee as hard as he could with the hammer, Cad looked away. The man's scream howled throughout the house. I wonder how many times they have done things like this, Cad thought to himself, wondering how they could remain so distant, so cold. They sat in silence whilst the man howled in pain, nobody moved, Cad felt as though they waited hours though in reality it was only a few minutes.

"Shall I bother to ask again?" Dyne asked, the man held back his gasps of pain.

"They will do worse to me." The man panted, Cad could barely make out what he said, he had said it so quietly.

"Who will?" Dyne asked. Cad was pleading in his head that the man would answer him. The man didn't. Cad heard another crack as the hammer had met the other knee. More howling, much more strained than before. His throat was probably hurting through all the screaming, he thought, although would he even notice it with the pain in his knees right now? When the shouting subsided, Dyne put down the hammer and picked up a sharp blade.

"They will punish me much more in death, than you can in life." The man said. Faendal twitched upright when he said it.

"I don't have time for riddles." Dyne said. He pushed the blade against one of the man's fingers, softly at first, then with force, Cad looked away again, he heard the sound of the blade hit the wood of the chair and the sound of the finger hitting the floor with a sickening plop. Cad looked up. There was no screaming this time. The man's head was drooped down in front of him limp.

"Is he dead?" Cad asked.

"No." Said Dyne, who had his hand on the man's throat. "Just passed out. He will be awake again soon, let's start on the next." Cad and Gwen untied the man from the chair but keeping him bound tight laid him down in the hall.

"What happened in there?" One of the figures panted and wiggled frantically. "I heard screaming. Have you killed him?"

"You're next." Gwen said, heaving up the quiet figure. She could have probably done it by herself, but Cad felt he had to help, as awkward as it was. He tried to remind himself that these would kill him when given the chance and have probably killed many people before. It did not help him feel any less sorry for the situation they were in.

"What are you doing, what's going on? Let me go!" The final man shouted, wriggling even harder against his restraints, Cad wished they could do him next to end his shouting.

The interrogation went pretty much the same as the first one, with a man refusing to speak and Dyne inflicting pain on him. Cad's stomach turned over as there was a lot more blood this time and the screaming was louder. He dashed out to the corridor and through the hall; he vomited just outside the building.

"You are not like them." One man said. Cad was surprised to see the man that they had interrogated first had already regained consciousness. "You know what they're doing is wrong, you're better than that. Please help me." the man said with a pathetic note in his voice. The sobbing man also joined in.

"Yes, please, please, we don't deserve this. Let us go." Cad looked at them, with worry in his eyes. It would be the right thing to let them go. He felt that they did not deserve this fate.

"I wonder if the families of the people you have killed feel the same way, do they think you don't deserve this?" Cad said.

"We were just doing as we're told, following orders, much like you are now. Do you think our families believe you deserve to be spared from a similar fate after what you have done to us? I will never walk unaided again. Please show mercy." The man was pleading with Cad. They had not put the bag back over his head, not thinking they needed to. His face was bloody and pathetic. His stomach continued to turn. He could hear more screaming coming from the room that they were using for questioning. "Or are you someone who does as they're told? Follows orders without question? Because that's what everyone wants you to do?" Cad looked at him with a frown. He walked up to him and put his foot on his chest.

"I am my own man." Cad had said, pushing his foot harder into his chest, causing the man to cough. Blood still filled his mouth and covered his face. "If I was to kill you now, it would be my choice. If I was to take you back in and torture you more. That too, would be my choice, don't think me naïve enough to not know you would probably do much worse to me if our positions were reversed." Cad said, removing his foot from the man. The other man remained quiet, unmoving.

"Ah so we are the same, you and I." The man said rasping, trying to keep his breath. "Except you pretend to be doing the right thing, at least I'm comfortable enough to accept that what I do is bad."

"We are not the same," Cad said sharply, He rolled the man onto his stomach and cut the ropes that bound him. "Get out now, the others won't allow you the same chance of mercy." The man tried to pick himself up a few times and failed until Cad realised, he was in no fit shape to move.

"I cannot," the man said feebly, "I cannot leave, but thank you." The man said with a smile. Cad was disturbed at the smile as his mouth was still bloody and stained. "Come, I have something that can help you, it is in my pocket." The man gestured his head towards his trousers. Cad knelt down to investigate the man's pocket as soon as he did the bandit launched his body upwards and grabbed Cad by the throat, choking him as hard as he could, laughing. The man was weak but refused to let go. In response, Cad grabbed him by the throat and choked him back. He pushed his head towards the ground as he did it. Not letting go until the man was well and truly dead. Cad realised he was crying, he did not know when he had started, Gwen was right, these are truly evil people. Faendal came and picked Cad up to his feet.

"How much did you see?" he sobbed, "How much did you hear?"

"It doesn't matter." Faendal said simply, embracing Cad awkwardly as he wept on her shoulder.

"You must think I am weak." Cad asked.

"You showed mercy when any of us would not. That is no weakness, that is a strength. I admire your heart." Faendal said, patting him on the back. "Gwen and Dyne have been bounty hunters for years, they have been in situations worse than this, more than we could count. They are hardened, don't think that they would have found it any easier than you for their first time and hopefully you won't encounter it so much that you will become hardened to it. Mercy is important." Faendal went quieter as she ended, "Mercy is important."

"What is a shadow fiend?" Cad asked, wiping his tears. "Orrick's last words, Shadow fiend. What does it mean?" The last man in binds stiffened as Cad said it, drawing Cad and Faendal's attention towards him.

"I think we can ask our friend here; he will know all about it." Faendal said as the door opened, and Gwen threw out the unconscious body of the man they had been interrogating.

"Anything?" Cad asked.

"Not much more." Gwen replied, "Just more riddles about the suffering worse in death than we could in life. I wonder if our final friend feels the same, I'm sure we could think of some things worse to do now."

"I told you I'll talk." The man said wriggling on the floor, "Just don't hurt me, please."

"Dyne will be disappointed if you don't let him have his fun. Make sure it's something useful you're telling us." Gwen said, hoisting him into the room, this time not waiting for Cad's help.

Cad followed Faendal and Gwen into the room. He had hoped that the man would talk; he assumed he knew something of the shadow fiends at least.

"So," Dyne asked, pacing back and fall. "How did you get out of jail?" Said Dyne, picking up the bloodied hammer.

"They freed us." The man said. "I do not know who." Dyne lined up the hammer to one of his knees and made a false swing. "I mean, I really don't know." The man said panicking. "He wore a hood, his face looked as though it had been burnt, and what was left of it, I did not recognise."

"So, a man with a burnt face breaks you out of jail, and you come here. Straight after an Elfkin attack so that you can loot without interruption?" Dyne said, shaking his head. He put the hammer down. "Well, that's good enough for me." He said looking back at Gwen. "Should we untie him?" The man sighed with relief; Cad flinched. He was not picking up on Dyne's sarcasm. Just as he sighed Dyne punched him in the gut, winding him.

"Morrigan" The man puffed. "He said Morrigan wanted us free. The Shadow Pact is back. I swear, I swear." The man said between breaths. Dyne looked at Gwen and Faendal, puzzled.

"Morrigan? The Morrigan?" Dyne laughed, "Or is someone trying to take his place?" Cad was confused, but he was sat at the edge of his seat. It made little sense to him, but he was glad someone was talking.

"I don't know, I swear I don't know. I didn't see him, just the hooded man. He told us to come here, to take the loot north. To Candor tower."

"What for?" Dyne asked gruffly, "And how are they controlling the Elfkin?"

"I don't know, I swear, please, I don't know. Please, just let me go, that's everything I know." The man began sobbing again, holding his head down in shame. Dyne looked at the others and shrugged.

"Candor tower." He said to them, "That abandoned pile of rubble. Could be worth investigating?" He said with a shrug.

"No." Faendal cut in. "We have a job to do. We need to get Cad to Mistpeak Mountains."

"But our homes are being attacked." Gwen said sharply, "and these people are the ones behind it."

"That is for the King to sort not us." Faendal and Gwen were glaring at each other, Dyne was looking between them not sure what to say. Cad approached the man sat in the chair.

"What are shadow fiends?" Cad asked.

"The men who rescued us, they said they were shadow fiends,

and if we joined them, then we would be too, but they're not real, he was just trying to scare us."

"Men?" Dyne asked, "You said there was just one?"

"Just one who rescued me." He said, "There were four in total, one was a woman I think, they are the ones who sent us. They are the ones who claimed to be shadow fiends, they made us swear the Shadow Pact."

"The shadow pact is reforged." Said Faendal to no one in particular.

"Well, wherever we go next, we've got a wagon, and some horses." Dyne smiled a toothy grin. "Plus, we can bring him with us." Nodding to the man in the chair. "In case he remembers anything else."

"I know nothing else, please, let me go." He said in a panic.

"Let you go?" Dyne said. "No, no, no. You know too much about shadow fiends and shadow pacts. You're going back to jail where they can interrogate you properly."

"No, I can't go back. They will kill me, please, just let me go."

"Take him to the kart." Gwen said. "The other one too, if he ever wakes back up." We need to talk about next steps.

"Aye." Dyne said simply, picking up the man almost twice as tall as he was and throwing him over his shoulder, carrying him with surprisingly little effort.

"I cannot leave this unchecked." Gwen said to Faendal. "Too many lives have been lost, and if Morrigan's name is being used, we need to stop it quickly."

"If Morrigan has returned," said Faendal, "Then it is more important that we get Cad to the World's Eye. It maybe our only hope."

"I'm right here." Cad said angrily. "It's my choice where I go. I will not be forced." He said staring back and forth at them both. "If I am this chosen one that you speak of, then allow me to choose what I do." Faendal looked annoyed.

"Very well, the choice is yours, but just consider the bigger picture. A lot more is at stake than you can imagine."

"Stop." Cad said. "Do not try to sway me. I will make the choice." It surprised him at how confident he seemed, taking charge of the situation. Frustrated at everyone talking over the top of him. "Before I make my choice, I need more information."

"What do you need to know?" Faendal asked.

"Who is Morrigan, and what are these shadow fiends?" He asked and Faendal exhaled.

"Let us wait for Dyne to return. I shall tell you all that I know, although it is not everything."

26

Cad and the rest of the team sat around a table in a nearby abandoned house. They had made some tea and had decided to eat. Although his stomach rumbled, Cad did not feel like eating. Every swallow he took was hard.

"Morrigan, master of shadows, traitor of the mages." Faendal began. "Centuries ago, when the mages were rising to power, they had become so powerful that people feared them. The kings had power of the lands and army, but if the mages were to revolt, they could easily take over and it was believed that there was a plot to revolt. It is said that the mages had mastered death. If one were to die, he would be reborn as another. This is more myth than fact, but they believed it to be fact back then. Morrigan had requested a meeting with King Ahkbar. It was them together that had plotted against the mages."

"But Morrigan was a powerful mage?" Gwen asked. "Did the king trust him?"

"Trust, I'm not sure if he was trusted, but Morrigan wanted to sacrifice the mages, for his freedom. It is said that the king agreed, thinking the payoff would be better. So, they designed a prison for the mages. A perfect prison where there could be no escape, a prison for them to last generations. A prison where until a few weeks ago no one had ever escaped. They called it Arcadia." Cad shivered, he had heard Arcadia called a prison before, now he knew why.

"But the mages that were imprisoned," Cad said and then quickly added, "if it is true." He looked at the others "They are all dead, no one is hundreds of years old."

"Like I said people were scared, a lot of the abilities the mages had were exaggerated, even worse back then, Morrigan set up the trap for the mages and they were all captured but Morrigan betrayed Ahkbar, he killed him and tried to take his place. The kingdom was in turmoil, some loyal to Ahkbar, some loyal to Morrigan. He had raised his own army. They called themselves shadow fiends." Cad nodded, engrossed in the story, but his stomach turned. Did this mean he was born in prison, his entire family?

"So, what happened to Morrigan?" Cad asked.

"He died." Dyne said bluntly. "There was a war, and they killed him, he was strong but was overwhelmed by numbers."

"And so began the exile of mages," Faendal continued, "They couldn't send more people to Arcadia, there was no way in or out, but the power of the mages didn't compare to those in Arcadia, anyone with any magical ability was exiled, tied to a raft and pushed out to the Cyclone Sea to the North of Midguard. No one can cross that and live to tell the tale."

"So Morrigan is back?" Cad asked.

"Possibly," Faendal said, "Or someone is putting on a show of him returning. Either way, it is bad news, but I'm afraid the time for talk is over. We must act soon before it is too late, we have already lingered to long. Cad, it is up to you how we should proceed." Cad looked between Faendal and Gwen, torn by what to do. He wanted to go to the Mistpeak Mountains, find out about his future, then again if he tracked down these shadow fiends then he may find out more about his past.

"I would have liked more time to think," Cad said quickly, cutting in before Faendal could protest. "Yet I know I can't. We should go North, to this tower, to see what we can find. Then we can go to the

Mistpeak mountains from there." Faendal did not look happy with his choice.

"Well, my mission is to accompany you there, even if we make," she paused, considering her next words. "unnecessary stops along the way." Gwen scowled at her.

"I will load up the wagon, we can go there pretending to be the bandits and see what we can find." Gwen said shortly, "Let us move now, they will already wonder what is taking us so long, it will be a full day of travel before we get there. We can eat along the way." Cad felt a little annoyed at Gwen, he had made the choice, yet she had taken charge, not that Cad would have known what to do exactly, but she barely looked at him. At least Faendal had come to an agreement with him. His mind was still racing with all the information he had just received. Morrigan betraying the mages, then the exile. He didn't understand most of it, but he could tell by the concern that if Morrigan was back, that this was a terrible thing indeed. He felt like he was pulling away from his destiny, he wanted to find out what it meant to be the chosen one, what he was chosen for exactly, but he was happy that he was the one in control, he was the one making the choices. Gwen startled him and disrupted his trail of thought.

"Are you coming? Or do you want to hang around here all day?" Gwen said sharply, he grunted and ran towards the wagon, he thought Gwen must be even more so disturbed by this news of shadow fiends, her face had taken on a scowl ever since.

"Something's wrong." Cad said to her. Not meaning to speak, but his thoughts had come out of his mouth, Gwen stared at him harshly.

"Of course, there is." She snapped at Cad. "Mass breakouts at jail, most of which I put there, they're now running loose. Shadow fiends, Morrigan and hordes of Elfkin seem to be working together. No matter what we do, the world is changing Cad, things are happening, and I feel out of control. People are dead and I can't help them." Her eyes filled with tears as she spoke, and her last few words came out in a choke. She slammed the supply sack down in the kart and walked back to the house.

"We've done everything we could." Cad said meekly, looking at his feet. He was not sure the best way to console her would be.

"I should have been in the city. Fighting, protecting them. Instead, I was brought into hiding, to escort you on some fairy tale mission about prophecies and chosen ones." She paused and sighed, looking back at Cad. "I'm sorry, it's not your fault. I'm just angry. Angry that they kept me in secrecy, angry that I don't have a choice. I doubt I could have saved them all, but it would have been right to die trying."

"You did have a choice," Cad said, "We all have a choice. Like where we go next, we choose that, no one else. No one forced you to take me." Cad saw the expression on Gwen's face. "You were forced, weren't you?" Gwen looked down, guiltily.

"Not exactly forced," Gwen replied. "Not by anyone around, anyway." Cad gave her a quizzical look. "We are bound together." She said simply. "Our fates are entangled."

"How do you mean?" Cad asked. "We are bound?"

"There are just many things you don't understand right now." Gwen said, exasperated. "Things you may learn in time, but not now. I need to be with you, to stay with you. That is all I know; I don't know why." She stormed back into the house and came back out dragging the bandit that had told them what had been going on. Sack over his head and arms and legs bound tightly, she picked him up and threw him into the back of the kart as though he was just another sack of supplies.

"Bound together." Cad muttered to himself, he wondered if that meant a marriage of some kind, he knew he still had a lot to learn about the ways and traditions outside Arcadia. Was it really such a bad thing to be bound to Gwen? He did like her very much. He blushed as his thoughts wandered and was brought to by a sharp pat on the back by Dyne.

"Put this on," He said, "Will help you blend in." He handed Cad a bloodstained cloak that he recognised was from one of the bandits, he did not need to sniff but the smell from it was unpleasant. He could see the rest of his team had already put theirs on.

"We are going to dress as bandits?" Cad asked, "Will that work?"

"Hopefully." Dyne replied. "We want to get as close as possible to whoever is sending the bandits out. That way we can find out more." Cad nodded in understanding. This was just like the tales his father used to tell him, of spies who would go undercover, finding secrets and hiding in shadows. He felt a small rush of excitement that faded quickly when he realised how real this was, not some adventurous story. He climbed into the back of the wagon with Faendal and the bandit. Gwen and Dyne sat at the front and started moving the wagon. There was a definite tension amongst the group, a silent battle of wills against Faendal and Gwen, Cad did not like it at all. He wondered if Dyne was oblivious to it, as he didn't seem to notice, or maybe he just didn't care. With little else said, Gwen kept the wagon moving, two horses pulling them, their other horses following behind.

Cad made himself comfortable in the wagon, he lay down, his head propped up on the side. Faendal was sitting there, a blank face showing no expression, he was used to Faendal looking like that but right now it unnerved him.

"I still don't understand these shadow fiends." Cad said. "Why are they here? What do they want?"

"Shadow fiends," Faendal began "Are our counterparts, from the shadow brothers, they also know of the prophecy, but believe they can manipulate it to their own ends. They believe it is more open to interpretation, they want the darkness to win in the end."

"Why would anyone want the darkness to win?" Cad asked. "Hell, what is the darkness? I still do not know."

"Fear or power are the major drivers for the darkness to win. Either they are too scared to fight back or believe they would hold more power if they served the dark. As for what the darkness is, some believe it to be a single person, others a group. I don't think its certain individuals, I think it's more of an idea, like a world ruled by force, rather than a diplomacy." Cad looked at her blankly. "A world driven by fear, torture and violence. Would be much easier to control and probably more productive than one with a compassionate leader."

"But a compassionate leader would make things more comfortable for everyone wouldn't they?" Cad asked.

"Yes, but it's not the follower's ideals that are being fought for here, it's the rulers. For you, someone innocent and kind, yes. A compassionate ruling would seem the obvious choice. The ruler who uses fear might be a more comfortable choice for others."

"Like Morrigan?" Cad asked, the hairs on the back of his neck stood up at the name. He didn't know this man, but he felt really uncomfortable just at the mention of his name.

"Yes, if he has truly come back. I am worried that he may be the darkness in the battle against the light. If that is the case, you are in for a hell of a fight." Faendal said, face still a stony expression. Cad did not know if she was worried or not.

"What makes you so sure that I am the one to battle the dark? I cannot rule anyone, I do not know how." Cad said glumly. The idea of leading an army in a great battle seemed exciting and fun. He felt proud thinking he was going to become this outstanding leader, but in reality, he had never even been in a proper battle. Not a war. He was not even the skilled swordsman that he had believed. He was still pretty good, but the best swordsman of Arcadia was just about average in this wide world, he had sourly learned.

"You have had the vision, you have seen the sister, and I believe you are innocent and too ignorant to lie about it." Cad stiffened at this, he blushed at the ignorance part. That was true, he had not even known about the sisters of fate, or even the visions let alone anything about the prophecy.

"How can I learn what to do in such short a time?" Cad asked.

"It is doubtful that you can." Faendal said, quickly continuing when she saw Cad's unhappy reaction. "But it's not about doing everything yourself. Sometimes it's about surrounding yourself with the right friends, sharing the skills of others. Something you have already proven more than adequate at." She said looking at Dyne and Gwen. "Even if we do not always see eye to eye, I cannot deny we make a good team."

"Then why can't you do it?" Cad asked. "Or Gwen, she would be great at it."

"It is not our destiny to have." Faendal said simply.

"Why? Just because some sisters say I must do something, doesn't mean I have to, there are many people better for this. I don't understand why me? I'm nothing special."

"Only the first person in history to break out of Arcadia." She said with a grin.

"I didn't break out. I told you it just happened, I kind of fell out. I find it hard to explain, but it was nothing I did. The walls are weakening, they do not maintain the shield anymore and it is obvious, the whole of Arcadia will be free soon, maybe then I can go back."

"You have some of the most powerful magic seen in generations, since before the exile of mages."

"Yeah, I can warm things up." Cad laughed at his own joke, Faendal did not show signs that she appreciated the humour.

"You have the potential for great things, you will learn soon enough."

"It's never soon enough, everyone says I will learn things soon enough, but when is soon enough?" Cad asked looking up at Faendal. She stared at Cad for a while, thinking of the answer.

"Soon." She replied. Cad clenched his jaw. That was not the answer he wanted but should have been the answer he expected.

"What is the exile of mages? I've heard that a few times now, is it to do with Arcadia?" Cad asked.

"Sort of. Back when Arcadia was built there was a faction of powerful mages, all trapped because of their overwhelming power and talks of betrayal. They were the ones imprisoned, to stop it from happening again, anyone who showed signs of being able to develop an affinity for magic were then exiled before they could learn to control it. Sent out to the Cyclone seas."

"Cyclone seas?" Cad asked.

"Yes, to the North of Midguard, the Cyclone Seas, the ocean is so deadly, we cannot even send fishermen out. There are what we call the wastelands beyond that, nothing can live out there, from what we can see is all desert, and no ships can cross the sea to explore. Even the pirate lords would not go out there. That is why they remain to the south." Faendal explained. Cad scratched his head. Every question he had answered, opened up another five questions for him. He did not think he could take anymore explaining. He lay back down in the wagon, rested his head against something hard on the back of it, until he realised it was the bandit's foot. He got up and apologised. He realised the bandit had not moved or struggled in a while.

"Are you ok?" Cad asked meekly, shaking him. There was no response. "Hello?" He said again, shaking more violently. Still nothing, Faendal crouched near them when she also noticed.

"He's probably passed out." She said removing the sack from his head. Cad gasped at what he saw underneath the sack and not for the first time today, vomited.

"This is old magic, ancient magic." Faendal said, looking at the disfigured face. The skin had all been burnt, leaving nothing but a blackened char. Some skin had stuck to the inside of the sack that covered his head and pulled away as they removed the sack, causing fresh blood to come from the open wounds. Gwen and Dyne both turned to look, mouth agape, Cad was trying his best to look away, but he could not, this would be another face to haunt his dreams. He still had shivers whenever he had thought of Linus, let alone all the deaths he had seen since.

"He definitely didn't look like that when I put the sack over his head." Gwen said in protest.

"He has broken the shadow pact." Faendal said. "This is magic I have only read about. Magic last used by Morrigan." Cad gulped.

"How?" Was all he could force out.

"When you become a shadow fiend, you swear an oath to the leader, not to betray or reveal. This guy obviously thought it was just a scare tactic. It makes sense why the others were so reluctant to talk." Faendal said.

"So, because he told us where we needed to go, somehow they knew and burnt him? Without us even knowing?" Cad asked. "He didn't scream, he didn't even..." Cad paused, he was about to say struggle, but he struggled a lot at one point, Cad just put it down to him wanting to unbind his restraints. The hairs on the back of his neck stood up on end. This had happened, and Cad had sat right next to the man whilst he died.

"Yes, I don't fully understand it, like I say, old magic. This is more of a myth rather than a fact, but the oldest myths often started from fact."

"Well, looks like Morrigan is back then. This should be fun." Dyne said sarcastically. "And we've wasted a perfectly good sack." He said in a huff as he dragged the man into the woodlands, throwing the sack that was used to cover his head next to him. "The wolves will eat well tonight." Cad was surprised at his callous attitude towards it, but then again, Dyne was always like this.

"It is said that those who break the shadow pact are often tormented in the afterlife too. I hope for his sake, that is not true." Faendal said.

"They will do more to me in death than you can in life." Cad said, remembering the words of the bandit they had interrogated. Faendal nodded slightly.

"Well, things just got a lot more urgent," Gwen said, "We need to get moving. It's less than a day's travel, but we need to rest up for the night soon, that way we are fresh when we get to the tower." Cad stared at the direction where the body lay as the wagon pulled off, not taking his eyes from it until it disappeared over the horizon.

His thoughts trailed, Morrigan, one of the most powerful mages of all time, and Cad was supposed to fight him. He did not know how it was he could possibly succeed; he could barely do any magic. It seemed that he had no choice though, that made him bitter. They keep saying there was always a choice.

27

King Rodderick sat on his throne, awaiting news on the repairs. He had slept little since the attack; he slept little before the Elfkin raid, but everything before that seems more of a distant memory now. So many in his kingdom had died, training his new regime of guards exhausted him. Businesses had collapsed and everyone was frustrated with rebuilding. Even worse was the fact that the farms were attacked too, leaving food supplies short and rations being used. Every day more and more refugees from the outskirt villages were coming in for help, shelter and food. The mood in the kingdom is tense, it would not be long before riots started, crime rate had shot up drastically and since they had had to rebuild the jail because of the recent breakout, they have packed the cells full.

The king leant forward and put his head in his hands. I need a miracle to rebuild this, that is, if I'm not disposed of as king in the meantime, he thought to himself. High-ranking stewards have been zoning in on him, expecting to use this disaster as an opportunity to take the crown. He clenched his fists in anger.

"No!" He shouted to himself, standing up and pacing his courtroom. He had energy he needed to get rid of. He knew what he needed to do. He grabbed a guard close to the door, "Assemble my council. I need them now." He said sharply, he felt slightly guilty of the tone of his voice, it was not the soldiers fault his mood was sour. The soldier looked quite abashed. The king kept his face stern, he could not let them see him doubting himself.

"Sire, I do not know..." he attempted to say before the king interrupted.

"Well find them, take help. I need all four of them in the throne room. No, in the library. As soon as possible. Now is too late." And with that the young inexperienced soldier ran off down the corridor, beginning his hunt for his council. He walked to the library, purpose-fully. Ordering a bottle of the finest brandy from the kitchen to be delivered with five glasses on his way. He sat there, picking up a book from the shelf, thumbing through it idly, not reading the pages. Just keeping his hands busy. A servant from the kitchen arrived first, he placed the five glasses on the table. Two guards stood at the door.

"Would you like me to pour now, sire?" The servant asked. The king nodded, looking through him at the doorway, waiting. It was not too long before all four members of the council rushed in. It was rare that he called them together like this, particularly to the library. Skorn was first in. Possibly my most trusted member, he thought. Followed by Randal. He was well educated, but as a mage his skills were below average, although still better than most. Aldrin came in next; he was the oldest, not as spry as he used to be, but his knowl-edge of the kingdom and the people are second to none, and finally Jared the leader of the military, one of the greatest tacticians he had ever known. They all stood around their drinks, staring at the king expectantly. He looked at the servant awaiting with the bottle to refill their drinks.

"You may return to the kitchen." He said, "Leave the bottle." He gestured towards the table. The servant looked at him with a confused look, but slowly placed the bottle down on the table before giving a small bow and retiring. He then went to the guards, "You are to wait outside. Stand at either end of the corridor. Ensure no one disturbs us. No exceptions." The guards nodded hesitantly and set off. It was part of his rule that they are to keep him in their line of sight, but he needed no ears listening through doors today. He closed the door behind them and greeted the council. He noticed they all looked tired and uneasy. They were working hard as well, he knew.

"First, I want to thank you all for your contributions on the rebuild. I want you to know that you four are my most trusted members of the kingdom, and I would not be half the king I was today if it was not for you." He looked around at them. He wanted to smile, to show his appreciation, but he couldn't. He was grateful, he just could not bring himself to smile. Instead, he raised his glass to them before drinking. They all followed suit. Skorn grabbed the bottle and poured everyone another. His council looked concerned. He was not surprised. "I am afraid my time as King will end shortly." There was an audible gasp.

"Sire, surely not." Randal started, but Rodderick just held his hand out to silence him.

"I will be handing the kingdom over to my son, I cannot hand him the kingdom in such a mess, so there are still many things we..." He paused, "Well, I need to accomplish first, and there are things my son must do too."

"Now is not the time for this talk." Skorn butted in. "We need an experienced lead. I apologise your majesty, but I cannot condone this at the moment, we are already stretched too thin."

"There is a great battle coming, something is stirring, I do not know where from or what the outcome will be, but I am not the one to lead the battle. Fenton is."

"Fenton will make a great king, sire." Randal said. "Someday, he is new to the battlefield though and has not experienced true conflict. He also has many more years of study to complete."

"I'm afraid we won't have time for that. Therefore, I have asked you here today." The king said pouring himself another brandy. He noticed the others had barely touched theirs since their first bolt.

"There is a reason the guardians were here before the attack. They were hunting the chosen one. I could not give him up."

"I did not think you held so much weight in that prophecy, sire." Aldrin said.

"I did not, I did not think it would happen in my lifetime, but I cannot ignore it no longer. Not when my son..." The king took a sip of his drink. "Not when Fenton has had the vision."

"He has seen the sisters of fate?" Skorn asked.

"Apparently so." The king said. "There is only one way to tell for sure, of course. He needs to go to the World's Eye, to seek an audience with them. I cannot send him alone, and I cannot send an army with him in case of another attack. That is why I have called you, you are to join him, escort him to the Mistpeak Mountains."

"But sire the kingdom." Jared exclaimed, and all the others started with their protests. "Sire, send the word and I can have my six best men escorting him. Twelve even, I cannot abandon the kingdom at this time. Not when there is so much to do. Not for a fool's tale." Rodderick eyed him sharply.

"This fool's tale can be our only hope in the coming months." He snapped. "I would trust no one else with this task. There are words of the shadow fiends returning, an uneasiness grows within my kingdom and with others as well. The pirate lords no longer communicate with us, and the guardians are more active than ever. You are the only four I can trust throughout my entire kingdom to do this job, and I trust you to do it with honour." The four men held their fist to their chest as a salute when the king said honour.

"Of course, sire." Randal said. "I will begin making preparations at once."

"Thank you," the King said. "You are dismissed." One by one they rushed out of the door, leaving their glasses of brandy untouched. All except for Skorn, who lingered behind.

"What about the Arcadian boy?" Skorn asked. "I must admit, when the guardians first mentioned a chosen one, he was my first thought."

"I have not seen him since the Elfkin attacked." The king replied.

"I fear he is dead. Or even worse was the one who had been controlling the Elfkin. Randal said he had great potential."

"Are you sure it is wise to send all four of us sire? Who will support you?" Skorn asked.

"I think it is about time I made these decisions by myself, now please, hurry along. I have a kingdom to rebuild."

28

The wagon had pulled up to Candor Tower. All four of them sat stiffly, cloaks above their heads to hide their faces. It surprised Cad to see an entire town built around the tower, and from the other's reactions he was not the only one. They had passed several farms and crudely built buildings on the way. No one had paid them any attention.

"So much for it being abandoned." Dyne muttered to them. Cad was worried, there were many people in this town, if they found out who they were, then they could not defend themselves if they all attacked. It surprised him that most of them looked like normal people. He had expected them to look fouler. A dwarf halted their wagon and guided them to a spot close to the tower. He stared at Dyne.

"I don't recognise you," The Dwarf said, "I thought I knew all of the dwarves."

"I don't recognise you." Dyne said. "Now where do we get paid." The Dwarf looked quite taken aback.

"Aye I suppose you'll be wanting yer money." He said nodding into the tower. "Go in and wait for them. Someone will be out to value yer..." He paused. "Load, I suppose. I would have expected more from Shoreville, wasn't it?" The Dwarf asked.

"It was a poor town." Faendal said, "Perhaps next time you can show us how it's done dwarf." The dwarf looked at Dyne expectantly, as though he wanted him to come to his aid. When he didn't speak, the dwarf simply said.

"I meant no offence. Off ya go, get yer money." They opened the door to the tower. Cad could see it was a work in progress, the tower had collapsed in places, he noticed that they had already cleared some of the debris. They were in the process of making a new roof, they had put a crude, temporary shelter up over the half that wasn't complete. The floor was dusty, and they could see footprints going in all directions. It was quiet. A man stood in the centre of the hall with two others, all of them had black cloaks on. Cad could not help noticing the colour, it was the darkest black he had ever seen, as though light could not touch them.

The three stopped talking and turned to acknowledge the four of them.

"Who are you to disturb us? Who let you in?" One of them asked, Cad noticed it was a woman, her golden hair fell from the hood as she pulled it back from her face, Cad couldn't help but notice how beautiful she was.

"We are here to find out why you sent the bandits to Shoreville." Gwen stepped forward, her voice tensed and aggressive. "And how you knew to send them so quickly after the Elfkin attack."

"The men we sent are dead, I suppose." Said another one of the figures, lowering their hood to reveal their face. He was an aged man, with no hair and a long-hooked nose, completely ignoring Gwen's questions. Cad thought at least this man looks foul enough to be a shadow fiend.

"Yes, they had escaped from jail. I could not take them back, so we took their lives. Now what did you have to do with it?" Gwen said again, stepping closer to them. The three did not move or look worried about Gwen's aggression.

"Shame, we had gone to a lot of effort to free them." The third person said, he had lowered his hood too. Cad looked at him in shock. His face was a blackened char, just like the bandit that was in the wagon. Only he was alive, even though his face was burnt, and he could only see through one eye. The other looked like it had been melted shut. Cad could feel his stomach turn.

"Answer the questions!" Dyne growled at them. The three robed figures stood there silently and looked each member of the group up and down. Cad's hand rested on the hilt of his sword, ready to draw it at a moment's notice.

"We may forgive you for your sharp tongues, as I do not think you are aware of who we are yet. It is OK. Few are. They will be soon, soon everyone will know of the rise of the cult of shadows. Here to serve Morrigan so that he can unite the world, as it should be." The woman said.

"Unite it by using the Elfkin to kill everyone?" Gwen spat. "If you believe that then you are as crazy as he is."

"Casualties are unfortunately necessary. Force is the only way we can bring peace. It is a small cost to pay for peace." She stated.

"Peace. You call this peace?" Gwen was angry. "You do not use force to bring peace. This was a peaceful place until you came and destroyed it."

"There was war, there was crime, there was poverty. We will stop that." The woman said. Gwen attempted to argue, but she cut her off, and Gwen fell silent. "We are not here to debate with people of no value, now what is it you came for." The woman asked. Gwen hesitated before stepping closer.

"We've come to stop you. To stop whatever, it is you're doing." She drew her sword. Cad pulled his out too. He noticed Dyne was already wearing his gauntlets and Faendal was backing away slowly, her bow drawn. The trio started laughing. Gwen hesitated at first before swinging her sword at them, as quick as a flash the woman had swiped the sword away from Gwen's hands pushing it into the wall, sending Gwen toppling to the ground. One man used his hand to rebound an arrow, Cad did not even see it shoot, let alone where it went after it deflected. Dyne was charging at them, but they pushed him back at what appeared to be nothing more than a flick of the wrist. This all happened within the same second, only Cad was left standing, he hesitated. All three eyes looked at him and approached. Cad swung his sword at the man with the hooked nose. The man's eyes quickly went from confident to fear as he held out his hand to stop Cad's attack. Cad's swing caught the top of his arm, cutting his arm off as the man staggered back. Cad brought his sword back again, digging it into the man's chest, driving it forward with as much force as he could before the other two climbed on top of him. The man with the burnt face clutching at his sword whilst the woman wrestled him to the ground.

"Our magic didn't work. Why not?" The woman panted.

"It's the boy, it's something to do with the boy." The burnt faced man said. They began calling others in. There was a commotion as others came rushing to their aid. Cad could hear them scuffling with the others.

"Bind them." The woman shouted. "Send them to the cells." Cad struggled against the ropes being tied around his hands, he panicked. Imagining how the bandits had felt when they had done the same to them. Was he going to go through the same fate that they did? Cad was panting, not because of the fight, but from panic. He did not want to go to a jail again, he did not want to be tortured. He needed to get out, he needed to be free. He could feel himself shaking, he couldn't catch his breath. He felt sick and could feel his heart beating out of his chest. He began shouting.

"No! Get off me! Don't touch me!" In between deep breaths. He struggled as much as he could, thrashing about on the floor with a new strength he did not know he had. He had barely made it off the ground before more people piled on him, pushing him back to the ground. He could hear muttering around him before something heavy made contact with the side of his head. Then all Cad saw, was black.

29

C ad awoke with his head throbbing. As soon as he realised where he was, a small jail cell, bars in front of him and cement walls all around, he jumped up in a panic. He started pulling at the door frantically.

"No, I can't be locked up, not again. I don't want to be here; I didn't do anything. Get me out, please, I need to get out." He was shouting, sobbing whilst pulling at the door. It would not move.

"Shh, shh, shh, we will be ok." Gwen grabbed him by the shoulders and pulled him away from the bars. Just sit down, you were hit pretty hard. She held her hand to his head. He winced in pain. "You've got a hell of a lump." Cad sat down but his breathing was still frantic, he couldn't seem to catch his breath. He was cold but sweat was dripping down his head. He felt dizzy so sat down when Gwen pulled his arm to sit him on the bed. "Slowly, slowly, concentrate. Keep calm, breathe in slowly, and then out, in and out." She repeated this several times, guiding Cad's breathing. He listened and followed. He could feel his heart calm down after some time and his breath coming back to normal, he still felt agitated, and his head was still hurting. He noticed Faendal and Dyne were also in the cell with them. He felt ashamed for looking so vulnerable in front of them.

Why am I getting like this? He thought to himself. He gripped on the side of the steel frame of the bed he was sat on and clenched his fists, the steel hurt his hands, but it gave him some control back in his mind.

"Are you ok lad?" Dyne asked, Cad nodded. He did not want to show that he was so scared, but he could not help it. "You gave them a hell of a fright; I think you might have killed one of em as well." Dyne said with a chuckle, "Weren't expecting that their magic wouldn't work on ya. That was some quick thinking." Cad tried to remember the events that happened earlier. His head was fuzzy, he vaguely remembered a fight and everyone else being thrown around like nothing. Yet when it came to him, they all jumped on him, physically restraining him rather than what they did to the others. He remembered his sword being driven through one man's chest. He panicked and reached for his sword, it was not there, they had obviously taken it from him.

"Were you using, magic?" Gwen asked. "To stop them?"

"No." Cad answered, shocked. "You know I can't do that."

"I know." Gwen quickly reassured. "I just wondered if you were doing anything to stop them, it just seemed odd they couldn't hurt you like that."

"I don't know why nothing happened." Cad said. "But I am glad."

"Well, however you did it, when it comes to getting out of here you take the hooded guys, we will take care of the rest." Faendal said, glancing over to him.

"We're getting out?" Cad asked.

"Of course." Dyne said, jumping down from his seat. "We will fight our way out if we have to, we're not just going to sit here waiting to die."

"Or worse." Gwen said quietly under her breath, but then looked up as though she had said nothing. "We just have to figure out the right time. Listen, I know you said you couldn't do it and I don't know if anything's changed, but maybe you can try heating the lock on the door, see if you can melt it."

"I've told you I can't do magic." Cad was getting annoyed at the requests to try all the time. How many times did he have to show them?

"Just try, maybe with them using magic on you, I had the idea that maybe you have absorbed it." Faendal said, guiding him to the cell door. She looked left and right to see if anyone was there. It was pretty dark, but she continued as if no one was. Cad thought she had a gift when it came to looking in the dark.

"Fine, I will try." Cad said, he showed them once more that he couldn't do it, but he was getting pretty fed up with it now, everyone expecting him to be something he's not. He held his hands to the lock and pictured heat in his mind, concentrated much harder than was necessary but he was going to give it his all even if he was sure it wouldn't work. He could feel the warmth coming from his hands, just slightly. He concentrated harder, scrunched his face up. He really wanted it to work if it meant getting out of this cell. He held his breath, as though closing his mouth and nose would hold in the magic and it would pop out of him faster and harder. Nothing happened apart from Cad's hands getting slightly warmer. Cad panted; he had really tried hard.

"I told you, I can't do magic. Not the kind you all think, anyway." He said flatly before sitting back on the bed. There was a silence in the room. They really expected me to do it, didn't they? He thought to himself.

"That's OK." Dyne said, rubbing his hands, "we stick to the original plan, we fight our way out!"

"How are we going to manage that?" Cad asked.

"We wait for them to bring us food, not a lot of people come down here, there're no guards or anything, they are probably arrogant enough to believe they don't need any, we'll grab them, get the key, grab our gear and fight our way out. You make sure you get the hooded ones if they're about. I don't fancy scrapping with them again." Dyne said, rubbing his head as though remembering the injury.

"And then what?" Cad asked. Faendal and Gwen spoke at the same time.

"Back to Roshir, report this to the king." Said Gwen.

"To Mistpeak Mountains. The eyes of the world." Said Faendal. They looked at each other and glared. "We need to get him to the sisters; it may be the only way to stop this." Faendal said through gritted teeth.

"This is real life. Not some story." Gwen said. "People have died, and more people are going to if we don't inform the King."

"This is beyond the King's control now, we must continue. We have already wasted too much time coming here." Faendal said.

"Cad?" Gwen said, looking at him. "We should tell the King, right?"

"Um, I don't know." Cad said, Gwen's face changed to anger and then quickly calm, Cad had wondered if he had actually seen the anger at all it was so quick. "I need to think." Cad said he did not want to be the leader; he was getting frustrated that they kept asking him where to go. Cad sat facing away from everyone and buried his head in his hands. He didn't know what to think. On one hand, he may learn about his past, his future, but on the other he could help people now in the present. He thought it was obvious at first until he remembered what Faendal had just said. This is beyond the king now. He remembered the prophecy about him supposedly leading them against the shadow. He couldn't even lead this group of four. What was he thinking, he tossed and turned the ideas over in his head, would it be better for the people if he went and learned what he had to do, if it was real of course? Many people doubted it. He was unsure if Gwen believed it sometimes, and Dyne, well Dyne liked to keep out of these sorts of conversations. He would always glance away and find something interesting with his nails or on the edge of his boot that required complete focus and attention.

"I think it would be best if I go to Mistpeak Mountains," Cad said with a sigh. "Though I don't expect you to come with me, I can go alone with Faendal and I can meet you back in Roshir when we come back, if we come back." He paused. "If we even get out of this godforsaken place." Gwen kept a scarily cool expression on her face.

"Fine." She said, "Dyne, you go with them, I don't want them getting killed in some stupid way." Dyne just nodded, inspecting his fingernails closely. "If any of us survive, we can all meet back up. But I cannot turn my back on Roshir when people need my help." Cad looked at Gwen, his mouth stood agape, he had given them the option to leave, but he didn't expect Gwen to take it, so much for bound together he thought bitterly. He lay on his bed and closed his eyes, not to sleep, but to think. What am I going to do? He thought to himself. Part of him wanted to stay by Gwen's side. Was he wrong to want to discover himself, would he do the same if it was Arcadia that needed warning? He tried to put himself in her shoes.

She was loyal to the king and Roshir; she had grown up there and she had only known him for a few weeks; he knew she was right to go. He still felt betrayed. He tried to justify in his head the choice he was making, it was selfish in a way, but he didn't owe Roshir anything. They imprisoned him, made him think that he was going to be executed. Then again, they took care of him after that, and he understood why they did that, even if he didn't like it. His thoughts drifted back to the original choice. What he wanted was right, it would be for the greater good, he was sure. He then worried about the implications if it was correct, the prophecies, his role in events. Being used like a puppet on a string, by some unknown entity, that had decided his future before he was even born, it made him angry. He almost said he would not go, but he knew that he needed to, just to make sure, it might not be true after all and if it was... Well, he would do what he wanted after that, they couldn't make him lead an army. How could he? He barely knew about war.

"Why has no one been down to question us." Faendal asked with a frustrated tone. "Or feed us, I'm starving." Cad picked himself up and looked around the cell frantically. She was right. They had been in here for ages, he hadn't seen a single person yet. He jumped down from his cell. He could feel the panic rising in him again. They were going to leave them here to die.

Cad rushed to the bars, began pulling at them frantically, he shouted.

"Hello! Is anyone there?" He could feel all the emotions flooding back, the panic. He hadn't even noticed that Gwen had grabbed him and pulled him back to the bed, calming his breathing down again, he was hardly aware of where he was or what he was doing, but as he breathed deeply, listening to Gwen's instructions in the background as though they were muffled sounds. He came back to normality, whatever that was right now and gathered his senses back. He noticed Dyne was pushing on the bars and Faendal was looking through them as though to spot some sort of way out. Cad could feel his mouth getting dry. They had no water and there was no one to bring them any. Cad lay down and closed his eyes. He was going to die in this cell, he knew it.

30

C ad tried to ignore the rising panic in the surrounding people. He knew that they were working hard to keep their cool, for his sake, but with his eyes closed it was as though he could sense their urgency and their panic. Throughout the night Cad could not sleep, nor could he move. He knew that if he got up to move, the panic would overtake him again; it was all he could do to focus on his breathing. In, out, in, out, he went over and over it in his mind. He focused so hard on his breathing that he did not notice the noise of footsteps enter the dungeon.

"Down here!" a voice somewhat familiar to Cad said, as he sat up abruptly. Into the room walked four men, Cad knew them, well most of them. He breathed an enormous sigh of relief that turned into a sob. It was Skorn from Roshir, as well as Randal the mage, he was surprised Fenton was there, he had only seen him in passing but he recognised him as the King's son, the other man Cad didn't know his name, but he too he recognised from Roshir.

"Skorn?" Faendal choked with what Cad thought was the first-time any emotion had shown in her voice.

"What are you doing here?" Skorn asked looking at the party, whilst the others searched around looking for a way to open the door.

"Never mind that just get us out!" Gwen pleaded; Cad could sense emotion in her voice too. In the end it took Skorn and the man that Cad didn't know to break the lock with heavy pikes that they had found against a wall whilst they all stood at the back of the cell. They were given water skins, which they all drank from greedily.

"How did you get through the town?" Faendal said. "They have powerful magic here."

"Powerful magic?" Fenton asked, "There is no one here." He said with a sneer. "How did you end up in that cell, and why are you here in the first place?" He asked. Cad looked at him oddly for a second, then realised he didn't know where they were going or why. Skorn did though, he was the one who sent them.

"They captured us, the night of the Elfkin attack," Faendal responded, "but what do you mean there's no one here, there's an entire village out there, or there was just over a day ago."

"There's no one out there now." Skorn said, "No one's left here either, I did not notice any tracks."

"Of course, there's people out there!" Dyne shouted, "You think we locked ourselves up for fun lad!" He shouted pushing passed them, they all clambered out of the dungeon and out to the village and was met with complete silence. Faendal began looking at the ground and checked the area.

"No tracks." She said simply. "There're no tracks, how is that possible? There was a complete village of shadow fiends out here."

"Shadow fiends?" Fenton said with another sneer, Cad really did not like him, he was so pompous and arrogant. Everything that was said to him was doubted to be the truth.

"Yes." Gwen jumped in to explain. "Shadow fiends have reformed; they had a community right here. At least 100 strong, mages too, three powerful ones, although Cad killed one."

"He did?" Skorn said with a raised eyebrow. Gwen explained what had happened from being "captured" to the fight in the tower and to the cell. Cad only listened with half an ear. He noticed a small stone on the floor. It looked like any ordinary stone, it was an ordinary stone, but it seemed like it sang to Cad. He couldn't figure it out. He walked over to pick it up. Held it in his hand. It was cold and felt just like any other stone would. He knew it was special though, he couldn't understand how. This stone was important.

"Cad?" Skorn said, bringing Cad out of his trance and back to reality. He shook his head and pocketed the stone before returning to the party, holding the stone in his pocket. "What have you found?"

"Oh, nothing." Cad said absent minded. It was just a rock, after all. "Just a nice stone, that's all." He reluctantly held it out to show it to them. He did not want them to take it off him. Most took one look at the stone and then went back to talking. He noticed Fenton rolling his eyes and mutter to himself.

"Well, we have to continue." Randal said to the group, "We have things to do out here, I suggest you all report back to the king. We can take care of business here, if there is any to take care of." The group come to an agreement and the four newcomers rode off without a moment's hesitation. Cad was dumbstruck.

"So now he wants me to go back?" He asked, "After coming all this way I just have to turn around?"

"No." Faendal cut in before anyone else could say anything. "We continue as normal. Skorn said that Fenton has had the vision. We will have to see for ourselves, we will camp here for a night or so then we will continue to Mistpeak Mountains as planned." Cad looked at Gwen, expecting to see her protest.

"Well, it seems like Roshir is not in the state that I thought, if it could send four of the most influential members of society out on this nonsense, looks like I will stick around after all." Cad could not tell if she was annoyed or not, she held a stony expression which made her difficult to read. "Plus, I told you Cad Cadderick, our fates are intertwined." She smiled warmly at him, the stony expression lifting off her face and replaced with warmth. He smiled at her; he was glad that they were a team once more.

The group combed through all the makeshift huts and farms, everything was abandoned, it made the hairs on Cad's neck stick up. How can an entire village full of people disappear? He wasn't much for tracking, but he knew the others were, and the fact that there were no tracks leading away frightened him. He wondered once or twice if they were hiding, but where could a whole village hide, and why? He idly played with the small rock in his pocket whilst he searched the huts. There really was nothing here. No food or supplies. If things were not so clean, he would wonder if it hadn't been abandoned for years.

"So where could they have gone?" Dyne asked. No one answered, no one knew. It made the hair on the back of his neck stand on end. "What's all this with Fenton being the chosen one?" Again no one knew, no one answered.

The longer they looked, the more he could tell people were getting frustrated. There was nothing that could lead them to the whereabouts of anyone.

"The only possible answers are that they have covered their tracks better than anyone I have ever known," Gwen said. "Or they have used magic somehow, but what kind of magic could make an entire village full of people disappear?" Gwen said to no one in particular, no one answered once more, no one knew. Night fell and they started setting up one hut to camp in, as they were loading the fire, Cad noticed something odd. Everyone stopped what they were doing, fell to the ground. Dyne was facing away, but Faendal's and Gwen's eyes followed Cad. He quickly dropped his bundle of wood. He felt the air go cold; he could see his breath. The surrounding land went darker, as though surrounded by a mist.

"So, you have escaped then." A voice behind him said. "I knew there must have been some sort of power in you." He turned to see one of the mages from the tower earlier, the one who had looked like he had been burnt. "You are something I had not expected, you are strong, yet you are so weak, you could become great." The man said slowly walking around Cad who was rooted to the spot. His hand gripped the hilt of his sword tightly. "Now there will be no use of weapons today." He said as the blade he was gripping got hotter and hotter, before burning his hand, he released it. "Do you know who I am, boy?" The man said.

"Morrigan." Cad said putting the pieces in his head together, it must be. The man let out a raspy laugh.

"No, no, but I am used to being in the shadow of the glory he held many years ago. I am Barnabas." He paused, looking at Cad, then scrunched his face up in frustration when Cad didn't recognise the name. "I used to be one of Morrigan's pawns. I was faithful to the shadow pact, until I realised my power surpassed his." Cad tried to grab hold of his sword again, but it was still too hot, his holster was smouldering from the heat and the sword started hanging at an awkward angle. "I know a lot of this world, and a lot of the magic, but I don't know why it doesn't affect you, Why?" He said with a snap.

"I don't know." Cad muttered, he was trying to come up with a reason why, to trick him, to scare him, but nothing came to mind.

"You will tell me." Barnabas said. "Or you will suffer." He pulled a small dagger from what appeared to be nowhere and pointed it at Cad's throat. "What are you doing out here, who sent you?" He glanced at Gwen and the others on the floor. Their eyes were wide with panic, but they were held stiff as though bound by invisible ropes. He was free to move, but he wondered what he could do.

"Ok, I will tell you." Cad said, holding his head high, his sword leaning away from his body now as it melted through the thick leather of his sheath. Barnabas narrowed his eyes at him and lowered his dagger slightly until he could see a small smile behind the blackened face. "No one sent me, I am my own man. I do what I want." He said, as he finished speaking the sword fell out of its sheath in one quick moment, he grabbed his sword gripping it tightly and thrust it at Barnabas, the heat from the sword burnt his hand, he could feel his skin blistering against the hot metal. He stabbed straight in the chest; he could feel the sword pierce through him, but it was as though there was nothing inside. It felt wrong. Barnabas vanished from where he stood, and Cad dropped the sword to the floor. His hand was in bad shape, severely burnt with a brand from the sword hilt. He was screaming, he didn't know how long he had been screaming, probably since he grabbed a hold of the sword. The red glow on the sword disappeared, but the pain in his hand remained. He looked around.

"Did you really think it would be that easy?" Barnabas said, appearing behind him. "I am not stupid enough to come here without knowing exactly who you are. Or what you are. I'll be there though, watching every step of the way." And with that, he vanished, the fog vanished, and everything seemed much brighter, Gwen got up and rushed towards Cad, quickly tending to his hands whilst Faendal and Dyne started scouting around the village once more. Cad winced as she soothed his hand with water from her waterskin.

"How did he do that?" Cad asked, looking at Gwen.

"I don't know, but you're safe, that's all that matters." She said bandaging his hand. "I shouldn't put a bandage on as it's going to stick, but to leave it out in the open when we are out here it would easily get infected. It's going to be painful for a while, I'd say use your other hand." Cad looked at his right hand. He couldn't use it as well. The sword felt odd in his right, as though someone else was controlling it.

"I won't be much use fighting." He said, "Then again, I wasn't much use with my good arm." He couldn't help but laugh. It wasn't long ago that they considered him the best. Now that he was no longer in Arcadia, he was below average. Things were not going well. He held the sword in his right hand and waved it around, it felt more like it was a wobble, he sighed and went to put it in his sheath only to find that it was no use, the sword went straight through.

"Think I would have been better off in the cell." He muttered to Gwen as he got up to search for a new one.

31

C ad was running through the field, a dark shadow was getting closer and closer, he ran harder. The black fog overtook him, surrounded him, he couldn't see. He heard Barnabas' raspy laughter.

"You can't outrun me boy." He said appearing in front of him, his charred face clearly visible even in the darkness that surrounded him. Then there were two of them, then three. Suddenly Cad was surrounded by more figures of Barnabas than he could count. They were all saying different things, "Burn him", "Kill him", "He's mine", "So weak" amongst other things. They kept moving towards him. Cad couldn't move, he couldn't fight, they got closer and closer.

Cad awoke with a start. He was sweating, his hand still hurt. He jumped up. Faendal was sat awake, she stared at him.

"You're alright lad." She said, "Dreams can seem so real."

"How did you know I was dreaming?" Cad asked.

"You were talking in your sleep, you have been for a while, I was worried you may have had a fever, but you seem ok. You were very brave for what you did."

"I did nothing." Cad said. "Nothing that mattered anyway."

"You stood in the face of defeat and still gave it one last shot. You have heart, sometimes that can be the difference between winning and losing."

"It's just a shame that this time I lost." Cad grunted, looking at his bandaged hand.

"Perhaps, but you have frightened him." Faendal said, bringing him a mug of tea. "He was too scared to face you in person."

"I don't know why though." Cad responded, "I'm nothing special. I'm no skilled fighter, and an even worse one now." He said holding his hand up.

"There is definitely more to you than meets the eye." Faendal said. "I think we will learn a lot from the sisters of fate."

"What if we can't get there?" Cad asked, "What if it is Fenton that is the one to find them. Then what?"

"There is no point in worrying about the journey unless it is the one that we are taking." Faendal said, "If we were to worry about the dangers on all the ones we may take, it would be too difficult for us to arrive anywhere." Cad sipped his tea. It made sense. One thing at a time, he thought. He had other doubts, other worries, he started a few times but ultimately decided it wouldn't achieve anything. "We will arrive at the mountains soon, then we can plan what happens next. It is almost morning. We had better make an early start." She gave Dyne a small kick and Cad shook Gwen's shoulder.

"That time already?" Dyne enquired gruffly whilst getting up, Cad could notice a big difference in him without his regular supply of mead or ale. He was more withdrawn, less bubbly. Still nice enough, but much quieter. The mountains were now less than a day away on horseback, and they grew more and more clear as they got closer. Cad could not see the peaks of the mountains as they seemed to pierce through the sky, but he could see that they were covered in snow which was odd as he wondered why the snow had not melted, it was quite warm as they approached the base.

"Hold." Gwen said sharply, causing Cad to jump in his seat. Her horse rushed off into the distance, Cad could see what she was approaching. It was a man, an oddly shaped man. It was only as he got closer, that he realised why. The "man" although lying on the floor, with multiple arrows sticking out of various places and slashes along his body, was more than twice the size of Cad.

"Do you think this was Skorn? And the others?" Cad asked.

"I hope so." Faendal replied. Best to keep your swords ready just in case there are more giants around. Cad felt for his sword before clumsily realising he held it on the other side now, his hands were still not used to this and he gripped it awkwardly as he trotted on. Leaving the giant's body behind. He was grateful that they didn't have to fight it, but Faendal said there could be more. He shuddered at the thought. He could barely fight someone his own size right now. They approached the foot of the mountain that was closest to them. There were several others surrounding.

"Which way do we go?" Cad asked. "Which mountain is it?"

"I don't know." Faendal responded, Gwen shot her a sharp angry look. "The others went around by the looks of it, I don't know why though." Cad looked around for inspiration.

"I know the way." Cad said, shocked that he knew, he didn't know why or how, he just knew. "We go up." He said pointing at the mountain in front of them. Faendal gave a glance towards the path that he said the others had gone down, but nodded and as a group, they climbed the mountain.

The incline was gradual enough that they could easily walk, but as they got higher and higher so did the slope. Cad could feel a pull in the direction. He wondered if he would have to climb the whole mountain. He could feel it getting colder. They had walked almost half a day and were less than half-way to the top. They camped in a little shelter for a while before continuing. Once again, Cad had nightmares about Barnabas, about the darkness, about the burning sensation.

Towards the end of the second day of climbing the mountain, they found a cave; he knew that this is where he must be. Although he didn't know why. When they had got there, it was just an ordinary cave; they set up camp for the night, but Cad felt like he was missing something; he paced around the cave, looking at the walls. Nothing stood out as different to any other cave, he just knew this is where he was meant to be. He didn't tell the others why, as he didn't fully understand himself. Come the morning he would try to make it further to the top. If nothing was there, then he would worry about that when it came, he thought, considering Faendal's advice.

They huddled around the fire for warmth, Cad was exhausted from all the walking, they had had to leave the horses in a cave further down when the paths became much more dangerous. He could feel himself drifting off to sleep.

Barnabas was there again. Laughing at him, chasing him. When he touched Cad, he awoke with a start once more. Only this time, when he had awakened, he was no longer where he fell asleep. He was no longer in the cave.

32

C ad found himself atop a mountain, he was not sure which one. What surprised him was that the air was still, and the temperature was warm when it should have been freezing cold this high up. In front of him stood three women, they were the most beautiful women he had ever seen, their skin was golden and smooth, they all looked freshly bathed and had a glow about them, they were all staring at Cad. What was peculiar about them was their hair colour. One had a shimmering blue hair that came down past her shoulders, the other a bright green, not a hair out of place on any of them. He saw the third with pink hair and instantly recognised her as the woman he had seen the night that he left Arcadia.

"You." He said pointing at her. His jaw dropped.

"Welcome Cadderick Storm-Bringer," The pink-haired lady said. "We have been expecting you." Cad had so many questions, but he did not know where to start.

"Storm-Bringer?" He asked dumb struck, not a question that he had wanted to ask, but it slipped out.

"Yes, that is your family name, before they were forgotten within the walls of Arcadia, you are a descendant of the once noble Storm-

Bringer family." He hesitated; he was even more confused now that he had asked the question. He thought it would be better to move on.

"Why am I here?" Cad asked. "Why have you been expecting me?"

"We are expecting the chosen one to reveal themselves. We have been watching you." The pink-haired lady was talking, but the two others were gazing at him.

"Why do you think that I am the chosen one?" He asked.

"We have followed your journey; you have heart, and you have courage. You could be the one to stop the darkness." She stated.

"And what if I don't want to be?" He asked stubbornly.

"It is not a matter of choice; it is a matter of fate. That is why we are here, as the sisters of fate we must see the prophecy come to." She explained.

"I think you should choose someone else." Cad said bluntly.

"We do not choose the person; destiny chooses the person." The blue-haired woman had now taken over. "It is up to you to see if you are, by peering through the World's eye." She gestured into a small pool that the ladies were surrounding. Cad edged forward towards the small pool of water. He glanced in. All he could see at the moment was his reflection. He looked haggard from the journey, and his stubble was rough and uneven. He needed a good shave and a bath. Shapes began to take form in the pool, he looked closer to make them out. Shapes were dancing around, as though trying to tell him something. He leaned in closer still, his nose practically touching the water. He felt himself fall in, but rather than hit the bottom he fell further into empty space. Water rushed around him, he couldn't breathe, in the same moment he was somewhere else.

He looked around him; he felt this place was familiar. He jumped when he heard voices behind him. There must have been fifty or sixty people here, wearing black robes, similar to the ones warn by the Mages at Candor Tower. Cad had nowhere to hide. Some were looking in his direction, but they appeared not to notice him. He looked around the people were panicking about something. They looked like they had been traveling; they had caravans of supplies with them and there was a lot of farmland around them.

"How can a fortress just disappear?" One figure said.

"No rubble? No debris? A powerful magic was involved here." Another said, "But we are the most powerful mages that walk the land, and it is even beyond our power."

"Why is Morrigan not here? He was the one who suggested we take over the fortress. Something feels wrong."

"What is this?" Someone asked, Cad walked closer to look, for some reason no one was paying any attention to him, he didn't think they could see him at all. They gathered around what looked like a small podium. Then Cad knew exactly where he was and what they were looking at.

They were in Arcadia. That was the podium the mages used to power the barrier. This was Arcadia before anything was built. He noticed the shape of the fields, and the places where buildings should go. As soon as one of the mages touched the podium, a purple spark emitted, hitting every single one of them. It did not come near Cad. The mages fell to the floor as it happened, none of them having any time to react. The barrier that Cad recognised shone around him. Once again, he was trapped in Arcadia.

Cad felt the water rush around him again. The scene changed around him; he was still in Arcadia but this time crude shelters were around him. Buildings were being built; he noticed the foundations of buildings he was familiar with. He realised that this was the beginning of Arcadia.

"There must be a way out, we shouldn't give up." A man with shaggy black hair said to another with a short, neatly trimmed cut. Wearing the same robes Cad had seen earlier.

"We've tried, since that thing absorbed our magic, and we have been working night and day to reverse it, we are helpless."

"Morrigan will pay for this." The man spat.

"That's if this even was Morrigan. This power is much greater than any I've seen before, hell, that any of us have ever seen. Besides, why would he do that to us?"

"He always was... Strange." The man said. Once again neither person paid attention to Cad, he had stayed rooted to the spot. "This was planned."

"By King Ahkbar, no doubt, he always was distrustful of us, thinking that we desired to take over."

"We didn't?" The man said with a laugh.

"Not yet, you know things would have been better when people with actual power are leading."

Cad felt the sensation of water rush around him. This time he was with a large group and all of them were looking at one man speaking.

"You can't keep us in this prison!" One shouted.

"Oh, but I can, this is the order from the king." the man said with a smirk. He was tall and handsome. Cad felt like he knew him but couldn't quite put his finger on it.

"Why?" Another asked.

"When Morrigan rises to power, there will be no one to contend with him. Only those who have sworn the shadow pact shall rule with him. I have sworn my oath."

"There must be a way out, if you are able to get in and out. Please, Barnabas, help us." Someone pleaded. Cad felt his blood rush cold. It was Barnabas, before he was disfigured. This was who had been following him, chasing him. Like everyone else, he paid no attention to Cad.

"Oh, it's easy to get out." Barnabas smiled. "You just need actual power."

"That thing, took our power from us." Someone shouted, he walked up to Barnabas angrily.

"Ahh yes, quite a clever artifact, I must admit. Do make sure you keep it powered don't you, it should have left you with enough magic to at least do that."

"And what if we don't?" The man said facing up to Barnabas.

"Then the town and everyone in it dies." At the same time, he had said that the man squaring up to him went flying backwards like a gunshot and in the same instant Barnabas vanished. There was a frantic chattering around the group.

"So that's it? Imprisoned forever? Or we can die? Some fine choices." Another man stood forward to the crowd.

"The barrier is large, enough for us to survive in. We can try to find a way out in the meantime. Maybe someone will free us."

"And until then?" A woman asked, cradling a small child in her arms. "I don't want my boy growing up knowing that he's been imprisoned forever."

"It may not be forever," The man replied. "In the meantime, we can just tell them it is there to protect us, from the outside."

"You mean live a lie?" someone asked.

"We may have to."

Once again, Cad felt the water rushing around him. He wasn't in Arcadia this time; only darkness surrounded him.

33

"So, you are from Arcadia?" A familiar voice said to Cad, "I have seen, just as you did. I was handsome once, wasn't I." Cad looked up to see Barnabas staring at him.

"You." Cad said, "You trapped them there."

"Oh, no, not I." Barnabas laughed. "I was just following orders. I soon learned to ignore my orders. It came at a price." He said fingering his charred face. "Do you know, I am the only one powerful enough to have survived breaking the shadow pact? Twice now actually, even Morrigan himself could not have done that, and he's the one who created it."

"Why?" Was all Cad could ask.

"Unrivalled power," He laughed again, "We will meet soon, Cadderick. I will be waiting for you. I have seen now what potential your power has; I cannot risk it." Cad could feel the darkness around him get brighter.

"You have no part in this Barnabas." A voice spoke. He knew it was one of the sisters, but he could not tell which one.

"Ah, Argona." Barnabas said, "So you are behind this, another puppet? Is it that time again?"

"Be gone." The voice said, and Barnabas began to fade.

"We will meet soon, Cad, I am above the prophecy." Then his voice faded, and he was gone. Cad felt the rush of water around him again and he was back on top of the mountain, with the three sisters looking at him.

"What happened?" He asked, gasping for breath. It felt like he had been in there for hours, but he couldn't have held his breath for that long.

"You saw the past, this will help you understand the future." The pink-haired sister said, although Cad was still unsure if it was her voice he had heard. Was she Argona?

"And Barnabas?" He asked. The sisters looked at each other.

"A fault in the timeline. He should not be here. He will be removed." She said bluntly.

"So, what now?" He asked. "What do I do now as the chosen one?"

"I'm afraid you are not the chosen one." The sister said. His jaw dropped, wasn't that the whole reason he came here. They practically summoned him.

"So, I wasted the journey. What now?" He asked shortly.

"That is up to you. You have power Cadderick, you will learn how to use it. The World's Eye will have helped you open that. Your future is up to you, I feel there is much of this world that could benefit from your power. You're not the chosen one, but I believe you can still play an important part."

"How?" He asked, dumbstruck.

"It is up to you. Find your friends, make your life. Live." Cad felt the earth move around him and when she said the word live, he was back in the cave.

"Quite an unusual tactic, why didn't you tell him?"

"Sometimes you have to give an illusion of freedom, to get someone to do what they must."

Cad lay in the cave; his friends sound asleep around him. It was still night; he was sure atop the mountains it was day, but then it was warm as well. He wondered if it had actually happened, or had it just been a dream, but it all seemed too real around him, and too unbe-lievable for him to dream it. He was tired, so rested his eyes and wondered what his parents would think of him up here, finding out he was not the chosen one. They'd probably want me back in town to be a mage, he thought. That's all they'd want, for me to stay in Arca-dia. He fell asleep. When he woke up, his surroundings had been changed once more. He was home.

34

Cad looked around, he was in Arcadia, but not in the past, this is what it looked like now, the surroundings he was used to. It was night, all the lights were out, everyone must be sound asleep. He walked to his home, worried by what he would find.

He gave his door a push and found his hand fell through it; he stepped through the door as though it was not there. I've died and become a ghost, was his initial thought. He tried touching a few things in the house. Again, it just went straight through, as though everything was just made of different coloured lights. He walked into his room; it was exactly how he remembered it, as though it was waiting for him to return at a moment's notice. He turned into his parents' room.

Both of his parents were asleep, his father snoring. His eyes filled up with tears at the sight. He tried to blink them away, but god he missed his parents.

"Mum, Dad, I'm home." He said with a choke. They did not stir. He walked up to them, about to gently rock his mother awake. His hand fell through her as though she was made of light too. "Dad, Mum!" He shouted louder, then louder. He wanted to wake them, he needed to speak to them. He was a ghost to them. He knew the noise that he was making would have woken them, his mother especially, and began to cry as he continued to call their names. He needed their attention. He so badly wanted to speak with them. He knelt next to the bed and held his head in his hands and wept.

"Are you real?" A small voice said as Cad felt someone poke his shoulder. He turned quickly, startled by the voice. There stood a boy, a child. He looked shocked as he continued to poke Cad. "I've never seen an actual person here before."

"Who are you?" Cad said jumping back, cursing at himself for being intimidated by this child. "What's going on here?"

"You can dream like me." He replied. "We're dreaming right now, no one can see us, it gets quite lonely. I could feel something was odd tonight." He said looking at Cad up and down. "You use magic, don't you?" Cad shook his head. He did not know what to say. "You must do. My Mum says I'm not allowed to use it, even if I'm really cross. It's hard because I enjoy using my magic." Cad opened his mouth to speak, then closed it again. He took in the odd scene for a while longer.

"Who are you?" He asked again.

"I'm Teague." He said, "What's your name? I'm not supposed to talk to strangers, but I've seen no one else here before, no one real anyway."

"I'm Cad." He hesitated. "No one real?"

"I think so," the boy said. "We can't touch anyone, see." To make his point, the boy jumped through the bed his parents were sleeping on. He passed through them, making Cad flinch. "But they can see each other, and you can see me, so you can't be one of them."

"How do you know all this?" Cad asked.

"I've been coming here for a long time." He replied, "Since I was five," He held up five fingers to show his point.

"How old are you now?" Cad asked.

"Ten." He said, bringing his other hand to join them. "Mum says I shouldn't be doing it, but I can't help it. I don't tell her anymore, but it gets boring."

"So, we are asleep right now?" Cad asked, "We're not dead?"

"Dead?" The little boy looked at him as though he said something silly. "No, I do this all the time, I don't come here much, it's pretty boring. The people seem nice though, not like the stories. Mum says I can't tell anyone I've been here though."

"How did we get here; I mean into Arcadia?" Cad asked.

"You just have to think of a place, and you end up there, you have to have been there first though."

"You haven't been to Arcadia though, have you?" Cad asked, surprised.

"No, the first time I had to walk here, it took a very long time."

"Walk?" Cad was surprised "From where?"

"From Roshir. The nights get boring, and I like to travel. Once I've walked somewhere once I can travel there the next night." Cad couldn't get his head around it.

"You do this every night?" The boy nodded.

"I wish I didn't, but I can't help it." Teague said, he looked sad about it. Cad felt sorry for him. He could imagine how lonely it would be to spend every night here alone. He then worried if this was his fate, to spend every night walking around as a ghost whilst he slept, and if so, why had it began now, he wondered if the sisters of fate had anything to do with this. He chatted with Teague throughout the night, the boy was pretty likeable, he tried to teach Cad how to travel, Teague could travel to different places by concentrating on them. Cad couldn't manage it, but Teague assured him.

"It took me a while too, first I did it by accident, now it's easy." Teague closed his eyes and disappeared. "Boo." He shouted behind Cad causing him to jump, he giggled. Cad found himself laughing too.

Eventually Cad started to feel a little light-headed. He looked at his hand and he could see through it, almost like he was fading.

"You're waking up now." Teague said. "See you soon." He waved with a smile. Cad returned the wave and was back in the cave, being woken by Gwen. He looked around, startled at the sudden change of scenery.

"You're alright, Cad, time to get a move on." She said he noticed Dyne and Faendal were already up and packing up the camp. Cad felt the bandage tight around his hand from the burn, he took it off to change it, when he undid the bandage it shocked him to see his hand had completely healed. When did that happen? He thought to himself.

"We might as well head back." Cad said, everyone turned to look at him. "I'm not the chosen one after all." He couldn't decide if he was sad or not.

35

Cad and his friends walked down to the base of the mountain in silence. They regarded him carefully when he told them the story of last night; he left out the bit of returning to Arcadia in his dreams and meeting Teague. No one asked questions, no one tried to object. He wondered if they were all disheartened.

"Either way, it's pretty impressive you got to see the sisters of fate lad." Dyne said, "I was always on the fence about if they were real or not, that's if it wasn't some crazy dream." Cad smiled weakly at him. He didn't want to argue, but he knew it wasn't a dream. They arrived at the cave where they had left their horses and began to mount them.

"What now?" Gwen asked, looking between Faendal and Cad.

"My pledge is to assist the chosen one." Faendal said, "If it's not you, Cad, I must find out who. I suggest we return to Roshir. If it is Fenton, I'm sure he will return with the news."

"What about you, Cad?" Gwen asked.

"I'm not sure." He said slowly. "Maybe I can stay with you?" He asked Gwen.

"Can I have some time alone with Cad?" Gwen looked at the

others, they nodded as they went outside. Gwen sat on the ground, not looking at him. "I think you need to find your own way, there's nothing to gain by sticking with me. Cad opened his mouth to speak, he didn't know what to say. I fear I have been leading you on, I forget how innocent you really are. I know why you want to stick with me, I have thought about it, and I know you think about it too, but this is not the life I want."

"I thought we could work together catching bounties." Cad said softly.

"And just have a professional relationship?" She asked, "What about when you want more than that, and please do not lie to me Cad, I know you do. Sometimes I do to, but it's not love. I am the only woman you've really spoken to since you've left Arcadia bar Faendal. There are many more women out there who would be lucky. I cannot stay in the same place for too long. My life is out there." She gestured to the opening of the cave. Cad looked at her glumly. He imagined spending a lot of his time with her, maybe even marrying her some-day. It was hard thinking that maybe he wouldn't.

"Well, I'm not the chosen one, I'm not stuck in Arcadia." The thought caught in his throat. He missed it though, his parents anyway. "I am free, it's what I've always wanted." He forced a smile. "No one to choose my future but me." Gwen smiled back at him and gave him a nod. It was what he had always wanted but he couldn't understand why he did not feel happy about it.

"For now, we will ride to Roshir together and when we get there, you can think about what it is you'd like to do. Possibly the king would like to keep you on as a bounty hunter, even if it's not with me."

"You have a part to play in this yet." The thought rang in his head, one of the sisters had said it, even if he wasn't the chosen one, they still wanted him to do something, they didn't tell him what. He shook his head and left the cave with Gwen, Faendal and Dyne were ready to go.

As they rode, Cad held the reins in one hand whilst he played with the stone he picked up outside the tower in the other. He didn't know why he liked it so much. A simple rock. He could feel energy coming out of it today as though it was trying to talk to him, a lot clearer than it had previously.

"Cad." Dyne called him snapping him out of the trance, he looked at him, "We're not going to all rush off when we get to Roshir you know, we will see you settled in first lad, we need to go drinking of course." Cad forced a small laugh. He was trying not to think of it, now that he was given the freedom, he realised he did not know how he was going to use it. He thought about something to do with the sword, but the thought of being in the army seemed pointless, just being sent out to fight until you're killed only to get replaced by another. Also, he was not as good as he thought when it came to the sword, that realisation had sucked the fun out of it for him, now he no longer felt the rush when he held it, more like disappointment.

He also wondered about joining Faendal, her plan to see the prophecy come true, if he wasn't the chosen one then he could at least work with them to see that the chosen one succeeds. If they lost it meant doom for everyone, maybe the thing he was resisting against this whole time was the right thing for him to do. His mind raced throughout the day, barely noticing what happened around him. They set up for camp and Cad laid down; it surprised him at how refreshed he was in the morning, considering how he spent most of his night in so many different places. He glanced at the stars above him until he drifted off to sleep.

He awoke in the morning, relieved to be in the camp he fell asleep in. He wondered why he had not joined Teague again; he wondered if it was a dream after all.

"Let's go through Candor Tower on our way back, it will only delay us by half a day at most. Something about that place makes me feel uneasy. I just want one last check." Gwen said to the party, no one agreed, but no one argued either, instead they all altered their direction slightly and went towards the tower. Cad had to agree with Gwen, something about that place made him feel somewhat queasy, the entire town disappearing with no tracks was so odd. Cad caught himself playing with the stone again, that's where he found this too.

What was it? He picked it up and looked at it, squinting with one eye as though that would make a difference. It felt cold in his hand. As they dismounted in the abandoned town, the stone become ice cold in his hand he tried to warm the stone up with what little magic he had.

36

Faendal considered Cad as they rode towards the broken tower. She was so sure he was the chosen one. He had potential for great power; he had also seen one of the sisters. It seemed odd to her that it didn't work out. She wondered if Cad had lied. In order to get his freedom, he knew he had some problems with being told what to do. She had hoped that Fenton was not the chosen one; she did not like him. He was arrogant and looked down on everyone because of his royal blood; she contemplated abandoning the pact to stay with Cad; she was sure there was more to be done with his story. She sighed; she was going to get stuck with Fenton; she knew it. At least Cad was likeable and could be trained in the correct way. Fenton would take every bit of advice as a challenge and resist it.

She noticed Cad playing with that stone again; she had meant to ask him about it. It seemed silly that it was just a normal stone. However, Cad had been holding on to it for a while now, he seemed to daydream every time he was holding it, as though it put him in a trance. From the looks of it, there was nothing special about it, although Cad held it like there was.

When they arrived at the abandoned town Cad held the stone up to his eye as though inspecting it closely, Faendal decided she was going to ask, his behaviour was strange around the rock. She got closer to him when suddenly a ball of flame erupted around Cad, when she got her vision back from the intense light. Cad was gone. The stone that he had contemplated for so long was lying on the ground, as ordinary looking and bland as it could be.

37

U rlwin walked through the town of Arcadia, the curfew worked well. That should put a stop to any more plotting, he thought as he walked into the mage hall. They had to have more holding cells built in order to contain the people who spoke out against him, but with the members of the town so loyal to him, any spark of rebellion was dealt with swiftly and harshly. The town lived in fear now; it suited him as they were much easier to control. The barrier was weakening. Any moment now he would be free, and he wondered what he was going to do with the rest of the town, spare them and keep them? Or let them burn with Arcadia.

He sat on his chair and propped his legs up on the desk; he leant back and poured himself a generous measure of whisky. Wil was acting suspicious, he had to know something to be sneaking around. What did he know, and what was he planning? He chose him to be part of the council because he was young, because he was easy to manipulate, but if anything, he was proving to be the most difficult. He would be dealt with soon. He was so close to getting what he wanted. He knew it would only be a matter of time. There came a knock on his door.

"Enter." Urlwin said.

"Urlwin sir. You wanted to see me?" Cassius said. He could not think of the exact moment people started referring to him as sir, he hadn't even commanded it. Once one person started the rest followed suit, they were like sheep. Little did they know he was not the shepherd, but the wolf.

"Yes, keep an eye on Wil for me." He said pouring himself another glass of whisky and one for Cassius, "The boy is up to something I am sure of it. I'm sure Gentar is involved somehow, but they are sly."

"I am not sure why you let him out of prison in the first place." Cassius said, quickly adding a "sir" on the end when he realised, he may have been speaking out of turn.

"We still don't know where Cadderick is. He has to be here somewhere. I don't know how he has kept out of sight for so long."

"Maybe he's dead?" Cassius offered.

"We would know, there would be some sort of body or remains. We are trapped in a gigantic bubble for heaven's sake, he can't just go wandering off. I have checked the tunnels personally and regularly. Someone in town must be hiding him. I just wish I knew who." Urlwin grated his teeth. He hated not knowing something. He knew there could be no way Cad left, so where was he? "You can go now." Cassius gave him a quick bow as he left. Sir and a bow? Some people may be worth saving after all. He grinned as he stood up to look out of the window. "I will find you Cad," He thought to himself. "And I will find out what you're up to Wil. This is my town after all."

38

Cad gasped for his breath when his feet touched the soft ground. He knew he was standing on sand. He'd never seen sand before, but he recognised the colour from the maps, and the fact that he was near the sea confirmed it. The sea was crashing, whirlpools crossed over each other, lightning crackled ferociously above it. Cad took a good step back in order to not be taken by a wave. He knew he was staring at the Cyclone Sea. He imagined all the lives cast away there; they sent anyone who showed an aptitude to magic to the sea to die. He could almost hear the screams in the storm. He tried to push the thought out of his head and tried to picture the maps he was so interested in during his time at Roshir castle. He remembered the Cyclone Sea separated Midguard, where Roshir was, and the Northern Wastelands. He knew that there was no way to cross the sea, and if this was the Northern Wastelands, he would have no way of getting back.

He tried to remember how he got here; he remembered the stone and trying to use magic. Only something else happened. It felt different somehow; he was getting fed up with appearing in different places. He stared at his hands and turned them over as though expecting them to look different. He could feel that he was hot, and the sweat was dripping from his forehead. I need to find some shade first; he thought to himself. He looked around, there was nowhere in sight. He couldn't see very far because of the light hurting his eyes. He thought to himself what Gwen or Dyne would do.

He began looking at the ground for tracks. It surprised him when he found some, leading away from the sea, quite close to where he was standing. They weren't footprints, but more of a small trench in the sand that looked like it could have been travelled some time ago. Apparently, no one knew much of the Wastelands. He wondered if he would be the first person to come here from Midguard and if so, how he was going to get home.

The Cyclone Sea disappeared over the horizon behind Cad as he travelled along the trail. If it was a trail at all, he was not as good as Dyne or Gwen. He could still hear the crashing of the waves and the thunder. It shocked him to see greenery in the distance. He knew little about sand or deserts, but he knew that grass rarely grew there. As he got closer in the distance, he could see one of the grandest fortresses he had ever seen. It was huge; it wasn't as nice as the castle in Roshir, but it was certainly bigger, as though built to be a jail rather than a home. There was a village surrounding it with farmlands and even a stream.

As he got closer to the village, a sudden thought struck him, causing him to jump and hide behind a rock. He did not know if these people would be friendly or not, even if they were, how would he explain how he had got there. The sun bore down on him hard; he had little choice, there was nowhere else to go, and he couldn't stay out here in the heat. He straightened himself up and walked to the village; he tried to hold himself confident. As he got closer people noticed him and stared, some stopped what they were doing to regard him. He regretted walking in so confidently but forced himself to keep it up now. A man came jogging up to him, Cad reached for his sword, but he saw that the man was unarmed and smiling.

"You must be a mage." The man said smiling.

"Uh." Was all Cad could say. He was not expecting such a warm welcome, or such a question.

"It's ok, there are a lot of us mages here. We've not had a new one in a while, though. They back to their old tricks again?" The man asked.

"Um." Cad did not know what he meant, but the man kept on.

"It's amazing how he continues to save us. Only Morrigan could guide us safely through the storms of the Cyclone Sea. They caught me too. Thought I was going to die until I ended up here. Now I'm stronger than ever, he lets us use our magic, you know? You don't have to hide it anymore." Cad flinched at the name Morrigan. The man was talking so fast and excitedly he didn't notice. He gestured Cad to follow him into the village. The people who were staring were now back at work, only giving him the occasional glance as he walked.

"Did they cast you out to sea? For being a mage?" Cad asked.

"Yeah, we all were. Some of us a long time ago, there's a way to live a lot longer when your magic. Morrigan can show you. I haven't learnt yet, I'm fairly new too. I say new, I mean just over a year. They don't send many out now. I was one of the unlucky ones." Cad was trying to get his head around what this man was saying. All of the people who were cast out to sea for being mages came here, because Morrigan saved them? Cad had so many questions, he knew Morrigan was evil, but if he was evil, what was he doing saving all those people. Maybe he had it wrong?

"We're getting strong now," the man continued. "Morrigan says we will leave soon to take back Roshir. I can't wait to get my revenge, I bet you will want a piece of that action to wouldn't you, leaving you for dead like that." Cad realised that this man thought he was cast out like other mages, he nodded slowly thinking this would be a good cover. "I'm not one for war, but they definitely deserve it. I used to live in Shoreville. Where are you from?". Cad hesitated for a moment. He knew he couldn't say Arcadia.

"Roshir." He said, being the only place, he was comfortable saying.

"Right under the king's nose, eh? I bet that upset him even more."

They walked into the fortress as the man, he realised he didn't know his name.

"Who are you?" Cad asked.

"The name's Erran," The man offered his hand. "Erran Hoard."

"I'm Cadderick." He replied, shaking his hand. "Cadderick Storm-Bringer." He couldn't think quick enough to give a surname, he remembered how Gwen reacted when he said he didn't have one, he remembered what the sisters of Fate told him. He noticed the colour drain from his face slightly, he kept his smile, but he could tell it was forced.

"You're a Storm-Bringer?" Erran asked, holding his expression.

"I uh, I think so. Is that bad?" Cad asked. Erran gave a slight chuckle, "Only if I've upset you, let me go tell someone you've arrived." Erran quickly ran off, almost tripping as he did. Cad wondered why he got so nervous when he mentioned the name. He looked around the fortress. The stones that held it were large, someone certainly built it well. People would have a hard time knocking it down if there was a war. The room was empty, no furniture or decoration. Erran returned with a Dwarf by his side. The Dwarf looked at Cad closely.

"Ahh you must be Master Storm-Bringer, correct?" Cad nodded. "I'm sorry, Master, but have we met before?" Cad looked at him closely. There was a certain familiarity about him. Cad shrugged.

"I don't think so, you look familiar though."

"Aye well, all you humans look the same to me, and I'm sure us Dwarves do to you too. Follow me, we have a meeting to attend, after that I will set you up in your room and inform Master Morrigan that you have arrived." The Dwarf gestured Cad through the fortress into a grand hall. Lots of other people came to join, they stood amongst the crowd that chatted amongst themselves, some looked at Cad, but none spoke to him, atop a stage stood seven robed figures. As they took their hoods down, Cad recognised one of them immediately. It was the female mage from the tower. The ones who had captured him and left him to die in the jail. The man who Cad stabbed wasn't there, he wondered if he had managed to kill him. The realisation hit

Cad that he knew the Dwarf from the village too. Cad could feel his legs turn to jelly; he kept his head down.

"There has been speculation and rumour." A voice boomed. Cad could see a man with a hooked nose and short black hair. His eyes looked like a hawk's as he studied the crowd when he spoke. "That Barnabas has defected," there were a few hisses amongst the crowd. He was not popular here. The sound of his name sent shivers right down Cad's spine. "I am afraid to say that is true, he left shortly after my people came from the broken tower, I do not know his reason or what his motives are, I know that he survived breaking the shadow pact once. He will not survive it a second time." There were cheers from the crowd, Cad continued looking at his feet, what was he going to do.

"Plans will continue," he continued. "The Elfkin attacks have brought us plenty of gold and valuables that we can use to buy our way back into Midguard once we establish, the prophecy is in motion, which means the Cyclone Sea will come to rest soon. Then we will cross and claim back what is rightfully ours." More cheers erupted from the crowd. Cad panicked; they were planning to attack Midguard? They did not know that the mages lived, they did not know that a small army sat on the other side of the Cyclone Sea. He needed to warn them, but to do that he needed to get back. "We will stand united under one banner, my banner, and if anyone disagrees, we make them change their mind, by force." More cheers. Cad could hear a noise behind a door to the left of the hall, a slight humming, less of a noise, more of a feeling. Cad recognised it. The stone! He thought to himself, it was the same feeling he had gotten from the stone he was holding before he appeared here. That must have had something to do with his sudden appearance.

Through Morrigan's speech, he began discussing ship building and progress with training, Cad edged slowly towards the door. Some people looked at him oddly as he stepped slowly passed them. He dared not take his eyes off Morrigan or the other mages at the front; he stepped over until he was at the edge of the crowd, there was around six foot of open space between the crowd and the door, if he moved, he would be out in the open. If he stayed and waited, he wasn't sure if he would get the chance to go in there. He did not know what to do once he had got in there. He hesitated for a moment before taking a giant sidestep out of the crowd, when he opened the door. It made a loud creaking sound that disrupted the speech. He swallowed hard, noticing all eyes were on him.

"I don't believe we've been introduced?" Morrigan said from the stage at the front. "Who are you and why are you wandering off during my speech, some would say that's very rude?"

"He's a Storm-Brother sir." He heard Erran shout from the crowd, "he arrived today." Morrigan narrowed his eyes.

"Impossible. He is lying." He said, pointing his finger at him, "Grab him." Several members of the crowd inched towards him to grab him, Cad panicked and jumped through the door. He grabbed hold of a small piece of wood. It sang to him like the stone, in his panic he tried to remember what he did. He used his magic on it, tried to warm it up, once more he disappeared. In the same gasp of air, he was back at Candor tower.

39

The trio were riding hard. Faendal didn't know what had happened to Cad, she didn't know if he travelled somewhere or if he had died. Deep down she didn't think he was dead, although the ball of flame that surrounded him before his disappearance was worrying. Gwen was carrying the stone, wrapped up in a handkerchief. No one dared touch it in case they endured the same fate as Cad. They had taken a detour; they were heading south of Shoreville, into a wooded area. Gwen pushed them on as quick as she could. With Cad away, the trio could travel a lot quicker as he was the slowest rider. Gwen claimed to know where to find out about this stone. Faendal was sceptical, but she knew she cared about Cad. Although she knew his journey didn't lie with him, she could at least do her best to find out his fate.

They arrived in some woodlands farther south. Gwen dismounted and tied her horse, Faendal followed suit and she could see Dyne do the same, Dyne hadn't said a word since Cad disappeared. She knew Dyne did not like to admit to emotions, but he had grown close to Cad. They all had. She guided them through the woods; she seemed to know where she was going and she was going there quickly, Faendal struggled to keep up, she noticed a tear in her eye once or twice although she knew Gwen would never admit it; they had an unusual relationship her and Cad. One minute it was mentor and student, another like lovers, then to bickering like an old married couple to a stony silence that made things tense, then they would repeat the cycle again.

"Ahh Gwen, you've returned, and with visitors, you know I don't like visitors." Her expression was calm throughout and the old lady did not look up from her cook pot, she was stirring a stew outdoors, hunched over it, long grey hair covered her face. Gwen didn't respond, instead she dumped the stone down out of her handkerchief onto the floor next to her. The lady didn't look at it, she continued stirring the stew.

"What is this?" Gwen snapped.

"A weystone." The woman replied, her tone was still calm throughout.

"Can you use it? Where does it lead?" Gwen asked. It impressed Faendal that she knew what a weystone was, she'd never seen one before, just read about them. It was old magic, items used to travel between points instantly, often small insignificant items that could hide in plain sight. If you had magic in your blood, you could sense them, must be why Cad was so obsessed with it, he wouldn't understand what he was looking at, Faendal breathed a sigh of relief at the thought that Cad was not dead, merely travelled.

"No, the song is strange, I believe you need a much stronger power than I possess to use it, I can send others, with no magical ability, but for someone who has the magic, they must be strong indeed. No, dear, I can send others, but not myself."

"Send me." Gwen added hastily, "I need to go."

"But I cannot bring you back." The lady responded.

"I can find my own way back." Gwen snapped; she was set on going. It was a one-way trip. Faendal hesitated, this could lead anywhere.

"I'm afraid not." She said looking up to regard Gwen. "He will find his own way back, trust me dear. He's safe."

"You know?" Gwen asked. "You've seen."

"Yes, just as I saw when I sent you to find him, it is clear to me, not much more is these days."

"You didn't tell me he was from Arcadia!" Gwen almost lost her cool, "That would have been useful to know."

"I did not know where he had been, only where he needed to be and that is with you, your fates are entwined together."

"So, you said." Gwen replied sharply. "But how? Why? Marriage? You know that's not for me." The old lady chuckled.

"Oh dear, not marriage no, there is more to the world than just you and Cadderick Storm-Bringer." Faendal choked.

"You mean?" Faendal started.

"Yes, he is descended from Morrigan, a long line, mind you. That is why his power is so strong."

"He isn't strong, and you didn't tell me he had power!" Gwen shouted, "Why do you tell me half-truths, why not let me know everything to begin with?"

"Because I only tell you what I know for sure at the time, I have learnt a lot since we last spoke Gwendoline. Power is returning to the lands, Cad will not be the only one with the strength, I fear that magic could be the end to us all. But I have not seen an end. Yet." Faendal saw Dyne shift uncomfortably and even felt the hairs on the back of her neck stood up. She wasn't sure if she liked this woman, she seemed strange. She could see things though, not clearly but a little. She wondered how she would have got a power like that.

"Cad can't use his magic." Gwen said. "He's been tapped."

"Oh, taps can turn on as well as off," she said simply. "He must have used power to use the stone."

"Will he be able to use his magic to come back? Back to the stone." Gwen asked.

"No, not the stone, but wherever you collected the stone from, there will be another weystone for him to find his way back. It will lead him back to the tower."

"Then we must head back." Gwen said getting up.

"No, I'm afraid it is too late. Cad's destiny lies somewhere else now. He has his own battle to fight." Gwen sat down slowly when she heard.

"So, you mean we are to stay apart?" Gwen asked sadly.

"For the meantime, yes. You will find each other in your own time, you both still have much to do."

"What must we do?" Gwen asked.

"I wish I knew," The woman sighed. "I wish I could see all, things would be so much easier."

"Where do I go now?" Gwen asked.

"That is up to you. For now, I suggest you stay the night. The stew is ready, our visitors can have some too I suppose." She said waving her hand towards them still not paying them any attention. Gwen mouthed sorry to Faendal and Dyne.

"I think Roshir will need you once again, dear, it would be better to head there."

"Thank you, Mother." Gwen said, and Faendal's eyes widened.

40

"Gwen!" Cad shouted, "Faendal! Dyne!" He marched around the abandoned village; he saw no sign of them. He tried looking for tracks to see which way they went, but it was a lot less obvious out here in the fields, and he had nowhere near the ability that the others had. From where he appeared he saw three robed figures appear. They looked around. He quickly ducked behind a cabin. He held his breath. They travelled back to look for him. He watched them look inside each of the cabins, he knew he couldn't stay here for long, he darted into the woods, keeping his head down as he ran, he sprinted as far as he could, not daring to turn back to see if he was being chased. Hi sprint turned into a run, which turned into a jog until Cad's lungs were on fire and his legs were heavy. He stopped to catch his breath. He was a good distance from the tower, but he did not know where he was. The darkness came on quickly. He was grateful the nights were warm as he had no equipment apart from his sword, no bedroll, no blanket. Nothing to eat.

He made a small bed in a ditch; he looked at it from all angles to see if it was well hidden. He couldn't keep watch all night as he needed to sleep. He made himself comfortable. His stomach groaned.

He would have to try to find some food tomorrow. He drifted off to sleep, thinking of the stew he had back in Arcadia. It wasn't the tastiest he'd had much nicer since he'd left, but the memories of eating it with his mother and father flooded him as he drifted off to sleep.

Cad was sitting in the kitchen of his home in Arcadia. It looked darker than normal, his mother and father were sat at the table.

"Do you think they caught him?" His mother said.

"I don't know, we shouldn't worry, if there are eyes on us it will be harder for us to get messages." Cad looked at them, confused.

"Mum? Dad?" he said. They did not look up to acknowledge him, he was dream walking again. Only this time, his parents were awake.

"This is getting dangerous." His mother said. "How can we trust Wil? He is working with Urlwin after all."

"He is the one putting his neck out, he approached me, I don't think he would go to these lengths if this was some sort of trick, they could easily jail me with the other half of the town." Cad's thought raced. Half of the town was in jail; Wil was involved with his parents. What was going on?

"Oh, nothing has been the same since Cad left." His mother said as she wiped the tears from her eyes. "He must be out there somewhere; god knows what's happened to him."

"He must have got out, must have." His father said, "Someone would have found him by now, I don't know where he went or how he did it, he always dreamed of leaving. We thought he was a fool, but it was us who were foolish. I wish we could have gone with him."

"A few months ago, I would have hit you around the head for saying such foolish things, but I agree. I would rather face the unknown dangers out there than putting up with life in here." Cad could feel his eyes stinging with tears.

"I will come for you Mum, and you Dad. You will love it out here. I promise." Cad fell to his knees and started weeping. Suddenly he heard footsteps rushing towards him. He twisted to see Teague burst through the wall like a ghost and stop. His face was terrified.

"Cad, we have to go. We need to hide. The bad man is coming." He grabbed Cad's hand and pulled; Cad stayed where he was.

"The bad man?" He asked. "I thought there was no one else here."

"He came the night after you did Cad, he's like us, he chased me, he hurt me." Cad stood and saw the fright in his eyes.

"Show me where this bad man is." Cad said to him bluntly, his parents were still talking but Cad had stopped listening now. If someone had hurt Teague, someone so small, Cad was angry.

"He's coming this way, I can't stay, I'm scared. Please Cad, run!" And with that Teague disappeared. Cad could hear his name being called out in the street. His parents didn't react to it, so he knew it wasn't a part of the actual world. He recognised the voice and swallowed hard; it was Barnabas.

"I know you're here Cad, there's no use hiding from me." Barnabas said, stepping closer to Cad's house. Cad walked outside to face him; he was angry. How could a grown man like that hurt a child as small and innocent as Teague? Cad had only known him for one night but felt very protective of him. Cad pushed all his fear down and brought up his rage.

"Maybe it is you who should hide from me." He said through clenched teeth, as he squared up to him. "I'm surprised someone with so much power uses it to torment small children." Barnabas smirked.

"Ahh yes the boy, well I needed information, and he wasn't forthcoming... At first." He gave a small chuckle. This made Cad angrier, the fact that he could be so coy about such a thing. Cad drew his sword and made a swing for him. The blade met air as he reappeared behind Cad. "I see you have not yet learnt the full potential of dream walking." He lifted his hand to Cad, freezing him in place. He felt as though rope had bound him, the only part of his body that could move was his head.

"Ahh yes, curious that the shadow pact stopped my magic effecting you, I have had to break it a second time, why is that?"

"Let me go and face me like a man. Or are you a coward?" Cad goaded. Barnabas just chuckled.

"I am not so proud that I would risk anything like that. You are the chosen one after all, certain precautions need to be taken."

"I am not the chosen one." Cad responded,

"Don't play games with me, I know you went to the Sisters of Fate, I know what you saw. You forget, I am above such things, above the so-called shadow prophecy. I control this world, not you and not the Sisters of Fate." Cad could feel the invisible rope getting tighter and tighter. He struggled to breathe. "You know, you cannot die in this world, this is but a dream after all. But do you feel that? The pain?" Cad's face was red, he was struggling to breathe. "That is what you get here, unlimited pain." Cad strained but he could not move, he was getting weaker and weaker.

His hands felt numb from where they were being squeezed, he tried to warm them up with his magic, relieve the pain a little. When he did, he felt a looseness around his binds. He could breathe again, he felt the magic course through his body, his hands glowed. He saw Barnabas' eyes narrow in fear. Cad could feel the energy burst through his hands. He aimed it at Barnabas, striking him in the midriff he buckled over on the floor.

"It won't be so easy in the actual world." He wheezed and at the end of his sentence he disappeared. Cad gasped and looked at his hands. He felt it, the magic, the magic he had inside him all this time. He could feel it course through his veins and into his fingertips. He glanced at the glow in his hands. After a few breaths he got it under control, the magic faded, and his hands turned back into a normal colour.

"That was awesome!" Teague shouted as he came running towards Cad. "You defeated him!" He laughed, holding out his hand for a high five. Cad reluctantly met his hand with his, "How did you do that?" The boy was bouncing with excitement.

"I'm not really sure." Cad said, looking at his hands once more. "It just happened."

"Well, you kicked his butt! It was amazing." He paused. "Please don't tell my mum I said butt. She doesn't like me using that word."

Cad could not help but laugh. He spent the rest of the night talking with Teague after discovering his parents had retired to bed. As he talked, he stared at his hands, wondering where this power had come from.

41

When Cad awoke the next morning, he checked his hands again. He wondered if he could only do that in the dream world. He tested it by setting a fire with some twigs, jumping back at the power of it. He could make a fire. No longer was his power useless, it could actually go beyond warming his hands. He smiled to himself, but it was quickly replaced with a grimace. He knew how people in Midguard reacted to powerful magic, they would send him to the Cyclone Sea, meaning that he would end up back at the fortress he had just escaped from. He suddenly remembered the fortress. I need to warn them; he thought to himself, getting up. He walked through the woods in a random direction. First, he had to work out where he was. Then he could start to make his way back.

He wandered through the woods, trying to keep going in a straight line. He moved quietly but with speed. He wanted to get out quickly, but he also didn't want to end up accidentally walking into someone; he didn't know if the Mages from the Wastelands were still looking for him. His stomach ached, he hadn't eaten in a while, he would need to find food and water. He had learnt by watching Gwen make traps for rabbits and other small animals, although he had never done it himself. He needed string though, and he had none. He was very unprepared. He climbed a tree and sat silently on the branch, studying the ground.

It wasn't long before he spotted a rabbit scurrying the ground, feeding on the grass. He studied the animal for a while before looking at his hands. He could use his magic to capture it, he thought. He held his palm out towards it and concentrated. He could feel the magic coursing through his body. He forced it towards the rabbit. The light that came out of his hands was so bright that Cad had to close his eyes. The force it came out scorched the ground below the rabbit and incinerated it, leaving nothing but charred bones. Cad could feel his head getting light. He passed out on the branch and fell to the ground.

He came to hurt and woozy. He tried to hold himself up; it felt different to what he had done in the dream, but then Barnabas said that it was easier in the dream world than it was here. He stumbled to the spot where the rabbit was incinerated; he pushed the carcass with his foot. Not a single bit was edible. He muttered to himself before sitting down holding his head in his hands. He still felt dizzy and the whole left side of his body ached from where he hit the ground. He tried to establish what went wrong. He felt as though he had overexerted himself. Like if he ran too far without resting, perhaps magic was the same. It drains you the more you use it; he gave it all against a tiny rabbit. Neither the rabbit nor Cad was of any use right now.

After his head had stopped spinning, he continued through the forest; he found a small stream; the water seemed clear, and Cad was desperate enough to drink it without testing. It seemed fine; he began lapping at the water before dipping his entire face in. The coldness of it was a shock, but it revitalised Cad a little. He shook his head before resting by the water. He spotted a small pond just off the side of the river; it looked familiar. It looked just like the one he had seen with the sisters; it looked just like the World's Eye.

He stumbled over to it, stomach still grumbling, and stared into the water. He could see a reflection, not his own but the pink-haired sister of Fate.

"Be ready. He is coming" Is all she said. Cad jumped, he didn't hear the voice come out of the well, more he heard the voice in his mind. He looked around him to see who was coming, no one was there, he looked back at the pond, it was gone. He felt a panic arise inside him, had he just imagined it, or was she sending him a message. Who was coming? Morrigan, Barnabas? He rushed into the woods, before stopping and listening carefully. He could hear no one either. His heart skipped. Right next to him was a bush containing some berries and a patch of mushrooms. It wasn't meat, but it would do. He began forcing them down him, his stomach felt cramped from the hunger, shocked that food was now entering his body, but he ate anyway. He had a good vantage point where he was, it would be difficult to see him, but he had a good view of the surrounding woods.

"I tire of this game of Cat and Mouse Cadderick." Barnabas' voice was clear in Cad's head. He was speaking in his mind. "It is time to end this, come face your death with dignity or suffer an unimaginable torment." Cad could feel him more than he could see him, he was close to the stream where he was just moments ago. He still felt a little light-headed and his stomach still ached. He thumped his chest to relieve some of the indigestion. If he can find me here, he will find me anywhere, Cad thought. Every night he will torment Teague and every night whilst I'm there I will have to deal with it.

He walked out into the opening. Barnabas stood there. He could see the smile on his lips under his charred skin. He was a horror to look at, but Cad was not afraid of him anymore. One of them had to die. He did not want to spend the rest of his life being chased around and hunted by this madman, and Cad knew he could not persuade him to stop.

"I'm tired too." Cad said, gripping his sword into a stance. He knew he could use magic now, but this was more comfortable for him.

"You don't understand the power you could hold; you cling to the sword. Why? You could be so much better than that." Barnabas said, circling him. They were both staring each other down. His eyes looked whiter than a normal man's, but that could be because of the burnt flesh surrounding them.

"This is who I want to be. No one can tell me what to do or who to be but me." Cad said and with that swung his sword to catch his midriff, as though Cad was moving in slow motion Barnabas side-stepped the swipe with ease, Cad span around to meet him, sword still pointing towards him. "Why do you hunt me?" Cad asked.

"You are a threat to me and my plans. If you only understood what you could do, as the chosen one you have power beyond many."

"I told you, I'm not the chosen one." Cad made another swing. He felt the sword fly out of his hands as though pulled by an invisible rope and hurled itself into a tree. Cad span to face him, holding his palms up, as though aiming ready to use the magic he tried to hold back.

"When I kill you." Barnabas said, gripping Cad in that magical constraint that he had used in the dream, "I will torture your dream walker friend, night after night." And threw his head back to laugh. Cad struggled, but again he could not move.

"No." Was all Cad could get out in a muffled sound, his jaw was bound shut.

"And your friends that follow you around, licking your boots, I will kill them too. Slowly." He laughed again. His face flushed. He thought of Gwen, where was she? Dyne and Faendal too. He had to stop him. Cad started concentrating. He could feel the magic through his body again. Not as strong as normal, he still felt weak. He wiggled his fingers. Barnabas had turned to pull Cad's sword out of the tree and walked towards him, swinging the sword in a mocking style towards his restrained body. He looked Cad in the eyes, Cad was still struggling to move although his hands felt looser.

"Those who live by the sword, die by the sword." Barnabas said, narrowing his eyes towards Cad before thrusting it straight into his Abdomen. His breath caught; every movement was painful. He fell to the floor, the magical restraints vanishing, and the sword became buried in him. Moving was painful.

"See what has happened to your chosen one!" Barnabas. "I am above your prophecy." Cad had pulled the sword out of his stomach. Blood poured, and the pain caused him to scream. He slowly got to his feet.

"No" Was all he could say. He was shivering. The pain was stopping his concentration as he put all of his might into focusing his magic and shot a sharp blast of energy at Barnabas. Before falling to his knees, writhing in pain. He heard Barnabas, howl in pain, Cad did not have the strength to look up, but he could hear him writhing about. He heard him fall to the floor, coughing.

"I underestimated you." Barnabas said in a slow croak, he was obviously in pain, "I am strong enough to recover though, but are you?" He laughed slowly with a croak. Cad knew that the pain was causing him to stop laughing. He tried to get up, but he couldn't find the strength.

"You thought you could hide from me." Cad heard the voice. He was clutching his wound, preventing the blood loss as tightly as he could. His skin was white, and he was shaking. The voice seemed familiar.

"Morrigan, I." Barnabas stopped. Cad could hear the fear in his voice. He knew Barnabas would be too weak to fight him now.

"You claim to be all powerful, yet here you lie at death's door defeated by a child."

"You don't understand." Barnabas rasped. "He is the chosen one."

"You fool." Morrigan snapped. It sounded like Barnabas was choking. "I am the chosen one, I will unite the land under one flag, me."

"I.... I..." Was all Cad could hear through the choking before he heard Barnabas' body crumple to the ground.

"What shall I do with the boy, sir?" Came another voice.

"Finish him, I don't care, my plans do not involve him. Now Barnabas is dead we can carry on, I will wait south of Arcadia, scout the tower first, make sure he had no followers before returning to me."

"Yes, sir." The voice said, Cad turned his head just in time to see Morrigan ride off.

"Sorry lad." The man said before holding his bow up and aiming it at Cad. He couldn't even move to avoid the blow. Even without the arrow, he was going to die, anyway. He could feel it. At least Teague would be safe now.

42

"You won't stay the night?" Gwen's mother asked. "There is no rush, I can assure you."

"No, I won't." Gwen said, strapping her bedroll to the horse before packing up. She looked at Faendal and Dyne.

"I'm going back, for Cad." She said to them. "You two continue to Roshir, I will return when I find him."

"You fool!" her mother shouted at her. For the first time in a long time, Gwen saw the emotionless mask that she always wore slip from her face. "You know that is not your destiny now, your destiny lies in Roshir."

"I know." Gwen replied. "Cad always had a problem with destiny, about doing what everyone thought he had to, and I think he might have been right. I'd rather do what I want to do, and right now I want to find Cad."

"This will not help, there are greater things at work than what you want."

"And if there is, I want no part in it." She jumped on her horse, all packed. "I will see you again, mother."

"Wait." Faendal called out to her, she turned ready for a scolding,

"I'm coming too," she quickly gathered up her belongings she had unpacked and crammed them on her horse.

"Well, I'm not going back alone." Dyne said. "The boy is more trouble than he's worth, but I've grown rather fond of him." He said strapping up to his horse. Gwen could feel tears filling her eyes.

"Thank you," She said, trying not to burst into floods of tears. She had hoped Dyne would accompany her she would need a friend nearby, especially if they could not find Cad. It surprised her that Faendal agreed, but she was happy, nevertheless. Without another word to her mother, who had stormed into her house, obviously angry at her choice, she galloped through the night to get back to the broken tower.

It was early hours in the morning when they arrived; she looked for clues, people had been here recently, she could tell by the markings on the floor. They had been in and out of the buildings.

"Do you think someone stumbled onto this place, or were they looking for something? Looking for Cad." She said to no one in particular.

"Here." Faendal said pointing at some light tracks heading into the woods. "Someone went away in a hurry." He said, it surprised Gwen at how good Faendal was at tracking, she had tracked many bounties before and was quite skilled at it. Dyne, too. Faendal knew a lot more than which direction they were headed. They rode their horses through the woods, following the trail.

"Someone has slept here," Dyne said, pointing at a ditch. They continued following closely, Gwen was sure it was Cad it had to be. She soon came to an odd scene. A scorch mark on the floor, and the charred remains of what looked like a rabbit.

"What happened here?" She asked.

"Magic." Faendal said looking around, "Someone has fallen here too." He was right. The ground and the broken branches someone had fallen out of the tree, recently too. "The trail carries on."

They came close to a small opening.

"Shh." She said ushering to the others to stop, I hear voices. "It's not Cad."

"Finish him, I don't care, my plans do not involve him. Now Barnabas is dead we can carry on, I will wait south of Arcadia, scout the tower first make sure he had no followers before returning to me." Gwen heard the robed man say. There were two crumpled bodies on the floor. One wore a robe, and she recognised him as one of the mages that had captured them in the tower which seemed like an age ago. The other was...

"Cad." She gasped.

"Yes, sir." The second man said as the robed one galloped away on his horse. "Sorry lad." He picked up his bow and aimed it at Cad. Before she understood fully what was going on, she was running.

"No!" She screamed as she jumped in front of Cad. The arrow flew and hit her straight through her shoulder. She fell awkwardly as she landed on the arrow, embedding it further inside her. She could hear a scuffle. Dyne and Faendal had obviously followed. She saw Cad's smile on his pale face; he was bleeding heavily. She tried to return his smile but passed out from the pain.

EPILOGUE

C ad walked stiffly. He had to use a stick whilst he healed. It had been a few weeks now since he had woken up back in Roshir. Dyne had told him what had happened, how Gwen had thrown herself in front of him. How they bandaged them both up and got them to safety. It was a miracle that Cad had survived; they said. The healer couldn't believe it when he recovered. They had crowned Fenton the new king after being declared the chosen one. Cad remembered warning him of the boats in the wasteland, they discounted it as a fever dream. He stood alongside Dyne in front of the king. The doors opened and in walked Gwen, clutching on to a stick of her own. She hobbled towards them with a smile. Cad smiled back, happy that she too had recovered. She saved his life, and he owed her his. The king looked down to them.

"The former King has granted you pardon for abandoning Roshir in its hour of need, in order to stop Barnabas. However, now that it is dealt with, I must find a use for you, Cadderick, I am sure they can find some use for you on the farms, I am sure you can use a hoe better than a sword. Gwen and Dyne, I am sure that Aldrin will accept you both as guards."

"Guards?!" Dyne snapped. "We are bounty hunters."

"And bounty hunters are glorified guards." Fenton snapped back. "I will also have no need for your cheek, you will find I have less of a tolerance than my father." He paced back and forth, "You are of course welcome to join Cad at the farm." He said with a smirk.

"I will not be working on the farm sire." Cad said respectfully.

"Oh?" Said Fenton, raising an eyebrow. "And what will you do to make money? You are welcome to be a resident of Roshir, but like everyone else in this world, you will have to pay for your way."

"I have spent my whole life being told what I must or must not do Sire." Cad bowed his head as he said Sire, trying to remain as polite as possible. "I think I am going to enjoy my freedom for a while. My destiny is mine to decide, not yours." And with that, Cad bowed low and turned to leave.

"Cad wait," Gwen said, Cad hesitated. He felt like he had left a powerful impression, and if he turned back now, it would be ruined. He couldn't resist Gwen's request. He looked back. She nodded at Dyne.

"We're coming too." She said turning her back on the King and walking towards him. "Sorry Sire, guard duty isn't for me, I'm not one to settle down." Dyne said nothing to the king but laughed. He was doing a rude gesture with his hands out of sight of the king and followed them too.

"Will you take one more?" Faendal called from her seat.

"Faendal, you will sit." Fenton shouted; his face was red from their lack of respect.

"Sorry, sire, I quit as well. I don't think I was born to be a, how did you put it, a glorified accountant." She walked to join them. Cad shook her hand and beamed.

"You will pay for your insolence!" Fenton shouted, sparks of unconcentrated energy erupted from him as he slammed his fists down in a rage. Cad managed to use his own power to deflect the energy that had aimed for them. Cad kept his smile the whole time, Fenton sat back on his throne pale from shock whilst the members of the hall all gasped in shock and muttered amongst themselves, surprised that the King was capable of magic.

"I'm sorry your majesty." Dyne said with a mocking bow. "Are we imprisoned? Is it a crime to refuse employment? Are we betraying you somehow?"

"Well, no."

"Then like the lad said. See you later. Don't get a cramp in your arse from sitting too much."

Cad left the castle with his friends. Excited to where they would end up next.

ABOUT THE AUTHOR

Nathan is a Father of two and his children's love of stories is what helped him discover his love for storytelling. Being a big lover of Fantasy he loves to write stories about the wild, the magical and the unknown.

You can follow him on twitter @NathScam or Instagram @Nathanscammellauthor. Escape from Arcadia is the first novel written into his creation of a new world and is available at most online book retailers

f 𝕏 ⬤

Printed in Great Britain
by Amazon

66905719R00144